Alfred Duggan was born in [...] American descent: his mother's father, Joseph Munro Hinds, was born in Illinois in 1843, and met the author's grandmother (born in Argentina of English parents) when appointed Consul General in Brazil. Duggan was taken to England at the age of two. After his education at Eton College and Balliol College, Oxford, he worked for the British Natural History Museum, collecting specimens. At the age of twenty-one he sailed in the 600-ton barquentine, *St George*, from England via Madeira, Trinidad and Panama to the Galapagos Islands, pursuing his job for the museum. In later years he travelled extensively in Greece and Turkey, studying Byzantine monuments, and in 1935 helped to excavate Constantine's Palace, Istanbul, under the auspices of the University of St Andrews. From 1938 to 1941, when he was discharged as medically unfit, he served in the London Irish Rifles (TA) and saw active service in Norway. For the rest of World War II he worked in an aircraft factory.

A prolific writer, Duggan turned out more than one book a year. His first was *Knight with Armour*, written in 1946 and published in 1950. Next came his novels *Conscience of the King* and *The Little Emperors*, the latter dealing in lively fashion with the decline and fall of the western Roman Empire as it impinged upon the life of a British civil servant. 'As one novel follows another in pleasant succession', wrote Thomas Caldecot Chubb in the *New York Times*, 'it dawns upon this constant reader of historical fiction that in Alfred Duggan he has found an extremely gifted writer who can move into an unknown period and give it life and immediacy.' 'A specialist in decline and fall', in *Lady for Ransom* he dealt with one of the great crises of Byzantine politics. 'Mr Duggan's characters are sharply drawn', wrote Chubb, 'and, as always, he keeps his eye on the flow of history'. His 'cheerful cynicism' and satirical view of men and politics 'have introduced a refreshing new element into current historical fiction'. Orville Prescott wrote in the *New York Times*, 'Mr Duggan looks upon the past with a connoisseur's relish of villainy and violence'.

Alfred Duggan died in 1964.

By Alfred Duggan in Phoenix paperback

Conscience of the King
The Little Emperors
Winter Quarters
Three's Company

THE LITTLE EMPERORS

ALFRED DUGGAN

PHOENIX

A PHOENIX PAPERBACK

First published in Great Britain in 1951
by Faber and Faber Limited
This paperback edition published in 2005
by Phoenix,
an imprint of Orion Books Ltd,
Orion House, 5 Upper St Martin's Lane,
London WC2H 9EA

1 3 5 7 9 10 8 6 4 2

Copyright © The Estate of Alfred Duggan 1951, 2005

The right of The Estate of Alfred Duggan to be identified as
the author of this work has been asserted by them in
accordance with the Copyright, Designs and Patents Act 1988.

A CIP catalogue record for this book
is available from the British Library.

ISBN 0 75381 826 4

Typeset by Deltatype Ltd, Birkenhead, Merseyside
Printed and bound in Great Britain by
Clays Ltd, St Ives plc

www.orionbooks.co.uk

CONTENTS

PLACE NAMES
IN THE STORY

Achaea *Greece*
Arelatum *Arles*
Augusta Treverorum *Trier*
Belerium *St Michael's Mount in Cornwall*
Brigantia *Yorkshire*
Burdigala *Bordeaux*
Calleva *Silchester*
Camolodunum *Colchester*
Colonia Agrippina *Cologne*
Corinium *Cirencester*
Deva *Chester*
Eburacum *York*
Gessoriacum *Boulogne*
Glevum *Gloucester*
Hellespont *Dardanelles*
Illyricum *Yugoslavia*
Londinium *London*
Lugdunum *Lyons*
Lycia *South-western Asia Minor*
Mauretania Tingitensis *Morocco*
Mediolanum *Milan*
Moesia *Austria*
Niduarian Picts *in Galloway*

Pontes *Staines*
Pontus *Northern Asia Minor*
Propontis *Sea of Marmora*
Rutupiae *Richborough*
Sea of Vectis *Solent*
Tingis *Tangier*
Vectis *Isle of Wight*
Venta *Winchester*
Verulamium *St Albans*

CHAPTER I

HONORIUS IMPERATOR
SEMPER AUGUSTUS

The climate of Britain is notoriously vile. But there are occasional fine days, and sometimes they come when they are wanted; otherwise it would be impossible to cultivate the soil of the island, instead of merely very difficult indeed. In the eleventh year of the Emperor Honorius, A.D. 405, the 10th of September was fine; C. Sempronius Felix, Praeses of Britannia Prima, realized that as soon as he woke, from the pattern made by the low sun on the ceiling of his bedroom. At once he thought of the harvest; a wet August had damaged the crops as they were reaped, but a few days of sunshine would dry the ground and enable the farmers to move their wagons between field and barn; they might save more corn than he had been counting on yesterday. He decided to go early to the office, and revise the provisional figures his clerks had made out during the storms of the last month. He threw off the bedclothes and clapped his hands for his valet.

In half an hour he was ready to set out. He was an African from the Mediterranean Sea, where men rise early to work before the heat of midday, and it pleased him to set an example; the provincials were too fond of lying in bed until this beastly island of theirs had warmed up after the chills of the night. He did not waste time on his toilet; it is the privilege of the head of any organization to dress as he pleases when his subordinates have to appear neatly turned out, and there was no one in Londinium who was his superior in rank. Besides, it was the custom of the ancients to bathe after the work of the day, and senior officials should follow ancient custom. He ate a bit of bread and smoked bacon while the valet fastened his tunic, and muttered a very short prayer to the Christian God while his hair was combed over the bald patch. On his way to the stairs he passed the stout door of the women's apartments, now standing open as the housemaids began their work; the eunuch whispered that the Lady Maria was not yet awake, and he did not enter. His young wife usually woke in a bad temper, and it was well to keep out of her way in the early morning; so the early-rising servants did their work very quietly. That was a good thing, though Felix did not really approve of a young lady who was always flogging her maids. However, he had not married Maria for her character, but for her family connections, and he seldom saw her except at meals.

Two footmen waited for him outside. They were hefty, fierce-looking Germans, dressed in what the Divine Gratianus had considered the sort of armour German chiefs would have worn if they had ruled a population of skilled bronze-founders. In fact, they were extremely meek, terrified of infringing a law they did not understand; real soldiers bullied them dreadfully. In the good old days the ruler of a Province was guarded by soldiers, but the Divine Diocletianus had totally severed the civil service from the army; now a Praeses, or even a Vicarius, might not give orders to the most junior recruit. Sometimes Felix regretted that he had lost the power of the sword which Legates had once possessed. But gentlemen were not allowed to join the army, and it was as well that everyone should realize he had no connection with the hard-drinking profligate boors who held military command in this degenerate age. He strolled along the sunny side of the street with his two attendants following, and tried to see himself as some magistrate of the Republic, a Praetor or a Quaestor, walking through the Sacred City with lictors in his train. It was his favourite daydream, for his education had taught him that the past was a great deal better than the present.

All the same, Londinium was looking very splendid on this fine September morning; architecture was one of the few arts that had improved since the days of the Republic, and this city, unlike most of those in Britain, had not been sacked in the Pictish War. It was very large, a mile long by half a mile wide, and since it had always been the financial capital of Britain (though not the military headquarters) it possessed a fine collection of government offices.

There were few citizens about at this early hour, and those he passed paid little attention to him; the lower classes backed against the wall and cringed in silence, and the more prosperous raised an arm in greeting; but nobody tried to hand him a petition. When he first came to this Province, ten years ago, everyone he met would thrust a paper into his hand, usually wrapped round a bribe; but now they had learned that he never did business outside the office, and that he only took presents after a transaction had been completed, as became an honest official.

It was at this morning hour, before the details of office work had altered the focus of his mind, that he liked to picture the whole Diocese, busy in the cause of Civilization. Here in the peaceful south the coloni grew corn and flax, on the northern moors sheep were sheared, from the western mines came lead and tin; stone must be quarried, fish caught, timber cut and charcoal burned, to supply the wants of the primary producers; there must be enough of every commodity, yet waste must be avoided. All this was the elementary work of the civil service. There should also be a surplus, after paying for defence, to support the sculptors, scholars and poets who were the embodiment of the Good Life of the Oecumene, the interlocking household of the Civilized World. It was much more difficult to find this surplus, and to keep it out of the military pay-chest.

The Treasury building was in the old style of the Claudian Emperors, and the columns had been clumsily fashioned by barbarous provincials when the whole place was rebuilt after being burned by the Iceni; that was more than three hundred years ago, and Londinium had not since been sacked by an enemy, though occasionally Roman troops had plundered it in civil war. It was quite an historical monument, though Felix sometimes wished the Picts could have destroyed it in the troubles of forty years ago; then he could have rebuilt in the latest style, with modern conveniences. Nowadays there was more paper work, and the files had to be kept longer; while as most trials were held in private there was no need for the great judgement hall.

The Praeses strode through the portico into his private room off the entrance lobby. Waiting beside his desk, holding a bundle of rolled papers, was Paulinus the freed-man, his confidential secretary. Instead of explaining the day's business he plunged into a discussion of the news: 'Good morning, sir. Have you heard anything about the campaign in Italy? or the Irish fleet in the Channel?'

'Nothing fresh, Paulinus. As I told you before, that is good news. If anything had gone wrong the rumour would reach us speedily; but when the army destroys a pack of barbarians that is an everyday occurrence which no one bothers to pass on. We must not gossip about soldiers. What have you got for me there?'

'Rough estimates, sir, of the harvest. The tax-gatherers valued it as it was reaped, before it was carried; so we must allow for loss during the late storms. One thing may upset our calculations. If these Irish land and ravage the open country we shall draw no revenue from the south coast this year.'

'Don't bother about that. The Comes Littoris Saxonici is paid an enormous salary to see pirates don't ravage there.'

Felix unrolled the papers, and studied particularly the summary of estimated revenue.

'I see you expect a small surplus, after paying the army,' he said briskly. 'In that case we can do something for education. The law says we ought to have teachers of grammar and rhetoric in large cities, and for the last ten years I have hoped to get them started. I don't like the way the Celtic language is spreading in the countryside; administration is more difficult if the coloni don't understand the instructions of the government. I know there are thousands of other things to be done, but it's hardly worth starting to repair a few roads, when at any moment we may have to stop for lack of funds.'

'Excuse me, sir,' Paulinus said gently. 'If there really is a surplus could we reduce the taxes, or at least forgive some arrears?'

'I certainly can't reduce taxes by my own authority, and the Vicarius would not allow it. For one thing, it would mean endless paper work, probably an application to Mediolanum, before I received permission. I might be rather more gentle in collecting arrears, but they must remain on the file. Have you any particular case in mind? Naturally, taxpayers who are well disposed to the government should be better treated than those who make trouble.'

Felix was a citizen of good birth, descended from a long line of civil servants; it was beneath his dignity to take a bribe. But he knew that freedmen must be judged by different standards. The machine would not work unless the subordinates were willing.

However, his clerk chose to be incorruptible to-day. 'Oh no, sir. I had no particular case in mind, although I know you will always protect my personal friends from the tax-gatherers. But the coloni are beginning to desert their land, especially near the coast where they are bothered by pirates. This Province is remarkably free from outlaws at present, but if we press them too hard we shall find Bagaudae starting up, as they have in Gaul.'

'Then the army will deal with them. I am not responsible for order. But I can't reduce the taxes, and you know that as well as I do.'

Paulinus was always trying to earn popularity by taking the side of the taxpayer. It was natural enough, for a successful freedman is loathed by every citizen; had he been harsh as well as successful he would have been lynched long ago. But taxation kept the Empire going; the more taxes were collected, the stronger was the government; and in these days it needed all its strength.

These broad decisions taken, as they had to be taken afresh every day against a perpetual nagging opposition, the Praeses settled down to give judgement on the most urgent of the smaller cases that his subordinates had sent up to him. What should be done with the daughter of a baker who had married a soldier twenty years ago, after the administration had lost track of her during a barbarian raid, and whose three sons now claimed to follow their father into the army? She had clearly broken the law, which made the unattractive calling of bakery strictly hereditary. She claimed the soldier had taken her by force. That was probably a lie, but it might be true, and it was so long ago there were no witnesses. One solution would be to make her husband put her away, and marry her to a baker on the waiting list for a wife; but the Church would make a fuss about the broken marriage vows. The law said she should be burned alive, now that her crime was at last discovered; but that would do no good to anybody. Of course the military authorities were delighted to find themselves with three prospective native-born recruits, so much cheaper than hired barbarians, and they backed the husband. Perhaps it would be wise to give in gracefully, and put the soldiers under an obligation. In that case the office must check the list of bakers at once, before others decided it was possible to escape their work.

As he had pointed out, Felix was not responsible for order in his Province. But he was responsible for practically everything else. Although Britannia Prima, in the south-east of the island, contained no mines of any metal more precious than iron, Londinium was the port whence most exports were shipped to the Continent; lead, tin and copper from the west came into the city by wagon or pack-pony, each ingot already stamped with the Emperor's name as a guarantee of weight and purity; small parcels were held in the Treasury until they made up a shipload, and then the chartered merchant ship was sent down river to the fortified port of Rutupiae, to await the right moment for a dash across the pirate-infested Channel. Every mine in Britain belonged to the Emperor, and most of the ore was used in the Imperial workshops and armouries; but for purposes of book-keeping it was convenient to fix its value as it left the Diocese, and this was done in the Treasury of Londinium. In fact, the price of a great many things was fixed in the Provincial Treasury, although for certain classes of goods this was done by the Fiscus at Mediolanum, so that the cost should be the same all over the Oecumene. Sometimes the authorities made a mistake, and the price was found to be uneconomic; this might have led to shortage of goods that were too cheap, but the administration had found a simple remedy. Every occupation necessary to a civilized life was hereditary, from farming to burying the dead; and no one was allowed to change his calling. An increasing proportion of the land was directly farmed by the State, either as the patrimony of some past Emperor or confiscated from an unsuccessful pretender, and the private landowners who remained were so heavily taxed in kind that they were practically in the position of share-croppers. The government took an enormous proportion of each year's income, and in theory saw it was spent in such a manner that the Province remained civilized and solvent. It was a great responsibility for the civil service, and they worked very hard.

But in practice things did not always go according to plan. In the first place, it was impossible to foresee military expenditure, now that all the barbarians in the world were on the march; if a Praeses saved a little money for next year the soldiers just came and took it, since you cannot make a scheme of defence so perfect that it would not be improved by more expenditure. In the second place, production decreased every year. Citizens were reluctant to marry and breed legitimate children, destined to step into their fathers' shoes; it was simpler to live with a slave girl, and produce offspring who could be sold to pay the tax-gatherer. Civilization is only kept in being by unremitting effort, and in the whole Diocese of Britain the citizens seemed to have lost the will to work.

After two hours with his secretary Felix had initialled every urgent paper, and he strolled into the main office to see how his subordinates were getting on. It was a nuisance that Paulinus, the most efficient member of his staff, was a freedman who could not take responsibility; technically he was not a civil servant at all, merely the personal clerk of the Praeses. All officials who had been regularly appointed and were empowered to sign documents were freeborn citizens, and that meant a good deal of work was done twice over. But to-day there was only routine business, which the most junior clerk could deal with; when Felix had done a round of the twenty or thirty desks that administered every activity of the Province of Britannia Prima his work was finished, and it was still only two hours after noon. He could spend the rest of the day bathing and dining, in accordance with the custom of the ancients.

At home he had a quick bath, for he had eaten nothing since his light breakfast at dawn, and though he was accustomed to working on an empty stomach he was always hungry by mid-afternoon. Then he sent to tell his wife he was ready for dinner; the evening could be devoted to social affairs.

The Praeses of a Province was an extremely important official, but of course he was not so well paid as the great nobles who held the more ornamental positions at the top of the service; if he was honest, as Felix was, he could not afford Greek wine and Spanish sausage when he dined alone with his wife. But the cook was a good old-fashioned Italian, and a simple meal was in accordance with the custom of the ancients. As there were no guests Felix reclined comfortably alongside the table, instead of end-on to make room for other couches. His wife, Maria, sat upright on a well-cushioned chair; respectable ladies did not recline at meals.

Maria sat silent, with her eyes on her lap; it was for her husband to begin the conversation, if he wished to talk at dinner. She was a handsome woman of twenty-five, with reddish hair and pale blue eyes; but frequent frowns were beginning to line her face, and the servants trembled as they waited on her. Felix ate his roast pork and cabbage in silence, and did not speak until they had reached dessert.

'My dear, has the household behaved well to-day?' he said at last. The household always did behave well, but it was the recognized opening; now she could talk as much as she wished.

'Everyone is behaving well. I went out in the litter this afternoon, and at the dressmaker's they were talking of nothing but the Irish corsairs on the south coast. A lot of citizens have gone north to get out of their way; do you think we could make an excuse to visit Eburacum?'

'Oh dear, are the local citizens panicking again? They seem much more jumpy in this island than they were in Gaul. But half the time, you know, it isn't genuine fright. They think that if they wander away as refugees the government will lose track of them, and then they can leave their rightful occupation for something less strenuous and better paid.'

'Yes, Caius. But a dressmaker has as good a job as anyone, and he wouldn't take his slave girls on the open road, where they might run away, unless he thought there really was danger. He talked of starting to-morrow, as soon as the gates open.'

'Thank you for the information, my dear. We shall see if Master Anthemius owes anything to the tax-gatherer, before he is allowed to go. But if his papers are in order I can't stop him; a dressmaker is free to change his place of business, so long as he sticks to the same calling. That is one of my handicaps. The Praefect of the Gauls expects me to manage this Province, yet people are allowed to move about.'

Of course, if citizens were free to change their residence it made planning more difficult, and Felix often grumbled about it. But he saw Maria was not listening. She could not keep still in her chair, and her fingers were fidgeting.

'My dear, you are not afraid of these pirates, are you?' he asked with concern. 'We are four days' march from the coast, and Londinium has never been sacked by barbarians.'

'I am afraid,' she answered indignantly, 'and so is everyone else in the city. They don't tell you about it because you think our troops can never be beaten, and anyway you have nothing to do with military affairs. This fleet is commanded by the King of the Irish in person, and you know how they ravaged Valentia and Secunda in the west. If they land a real army by the Sea of Vectis what force is there in the south to stop them? A lot of our soldiers went to Italy three years ago, and the Comes keeps what's left of the cavalry round Eburacum. He will march south when they land, and I suppose they won't face a pitched battle; but will Londinium hold out until he arrives?'

'Really, women don't understand these things,' Felix said as politely as his indignation would allow. 'The walls of this city are extremely strong, and we have regular soldiers in the Praetorium, who will show the citizens how to man them.'

'But I tell you they don't want to man them.' Maria spoke rapidly, with a hysterical note rising in her voice. 'You sit in your office, and read reports and make calculations, and you haven't the slightest idea of what people are thinking. No citizen would face barbarians, even with a wall to help him. Those who have money will take it north, and the humiliores think they will be no worse off under the King of the Irish.'

Felix was shocked. The Emperor was the father and guardian of the humiliores, the lower classes; the civil service spent laborious hours arranging every aspect of their lives so that the feckless creatures should have food, clothing and the amenities of civilization; without such guidance they would soon be wandering naked through the woods, grubbing for acorns. The least they could do in return was to put their brainless strength at the disposal of the Empire when a wall had to be manned. But he knew that his wife was right. She had been born and lived all her life in Londinium, and he often complained that she spent her time gossiping with tradesmen. Yet his duty was clear.

'My dear,' he said stiffly, 'there can be no question of the Praeses leaving the capital of his Province for fear of barbarians, and it would look bad if I sent you to safety alone. Since you seem to be nervous I shall ask the commander of the garrison to arrange lodgings for us in the Praetorium. Perhaps this long circuit of walls cannot be held by untrained citizens, but obviously the soldiers will defend their own fortress. Besides, the pirates will be looking for undefended villas, and won't besiege a strong town. Let us talk of something else. I shall remember what you have told me, and consult your father; you were right to let me know what is in your mind. But the wife of an official should not discuss even the possibility of a Roman defeat.'

Naturally, that killed what little conversation a well-bred wife may hold with her husband after he has done a hard day's work, and soon Maria kissed him good night and went to her own apartments. Felix lingered over his wine, with a book on the table. But he could not settle down to appreciate Vergil (he was trying to write an epitome of the Aeneid in five hundred hexameters, leaving out the supernatural element; it was a poem that had not yet been epitomized, and his version might be approved for use in Christian schools). So the citizens could not be trusted to defend the wall the government built for them! They cared so little for all the work of the civil service that they would not even shoot arrows at barbarians who threatened to destroy civilization in the island! Well, that made no difference to his duty, which was to administer the affairs of his Province until the soldiers took over responsibility. He forgot Vergil, while his mind ranged over the latest figures of the revenue.

It was late when he heard a horseman gallop up to the door. There was a porter on duty all night in this official house, and Felix pulled himself together to receive the messenger. A man who rode at a gallop must carry a message from the army; there was a law against riding fast in narrow streets, and his own subordinates obeyed it; but soldiers never did. Probably it was only a request for extra rations, and it amused the orderly to pretend it was urgent.

But the man who was shown in was a young officer. He looked very stiff and tired, but there was no mud on his armour; of course, he would have reported first to the Praetorium, and they would have looked after him there. No need to offer him more than a cup of wine.

The young man stood at attention, and announced himself formally. 'The Tribune Marcus Julius Naso, sir, with despatches from the Comes Britanniarum to the garrison of Londinium, and an urgent message to the Praeses. Here it is.' He handed over a rolled paper, marked 'Immediate'.

Felix signed the cover, and added the time of receipt. He saw it had been despatched before dawn on the 8th, and now it was only midnight of the 10th. It must be very urgent indeed. When he opened it he recognized the meaning at once, for it was common form. It was the official intimation that his Province was at war, and that military authority was supreme.

'Very well, Tribune. I understand and, of course, I shall

make no difficulties. Is there anything you want me to do at once? No? Then perhaps you will tell me where the war is, and who is attacking us.' Soldiers were always trying to get this state of emergency proclaimed, and they might have bullied that incompetent Comes into issuing it without adequate reason.

'Why, sir, the Irish invasion, of course. The King of the Irish is in the Channel with a numerous fleet. He should land on the south coast any day now, if he hasn't landed already.' The officer seemed surprised.

'You know about these things, and I don't. But there have been Irish at sea ever since I came to Britain, and they seldom come so far east. They raid Secunda, and Valentia; but here in Prima we have all those defences against the Saxons, and they usually leave us alone.'

'Yes, sir, we can repel pirates without bothering the civil authorities. But these aren't wandering Scots; this is their King, with all his army. Perhaps you will let me describe the situation, as we see it in Eburacum.'

'Of course, Tribune Naso. Sit down and have a drink.'

'Thank you, sir. They generally call me Tribune Marcus, by the way; half the army in the north are Julii Nasones. What really worries the Comes is the way troubles come from every direction at once. You know we have been under strength for the last three years, since we sent troops to Italy. We have to rely on King Coroticus and his foederati for the defence of the Wall, and King Cunedda is in charge of Valentia. Now we must mobilize the field army and march south. We can just manage it if everyone does his best, though it will be a tight squeeze. The question is, will these foederate Kings defend their districts, or will they make an alliance with the Irish? Normally they would be afraid of reinforcements from Gaul; but they are well informed of what happens abroad, and they know the whole Army of the West is concentrated in Italy to fight King Radagaisus and his Germans. We can expect no help until that war is finished, and it is just within the bounds of possibility that Stilicho may lose a battle; in which case there would be no Army of the West at all.'

'That is absurd,' Felix put in, hotly. 'Surely our main army can defeat any number of barbarians.'

'Well, there was Adrianople, years ago, when the Divine Valens was slain on the field. You civilians don't realize what a very narrow margin we have.'

'But Stilicho is the greatest general in the world.'

'Yes, he is. That is in our favour. I don't think his army is any better than the Germans; in fact, it is also a German army, most of it. However, I suppose he will conquer again, as he has in the past. But we must keep this Diocese quiet until he can spare troops to reinforce us. That is why the Comes has proclaimed a state of emergency. Automatically the foederate Kings now come under his orders. I have been commanded to withdraw the garrison of Londinium, and of the other cities in Prima and Secunda; they will concentrate to watch Cunedda in Valentia, to see that he stays loyal. You will still have the troops of the Comes Littoris Saxonici, and the citizens must man their walls. Can they be relied on to do that?'

Felix felt his heart turn over; Britain was an exposed Diocese, and pirates who raided and went back to their ships were to be expected every autumn. But this talk of the garrison withdrawing from Prima to concentrate against their own foederati was as though the walls of his house suddenly ceased to keep out the weather. As a youth he had heard of the great defeat at Adrianople, but since then the Goths had been held in Illyricum; it was against nature for the Roman Army to be unequal to its task. All the same, it was the custom of the ancients to hear tales of disaster unmoved, and he answered quietly:

'Oddly enough, my wife, who knows more about the feelings of the local citizens than I, said only this evening that they would not defend the wall. Quite possibly they don't want to. But when the Irish arrive they will have no choice. You can't negotiate with savages, and they will make an effort to defend their property. Whether such an unwilling defence will be successful is another matter. But this is only gossip from my wife; they may be full of the most bloodthirsty resolution, after all. Now you must be very tired. Go and rest in your quarters. In the morning I shall see my father-in-law, the Senator Gratianus; he has lived in Britain all his life, and he knows the local citizens.'

Marcus left, and Felix retired to his bedroom. This intrusion of military affairs into the government of his Province was extremely annoying; he might have to give an opinion about matters of which he was ignorant. But it was absurd to imagine that the Roman Army could be permanently worsted by barbarians. He slept soundly.

Since a Senator was technically an officer of the Republic, senior in rank to any servant of the Emperor, protocol made it impossible for the Praeses to send for Gratianus; accordingly the conference was held at the house of the Senator. When Felix arrived, an hour after sunrise, he found the party assembled. Marcus was there, looking more tired than ever after a very short night's rest, and he had brought T. Flavius Constantinus, commander of the local garrison. Paulinus stood in the background, in case they needed any figures about money or supplies, and the chair was taken by the Senator Tib. Claudius Gratianus, father of Maria.

Gratianus was about fifty-five, the same age as his son-in-law. It was irregular that a Senator should live in Britain, instead of attending the meetings of the Senate in Rome; but as the Senate was never allowed to discuss anything of importance the irregularity did not matter very much. What was much worse was that he should be a Senator at all, and in spite of their relationship it irked Felix every time he thought of it; for Gratianus had been born a Curialis, and had escaped from the expensive obligations of his birth in spite of one of the most stringent laws of the Empire. By rights he should forfeit all his wealth to the Treasury, and go back to the council of his city, where he would be responsible for collecting the taxes of his fellow-citizens. But even an honest Praeses was powerless against the after-effects of civil war. When the Divine Theodosius sent him to this Province he had found the most prominent citizen of Britain in an equivocal position. By methods into which it was better not to inquire too closely, Gratianus had become very rich indeed; Magnus Maximus had conscribed him into the mock Senate which that usurper carried in his train; but he was unquestionably a civilian, he had never worn a sword in his life, and if he had contributed money for the civil war he had been in no position to refuse what was demanded of him. He had quickly recognized the new state of affairs when the tyrant was defeated, and his money had been useful to pay off the local levies. The great Emperor had personally considered the case, and had decided to leave the upstart in possession of his honours; better to allow a little irregularity in the Census than to make enemies of all the prominent men in the island. It was understood that Gratianus would never go to Rome to take the seat to which he was so doubtfully entitled. The later defection of the Magister Militum Arbogastes had hardly caused a ripple in Britain. The provincials continued to send their taxes to Lugdunum, but they had accepted with relief the verdict of the Battle of the Frigidus, which restored them to the undivided Empire. During this second usurpation Gratianus had behaved correctly. He had subscribed to the forced loans, but as a civilian he could do nothing else. He had again been confirmed in his rank.

He must either be broken, and his property confiscated, or Britannia Prima must be governed with his assistance. Felix was poor, yet he wished to be honest, and if he was not to take bribes he must marry money. Gratianus, a widower, had an only daughter. It had seemed a stroke of genius for the Praeses to marry Maria; a government that was too weak to enforce its laws appeared to break them for family reasons.

It had worked fairly well up to now; Gratianus knew that he had been very well treated, and he went out of his way to help the Praeses and the rightful Emperor. His wide knowledge, not only of Britain but of surrounding barbarian lands, was at the disposal of the government, and he had once or twice delated dangerously popular officers or influential landowners to the agentes in rebus, the political police. It was unfortunate that he always knew what was wanted from him before he was asked, but he was firmly on the right side. Now he opened the meeting.

'Good morning, lord Praeses. These officers want to know whether in my opinion the citizens will make a stout defence against the pirates; and my answer is No. But that does not mean they are on the side of the Irish against the government. I should put it this way: they none of them like the government, but most of them don't like the Irish, either. When the pirates appear outside the city you must hunt up the respectable shopkeepers, good guildsmen with a little property to protect. They won't volunteer to fight, and they won't be very good at it, but they don't want to see their homes plundered. Put them on the wall where they make a good show, and perhaps the Irish won't dare to attack. Of course, if they do the shopkeepers will run away, but you may hold the city by bluff. With your permission I shall move my wealth, and, of course, the provincial archives as well, into the Praetorium. We can hold that little fortress when the town has fallen. Then we must make up our minds what to do next. Perhaps there will be an army of relief, or perhaps we can buy the retreat of the barbarians. It may be that King Cunedda will send his foederati when he sees a Roman army on his borders, but I don't really know the feeling in the west.'

So the Senator knew already that the garrison was to march out and where they were going; he always knew every state secret, which was why it was a good thing to call him into conference and show him that he was trusted.

The garrison commander spoke next. He was a middle-aged man with no manners, who had obviously risen from the ranks; but at least he was not a barbarian. 'That's right. The citizens won't fight, and anyway the wall will fall down if an Irishman gives it a dirty look; to my certain knowledge it hasn't been repaired for thirty years. But my savings are inside the Praetorium, and I have seen to it that the stakes are sharp, and the bank steep. A few of you can hold that, if you are in earnest about it. I shall leave you a dozen veterans, unfit for long marches, to show you the routine of holding a fort in the face of the enemy. Relieve the sentries punctually; don't trust anyone else to do it, but see for yourself; otherwise there's nothing in it. One other point. My men may not want to leave for the West, since they look on Londinium as their home. Remember they are only limitanei, second-line troops for sedentary garrison duty. It would put us all in an awkward position if they refused to march.'

Every man at the table stiffened and looked up keenly. Constantinus might talk of his men refusing to obey orders, but, of course, a mutiny would involve more than that; when soldiers disobeyed the orders of their superiors they could only save themselves from the death penalty by setting up another Emperor; this was a hint of approaching civil war.

Civil war, or the threat of it, had been almost the normal condition of the Empire since the death of Nero, more than three hundred years ago; civil war had made Gratianus a Senator, and Felix a Praeses; the officers could remember Magnus Maximus and Arbogastes, and all the desperate fighting in the eastern Alps; like other soldiers and government servants, they had been compelled to choose a side when the Empire was divided. But nobody likes to choose sides suddenly, on the spur of the moment and without adequate information, as they must do if an Emperor were proclaimed in Londinium during the next few days. Gratianus replied smoothly:

'Limitanei never like marching; that is well known. But we shall make things easy for them. Luckily we have a solvent Treasury here in the city. Pay them up to date, send their wives and baggage ahead, and don't allow them time to think it over. They will be marching away from the enemy. Besides, there is no one in the neighbourhood who would make a suitable Emperor; Tribune Marcus is a stranger, and you, Constantinus, if you will forgive me, lack the flamboyance of a leader of revolt. Let us forget politics, and assume that the troops will obey orders.'

Paulinus produced a list of leading citizens, and they settled down to discuss how these unwilling men could be induced to defend their property. One trouble was that by the settled policy of the State no man of local influence was allowed to join the army or receive military training; even the guilds were so closely supervised that their leaders had no chance to display initiative. The citizens were treated as machines to produce taxes and obey regulations; it was difficult to regard them as potential heroes. But Gratianus was acquainted with everybody, and Constantinus had a sound knowledge of the neglected defences; Felix left it to them, though Marcus had to show his superiority by raising a few objections. At last they drew up a provisional list of possible leaders, and it was agreed that the garrison should remain for one more day, to push them into their stations on the wall.

That morning the Treasury was closed, for the clerks were one of the most reliable sections of the population; they had been formed into a unit to defend the North Gate. Felix spent the afternoon standing about, uncomfortably trussed in a breastplate, watching his subordinates learn their places in the ranks. Constantinus managed his difficult task well; he was not a particularly intelligent officer, but he had trained a great many recruits in his time. Everyone felt a tremendous moral superiority in standing on top of the wall, looking towards open country; the wall itself seemed much higher than from below; it was quite possible the citizens would make a good defence after all.

The Praeses was more worried about the risk of a rebellion led by the local garrison than about the threatened barbarian attack. Barbarians were always attacking prosperous cities; sometimes they sacked them, though they were always driven away in the end. But a civil war now would be disastrous.

Felix had begun at the bottom of the ladder. Though his ancestors, the Sempronii, had served the State in Africa since the days of Julius Caesar, his father had been only a junior clerk in the Treasury of Mauretania Tingitensis, the westerly Province that was administered as part of the Praefecture of the Gauls. There he had sat at a desk, collecting taxes and forwarding them to the western Treasury at Lugdunum, not caring which soldier had the spending of them as Emperor in the West. He was honest, for an official, but when his only son came of age he could buy him a place in the Treasury at Lugdunum, which was a rise in the social scale. That was thirty-five years ago, when Valentinianus was Emperor; but the talk in Gaul had been of Theodosius, the great Magister Militum, who was driving the Picts from Britain. Felix had seen him as he passed through the city on his way to a ceremonial welcome at Mediolanum, returning with his troops to render account to the Senate and People like some Triumphator of old.

The effect on Felix had been almost that of a religious conversion. Previously he had written minutes and made up accounts mechanically, because that was the way his ancestors had earned their bread; now he felt himself part of the majesty and dominion of Rome. Henceforth Theodosius was his master, whoever ruled in the Sacred Palace; and this devotion was transferred, on the death of the great soldier, to his son and namesake; for no true Roman could love the Sacred Gratianus, friend and patron of barbarians, who had succeeded his father as Emperor in the West. When Magnus Maximus rebelled and slew Gratianus, he had been tepidly pleased that a regular soldier had replaced that exotic and untraditional young man; but as a servant of the Empire he could not be enthusiastic for a rough warrior who seemed content that Rome should be permanently severed from the East. After he had worked for eighteen years at his desk, doing what he was told without expressing political opinions, in 388 he heard that his young hero had moved; then he had, very bravely, taken a side. He had been able to lay his hands on a large sum of money destined to pay the troops; he fled with it, and lay hidden in a Gallic forest until after the great battle on the Frigidus; Theodosius the

Younger was victorious, but quite possibly the battle would have gone the other way if that money had been in the pay-chest of the Western Army. When Valentinianus II was set up again in the West Felix had come out of hiding and handed over his treasure. Theodosius had rewarded him with a post in the Sacra Largitio, the travelling treasury of the Emperor; Felix journeyed all over the eastern parts of the Empire in his master's train, and fell all the more in love with the intricate and never-resting Imperial machine when he saw it working among the wealthy and cultured cities of Asia. In 392 came the rebellion of Arbogastes, Magister Militum per Gallias, and his puppet the pagan Eugenius. When Theodosius marched to avenge the murdered Valentinianus it was as the protector of Christianity, the official religion of the Empire, and Felix decided that it was his duty as a loyal Theodosian to undergo the ceremony of baptism; of course, he had been brought up to worship the Genius of Rome, and especially the Lares of the Gens Sempronia; but though it was his duty to worship them he was also an educated man, and no one expected him to believe in their existence. Now he must go to church on Sundays and repeat that version of the Creed which was in favour at Imperial headquarters; he continued to believe in nothing but Rome and Civilization, and the Stoic duty to aid mankind.

He accompanied Theodosius on his last Gallic campaign, and when the great Emperor died in his bed a year later he was returned to the staff of his original Praefecture. This was his tenth year as Praeses of the wealthiest Province of Britain, and practically its chief ruler; for the Vicariate was a sinecure, held by an indolent noble in Gaul.

During those ten years his chief problem had been the danger of civil war. Britain was a tempting Diocese for a military pretender; the soldiers, whose ancestors had been stationed in the island for anything up to three hundred years, felt themselves as much British as Roman; any insurgent could count on about a year before troops from the Continent could be mobilized and ferried across the Channel, and the civil population had a tiresome tradition that they had been prosperous under the rule of Carausius long ago, because the money they paid in taxation stayed at home. In any case, men of spirit and ambition looked forward to civil war as the only means of climbing to the top of the tree. Felix himself would have remained a clerk at Lugdunum if he had not chosen a side in 388. But now he had climbed, and he did not want any storms to shake the branches.

So he stood on the wall, watching his clerks trying to bend their bows, and hoping that the feel of a weapon in the hand would not give them dangerous ambitions.

At sunset, when the drill ceased, Felix invited Constantinus into the Treasury for a drink, and to discuss their chance of withstanding the threatened assault. He thought it imprudent to speak to an officer, even such a junior and elderly officer as Constantinus, about the danger of revolt. But the latter guessed what would be in the mind of an official who had been watching armed civilians.

'Those pen-pushers of yours will be glad to finish this job, and get back to their leather cushions. It must be a long time since any of them spent a whole afternoon on his feet. They won't take their swords into politics. Neither will the citizens, at least those who have received arms from the Praetorium. But I was looking up in the regulations how you ought to go about arming the citizens of a threatened town, and it says you should consult the Curia. I inquired for the Curia of Londinium, and they tell me there isn't one. I've lived in garrison here for years and never noticed that before, which shows I keep clear of politics. But why is it?'

Felix frowned. It was an irregularity that worried his tidy mind.

'I noticed it as soon as I came here,' he replied, 'and I recommended that one should be set up at once. I have to deal with the individual taxpayers myself, instead of making up any deficit from the Curiales, as we did in Gaul. But the authorities at Lugdunum referred the matter to Mediolanum, and I have not yet received a definite answer; it was only eight years ago, and these things have to be looked at from every side. The reason is interesting historically, though, of course, it results in a tiresome anomaly. This city was never founded, and from the administrative point of view it ought not to exist. Eburacum is the chief town of the Diocese, and Camolodunum of the Province of Prima. That is how things were arranged when the island was brought into the Empire. But Londinium was a market when the Divine Claudius landed, and it has continued to grow. This is an untidy Diocese, and the people delight in upsetting the plans we make for their welfare. In law Londinium is nothing but a prosperous village. But there it is. I hope I am right in recognizing its existence.'

'Odd,' said Constantinus, looking hard at the wine-jar, and twirling his empty cup. 'Civil affairs have nothing to do with me, but the Army recognizes it as a city. Why, we have a whole numerus in garrison, six hundred men. That's as many as you get in any one place, now we are so under strength.'

'When Radagaisus has been chased out of Italy our troops will be sent back immediately. Things are working up to a climax over there, and the campaign must end soon.' Felix said this soothingly; every day he had to comfort someone about those missing soldiers, and he was getting rather tired of it. It was wrong, in any case, that he should have to remind an officer of the exigencies of the military situation; but every soldier hated to see his own army diminished by reinforcements to another part of the Empire.

'Will you lead out the garrison to-morrow?' he continued. 'My clerks are not very efficient with their weapons, but I don't suppose one more day will make them any better.'

'To-morrow evening. I shall give the order in the morning; it would be foolish to tell them to-night, when they have hours to get drunk in the taverns and prepare a revolt. I shall announce it at the morning parade, then they can spend the day loading baggage and get a few miles beyond the walls by dark. The officers will be free to help your civilians most of the day.' Constantinus was taking the whole thing calmly; he spoke of the chance of revolt as though it was never out of his thoughts, but did not worry him. Without changing his tone he continued: 'I should be honoured if you would sup at the Praetorium this evening; I shall invite the Senator, and perhaps the Lady Maria could come also. I am handing over the defence of the city to the civil authorities. It is only right they should consult with the officer commanding.'

Felix looked worried; but after a moment the slight frown left his face, and he accepted with a smile. If they heard at the Praefecture that he had been supping with an officer in command of troops they would suspect him of plotting treason; for one of the strictest rules of the Imperial Government was that there should be no contact between soldiers and civilian officials. But he would write at once, and get in his explanation before he was suspected; they knew him for a loyal Theodosian, promoted for his loyalty. He called his litter, and went home to tell Maria to cancel their own supper.

*

Londinium was essentially a walled market containing government offices, and had never been an important military centre. The Praetorium was only a small enclosure in the south-eastern corner of the wall, protected by a ditch and a stockaded bank; it contained wooden huts for a thousand men and a small brick building, the Praetorium proper, the office and quarters of the officer commanding. Felix had never been inside, in all the years he had been Praeses of the Province, and he looked about him with interest as the big family litter was borne through the gate in the palisade. It was dark, two hours after the lingering September sunset of this northern Province, and the huts were unlighted, for the troops mostly spent the evening in the farms round the city that had been assigned for their support. Two torches streamed in the rising wind outside the brick building and nearly scorched him as he descended backwards from the litter. That was typical of the army; they lived in one place all their lives and treated it as a camp they would leave to-morrow; no one had yet got around to fixing proper lanterns before the door.

But the house was warm and well lighted inside, quite surprisingly civilized for the dwelling of an uncouth soldier. The guests were lined up to be presented to the ruler of the Province, and Constantinus had put on his decorations as though this were an official ceremony. There were present the Senator Gratianus, Marcus Julius Naso, evidently waiting in Londinium until his orders had actually been carried out, G. Flavius Constans the son of Constantinus, and Paulinus the freedman from the Treasury. No gentleman would have invited a freedman to supper; it was embarrassing for Felix, his official chief and the representative of his previous owner; but soldiers could be relied on to make these blunders when they tried to move in society.

So there were six couches and a chair for the lady, quite enough for a supper party that intended to talk business. Three couches filled a table, and Maria had a smaller table to herself, since there was no other lady present. The footmen were clean and well dressed, and the food, though rather too lavish, was good and well cooked. Altogether Felix was relieved to find the party less uncouth than he had feared.

At first they talked commonplaces, but soon the wine bowl was placed before Constantinus and the slaves withdrew. Then Gratianus broached the serious business of the evening. 'Marcus, you have seen our preparations for defence, and you are a stranger with a fresh eye. Do you think we can hold the city?'

'That's very hard to answer,' said the young officer, though there was no doubt in his voice. 'You have plenty of men, and enough armour to make a good show. These Irish are utter savages, knowing nothing of siege-craft. They may decide the wall is too strong for them, and go away without trying an attack. That is looking on the bright side. Or they may feel fierce, and willing to try anything, since there is no accounting for barbarians. If they make an escalade I suppose they will get in, for your men won't really fight when it comes to the point. That is the worst that can happen. But neither is likely. These barbarians want plunder, not fighting; probably they will hang about and ask for a ransom. Then you keep them talking until we have persuaded the western foederati to move, and when Cunedda comes up they will retire to their ships. Cunedda has beaten the Irish before, and he's not afraid of them.'

'That seems reasonable,' said the Senator. 'We can keep them talking a long time; barbarian armies have dozens of leaders, and each one has to be consulted separately. If Cunedda won't come up to scratch, for some barbarian reason of his own, there is money in the city to buy them off honestly, though it will leave us poor.'

It was like Gratianus, Felix reflected, to discuss serious affairs of State in metaphors drawn from cock-fighting; 'come up to scratch' indeed! The Emperor's foederate allies must do as they were told, or feel the weight of the Roman sword. But his father-in-law had no fine feelings; he deliberately used low expressions to deflate a serious subject.

'You talk as though the Irish had only to beach their ships and march here along the main road,' he said angrily. 'What will the Comes Littoris Saxonici be doing while this goes on? We pay to support enormous defences on the coast, and when invasion comes you soldiers assume the barbarians will march straight through them.'

'My lord Praeses,' said Constantinus, trying to keep the conversation on the plane of a formal discussion between civil and military authorities. 'Londinium is not part of the Littus Saxonicum, or I would not take orders from the Comes Britanniarum. The forts on the coast were built against raids from the east, and their Comes cannot leave his territory undefended and march to our assistance without direct orders from higher authority. The Comes Britanniarum is senior in rank, but I don't think he has the power to give him direct orders. Probably he could refuse, and refer the whole matter to the Magister Militum.'

'I'm not sure of that,' put in Marcus. 'The Comes Britanniarum is the highest military authority in Britain. At least that is what we think at Eburacum. But he may be reluctant to give orders that would be queried. It would be an unnecessary humiliation, and might cause bad blood between the two headquarters.'

'Good God!' said Felix, who often lost his temper with military men; he had a theory that they never listened to a civilian unless he shouted and blustered. 'Good God! Do you mean to tell me there is no undisputed head of the Army of Britain? How can Stilicho plan a campaign here when he is busy fighting in Italy? I shall complain to the Praefect of the Gauls that there is no military officer for the Praeses to deal with.'

'My dear Caius,' said Gratianus, 'the military affairs of the Empire have been arranged as they are, deliberately and after much thought. The Praefecture might think it odd if the governor of one Province has intimate dealings with the army.'

A Senator was a greater man than a Praeses, and a father-in-law can always snub the husband of his daughter. Felix subsided at the hint that the Praefect of the Gauls might suspect him of ambition.

Marcus summed up, in the flippant tone he had caught from Gratianus. In spite of Constantinus, the conference was becoming very informal, and slightly disaffected. 'It would be much easier to defend this island if all the soldiers obeyed one commander; it would also be much easier for that commander to make himself Emperor, so the Magister Militum has provided otherwise. My Comes has given orders which will be obeyed here in Londinium, but we know the limits to his power. Cunedda and Coroticus must be persuaded, or threatened, before they fall in with his wishes, and he is reluctant to give the Comes Littoris Saxonici a chance to appeal to higher authority. It means that we have three separate armies, counting the Dux in the north. Things were easier when I was a child.'

'My dear Marcus,' said Gratianus, with a grin, 'you have dared to say what is in the hearts of a great many civilians. The Divine Theodosius was a better man than Magnus Maximus of evil memory; a better man, a better soldier, and a much better ruler. But things *were* easier when you were a child. An Emperor of Britain alone, or even an Emperor of the Gauls, would defend us with more success than a Magister Militum who is working night and day to keep the Germans out of Italy. Do you think, Caius, that if we sent a united petition to the Praefect of the Gauls, and got that idle Vicarius to back it, they would appoint a Caesar to rule the Diocese? We are in real danger from the barbarians, and we ought to have an undisputed head.'

'I dissociate myself from that,' said Felix firmly. 'This Diocese has a record of rebellion, and it would seem disloyal to the sons of the Divine Theodosius. I was born in Africa, and I never knew Britain under an Emperor of its own. But remember how it always ends. The ruler of Britain is never content; sooner or later he takes his army to Gaul, and then on to Italy if he is successful; in the end Britain is worse defended than before.'

'And the taxes are very much higher, to satisfy the soldiers!' Paulinus added, now that his chief had given a lead. He knew the situation of the Province better than anybody, but plans for the future did not interest him. Whoever ruled in Londinium he would remain chief clerk of the Treasury, because his experience was irreplaceable; but he had already climbed as high as a freedman could, and he took no interest in politics.

Marcus brought this conversation back to reality. 'Then I can tell the Comes that the citizens will man the wall,' he said in a businesslike voice. 'But you think if the barbarians try an assault it will be successful. If you are blockaded you will negotiate, and ultimately offer money. So we can take our time raising the army of relief, and inflict a really crushing defeat on the invaders. That fits in with our plans.'

Felix rose to go. It was absurdly early to break up a supper party; but the sooner he got away the better. The Imperial Government was right to look with disfavour on intercourse between civilian and military officials; they could not meet, even to discuss the most urgent affairs, without talking treason. Maria and Paulinus went with him. It left Gratianus with the three soldiers, and they would undoubtedly consider among themselves whether the Diocese would be better off under an Emperor of its own. But what soldiers discussed was the concern of the military authorities, and the Senator, with his record of past disloyalty and his great wealth, would not dare to compromise himself.

Outside the weather had worsened. The wind had risen to a howling gale, and a light rain drove horizontally against the curtains of the litter. Felix spoke only once, to compliment Maria on her manners. Throughout the supper she had not opened her mouth except to eat and drink, which was how a lady should behave in the presence of strange gentlemen.

Next morning the gale, which had been strong enough to dislodge roof-tiles, subsided into heavy rain. This weather was unfortunate, for the troops would be reluctant to set out. Presumably they had received their orders at the morning parade, and if they made a disturbance, rumour of it would soon reach the Treasury. But all seemed quiet, and after reading a few urgent papers Felix gave orders that the staff should once more muster by the North Gate with the arms they had received yesterday.

Marcus was there to give another period of instruction, and everyone seemed willing and even rather gay. It was exciting to be out of doors in such an appalling storm, and rather pleasant to peacock about in breastplate and shield before the frightened refugees. For country people were beginning to come in, even from the north. There was a solid column of ox-carts and pack-mules pressing through the gate, and the wet and bedraggled families that walked beside them were directed to camp in the north-western corner of the city, where there was waste ground.

Marcus was worried by the number of refugees.

'This is something I didn't allow for,' he said to Felix in an undertone, while the clerks were throwing javelins at a dummy scaling ladder. 'The baggage and families of the Barcarii Tigridenses are due to march north before sunset, and there will be a nasty mix-up at the gate. They may even take fright, and refuse to march at the last minute. Up north the country people usually hide on the moors when raiders are about, instead of crowding behind walls.'

Felix saw an opportunity to boast of his Province.

'Londinium has never been sacked by barbarians. Besides, our coloni have goods to be saved as well as their lives. But there will not be many more from the north. The walls of Verulamium are only fourteen miles away. We shall only get the peasants from six or seven miles round, and if they started at cock-crow they will be inside by midday. I expect the Bridge will be crowded until the barbarians appear, for there are few cities beyond the river. But the northern districts are well fortified.'

Marcus grunted absent-mindedly, but one point in his previous speech had caught the attention of the Praeses.

'Who did you say would march out? What is the name of the numerus?' he asked.

'What? The Barcarii Tigridenses? Second-rate limitanei; infantry with bows and light armour. They were on the Wall before we handed it over to King Coroticus.'

'But surely they are not boatmen from the Tigris?' Felix persisted.

'Of course not. Their ancestors were, three hundred years ago. But a numerus never changes its name. Their standard-bearer wears Persian costume in full dress, and they have a regimental dance that has been handed down from the original boatmen. But by now they are just as British as I am, and I am pure Brigantian. Their ancestors did not bring women from Mesopotamia.'

Felix had hoped that this numerus might really come from the eastern parts of the Empire, which was more loyal to the House of Theodosius than the West. He might have known, he told himself, that its exotic name was only part of the elaborate make-believe which the Army took so seriously. Also he did not like to be reminded that the Wall was now in the hands of barbarian foederati.

'Were they willing to march when they got their orders this morning?' he asked politely, to change the subject.

'Oh yes, most obedient and well behaved. The older ones, who usually start trouble when they have to move, are not really settled here. Their homes were in the north.'

Felix edged away, to end the conversation. In this emergency he always seemed to be talking to soldiers in public; already every secret agent in the city would be reporting his suspicious behaviour.

The refugees from the north were all inside the gate when the baggage-train of the garrison prepared to march out, and everything worked smoothly. Felix was surprised to see such a large column. According to Marcus the numerus was between five and six hundred strong, but their families made up about four thousand persons. That must be looked into. Soldiers, and their sons who would become soldiers, as well as their daughters who must marry soldiers, were exempt from direct taxation; but they were not supposed to take servants from among the industrious classes. In peace time the Treasury would have been entitled to check the military status of everyone in the column; but with the emergency regulations in force the army was probably taking the opportunity to gather unauthorized recruits.

An hour before sunset the convoy was clear of the gate, and Marcus took leave of the Praeses to join the garrison on its march. Felix remained at his post, with a few of the more imposing clerks, to give a salute and close the gate when they had withdrawn. It was then that the news came.

First, there was a stir and a muttering in the south, where the endless throng of frightened peasants still pressed across the Bridge. Paulinus came quickly to his master, with his sword drawn and a posse of German slaves behind him. (Paulinus was the most competent assistant he had, but he could not command free men.) They both listened anxiously to the tumult which was spreading northward through the city. Perhaps the humiliores were starting to plunder as the government's forces withdrew? In that case they had started too soon, and the numerus must be turned back to teach them a lesson. Yet the strange murmur was not the angry roar of a riot. It reminded Felix of the cheers when Theodosius the Comes led his victorious army through Lugdunum, long ago. That was the last time he had heard a crowd rejoice, for nowadays good news was rare. Then he saw an orderly riding up the empty North Street, while behind him citizens ran out of their houses shouting and cheering. The messenger, a trooper from a strange regiment, trotted up (much too fast for the streets of a city), and halted with a savage jerk at the mouth of his unfortunate horse.

'Greeting, lord Praeses,' he called, in the cheeky tone so many soldiers used to a civil servant; he was grinning all over his face in a disrespectful manner. 'Message from the commander of the garrison at Venta to the Comes Britanniarum, repeated, for information only, to the civil authority in Britannia Prima. The Irish fleet was destroyed by the storm, at the entrance to the Sea of Vectis. Prisoners say their King was drowned, and what ships remain are returning to Ireland.'

He gave a most unmilitary whoop of joy, and galloped up the North Road to spread the good news to Verulamium and beyond.

Felix turned to Paulinus, with no emotion on his face; he was once more an ancient Roman receiving good news and bad with equal fortitude. 'Tell the clerks to hand in their weapons and armour at the Praetorium, and get a proper receipt for each article. In view of the late hour I shall not open the office to-day, but they must be at their desks in good time to-morrow, sober, clean, and in civilian clothes. I should be pleased if they would join me in the church, where I shall give thanks for our deliverance and pray for the safety of the Empire. But that is not an order.'

In his heart Felix still thought the true guardians of Rome were Jupiter Optimus Maximus and Venus Genetrix, mother of the Julii; but the Divine Theodosius had been head of the Christian party against the pagans, and a loyal Theodosian must give thanks according to the Christian ritual. The new religion had started as an anti-Roman movement, but now the Emperors and the majority of their subjects were Christians while all barbarians were pagan; if you looked at it like that the Church could be considered an Imperial institution.

He saw, as he walked home, that the citizens intended to celebrate their marvellous deliverance all night; people would be dropping into the church at any hour, and he need not go there until he had bathed and eaten.

It was nearly midnight when he set out in the family litter, Maria by his side; as her name implied, she came of a Christian family and had been baptized in infancy; he relied on her example and guidance in what to him was still a strange environment. The city gates had been left open through the night, that the refugees might start for home as quickly as possible; besides refugees, a number of citizens were passing out of the West Gate, on their way to the church. Felix was set down at the west door, and entered the building quietly and unostentatiously, leaving his servants outside with the litter.

The Church of St Augulus, Bishop and Martyr, stood beyond the western wall of Londinium in open country. It was a large brick building, without architectural pretensions; although within it was as gorgeous as the bad taste and limited means of the clergy could make it, and Felix, who had seen Constantinople and Mediolanum, shuddered every time he entered. Luckily, the Christians could not afford the very expensive and laborious task of covering the walls with mosaic, and the colours of the wall painting were beginning to fade.

A choir was singing in a gallery while a priest read from a holy book, his voice drowned by the music. Felix led his wife up the nave and sat down in one of the carved chairs reserved for important officials. He hoped that at that late hour the leading clergy would be in bed, and that he could show his gratitude for the deliverance of the Province, and his support for the official religion of the Empire, without a tiresome interview.

He intended to stay for an hour, to set a proper example to his clerks. But he had only been in his seat ten minutes when the Bishop emerged from the vestry door, accompanied by his deacon. Felix groaned; the pompous old man must have been lying in wait for him.

Maria went down on one knee as the Bishop stood over them. This was really making too much of him; Felix half-rose from his chair, and promptly sat down again, leaving the Bishop to stand. His wife blushed, looked from her husband to her spiritual pastor, then sat down also. But the Bishop was used to snubs from the secular power and did not retire in a huff, as Felix had hoped. On the contrary, raising his voice above the noise of the choir, he began to complain of his injured dignity.

'Lord Praeses, I have been insulted by the military authorities, and neglected by your subordinates. I wish to make a formal protest. When we heard the Irish were coming I approached the commander of the garrison, that this church might be protected from the barbarians. I received what I can only describe as a frivolous answer, suggesting that I sprinkle holy water on the Irish pagans, since it was well known that holy water burned devil-worshippers as though it were boiling oil; or that if I wished to leave the city with the numerus they would put one cart and one riding mule at my disposal. I at once applied to the Treasury, as the civil power seemed to be taking over the defence. I received a written answer, as was proper. But it was signed by a freedman, one Paulinus, which is not in accordance with the dignity of my office; and it merely offered me a breastplate and sword if I wished to use them, or a vacant plot by the North Gate where I might pitch a tent during the siege. I inquired whether you had person-ally considered my letter, and this same Paulinus answered, in a scribble on a wax note-book, that since you and your staff were taking over the North Gate you could not spare time to give instructions to the clergy. That was irregular in two important aspects. In the first place, as Bishop I am a vir spectabilis (though humble and unworthy); my letters should be answered by a senior official, not by a freedman. In the second place, although the Church obeys the Sacred Emperor, we are not humiliores to receive and carry out instructions from the Praeses. We are, in our temporal aspect, a branch of the Imperial administration, bound only by our own laws. I must have a formal undertaking, under your signature, that the Bishop of Londinium will in future be consulted in all things that concern the defence of the city; otherwise I shall be compelled to forward my complaint to Mediolanum.'

Felix had stretched his face into an expression of sorrow at the misplaced humour of the soldiery, and concern at the breach of etiquette in his own office. Inwardly he was raging at the pomposity of this silly old man; but he was an experienced official, and he knew that anyone who was fluent on paper and not overawed by high rank could cause an infinity of bother to a government department. To-morrow he must compose a graceful apology, on the best paper, in which he would promise to consult the Bishop on all matters concerning the city. Then he would carefully lose the office copy, so that it could not be brought up as a precedent next time. Now he must pacify the old nuisance by word of mouth, and he was not as ready with his tongue as with a pen.

But Maria, a Christian from infancy, came to his rescue. 'Holy father,' she said, 'don't take it to heart that ribald soldiers and freedmen mock your sacred office. Why worry about the command you should hold in a siege, when by your prayers the city is delivered before the gates are closed? Were you not praying all yesterday before God's altar, and did not the winds arise and scatter His enemies? My husband will write an official account to the Bishop of Rome, explaining that Londinium owes its safety to your supplications.'

The Bishop preened himself, and looked at his deacon with a satisfied air. 'We spent the hours of danger in prayer before the altar,' he said in a more friendly tone, 'and it is possible our humble petition reached the ear of the Almighty. But it would be presumptuous and over-weening if I wrote that to Italy myself.'

The deacon intervened to clinch the bargain. 'I would

suggest,' he said smoothly, 'that if the Praeses will write an account of what actually happened, properly sealed and witnessed, the Bishop, from the overflowing charity of his heart, will wipe out all recollection of the discourtesies he suffered.'

The Bishop blessed his faithful subjects and retired to bed. Felix remained in the church a few minutes longer, sitting in his chair while Maria knelt beside him. Then he too went out, after glancing round to see how many Treasury clerks had the good manners to come as he had suggested. In the litter he thanked Maria for her intervention.

'You were quick-witted and tactful with that old windbag, my dear. I did not have your upbringing, and I would never think of that way of dealing with him. The trouble is that though he stands on his dignity he is not avaricious, and it's no good offering him money. The law excuses him most of his taxes, so I can't even let him off those. Yet if he complained to Mediolanum he could make himself a great nuisance. You have been very helpful, and I would like to show my gratitude. Would you like to visit the goldsmith to-morrow, and choose a not too expensive bracelet?'

'Dear Caius, that would be lovely,' she answered, with the appealing and submissive look of a dutiful wife (she had very good manners, for a provincial). 'But there is another reward I would like even more. I know a young man, in fact he's a distant cousin, C. Flavius Valens. He is a shipowner, and he wants to marry the daughter of a Curialis of Camolodunum. Both families approve, but of course it is against the law. Could you give them permission, to please me?'

'H'm, I suppose your father put you up to this. As you say, it is utterly against the law, one of the fundamental laws of the Empire. Curiales must be succeeded by their sons, or where would the taxes come from? And those sons must wed the daughters of other Curiales, for no one else would allow his daughter to marry into such a depressed occupation. Shipowning is also a hereditary calling, though as a rule those concerned are fairly willing to stick to it. But you did me a service, and it will bring you respect if people see you can reward your friends. Let them marry, and the Treasury will take no action while I rule this Province. You understand I cannot give them formal permission to break the law, but I shall not prosecute. Tell them to be married in church, by the Bishop, and to make sure there is a written record. Then they will have the support of the clergy if another Praeses tries to separate them. Of course, sooner or later someone will pay a fine for such a serious offence. But that may not come for several generations.'

One of the difficulties of his office was that the law was too severe to be kept in its entirety; he must continually make exceptions, or the whole system would break down. Yet his decision was never final. In theory a Praeses had no discretion, and any case where he had omitted to inflict a punishment could be reopened to the end of time. But a wise official accepted that his predecessor probably had a good reason for leniency; the only way of running a Province was to create a privileged class, loyal friends of the administration, who used their influence to make others obey the law and were themselves excused obedience as a reward.

In his lonely bedroom Felix worried himself to sleep. He could not afford a gold bracelet for his wife, but the favour he had allowed her instead was also expensive. It was all very difficult. The Imperial Government was not as powerful as it pretended to be; he could admit that to himself, as he lay in bed alone, though in public he must conceal it always. By enforcing the division of labour, which meant making nearly every occupation strictly hereditary, he kept in being a rather poor sort of civilization in this fundamentally barbarous Province. Round the Mediterranean the citizens co-operated, partly because they were used to doing as they were told, partly because they wanted the services of bakers and mine-workers, though they preferred those services to be rendered by someone else. But in Britain, even in this settled Province of the south, the inhabitants would be quite content to fall back into barbarism; if his restraining hand were withdrawn they would settle down in self-supporting farmsteads, baking their own bread and weaving their own wool, while the mines fell into decay, letters were forgotten, and no taxes reached the central administration to pay the soldiers on whom all depended. He was continually struggling against passive obstruction, and he had only grudging and reluctant support from the Comes at Eburacum. The Emperor felt more secure if military and civilian officials were at loggerheads, and the government at Mediolanum never interfered to settle a dispute finally in favour of one or the other. The actual soldiers in the ranks, though soldiering was a hereditary calling, were allied by ties of blood and long acquaintance with the peasants who paid the taxes, and could not be trusted to harry them thoroughly. Only once had Felix, after several humiliating applications to the Comes, sent out a numerus to collect arrears of tribute. The soldiers deliberately slowed up their march so that the coloni could get away; then they burned the crops, against orders; in the end the Treasury had been out of pocket after paying the expenses of the raid.

Every government official who had anything to do with finance usually worried himself to sleep; but if he had not the habit of waking up in a cheerful mood he would long ago have gone mad. Felix entered the Treasury next morning with a pleasant smile, for things were better than they had been. The last of the refugees were leaving the city, to go back to their farms and grow corn to pay the taxes; the weather had improved after the storm; and there was no sign of military activity. He actually whistled and rubbed his hands as he greeted Paulinus.

But the freedman, with less responsibility, was still unhappy. 'This emergency has spoilt the estimates,' he explained. 'The Barcarii Tigridenses seized all the ox-carts and baggage mules in the neighbourhood and put the expense down to us. Their baggage actually left the city, although they themselves were stopped in time; it will take weeks and months to get all this transport returned to its rightful owners. Apart from that, the flight and return of the refugees will mean no work done on the land for ten days. I tell you again, sir, this Province cannot pay its assessment after the soldiers have proclaimed an emergency and laid hands on all the ready cash.'

Felix was still feeling cheerful, and he brushed this aside. 'We can borrow from the Senator Gratianus for current expenses. He is a member of my family, and his past record would condemn him if we complained to Mediolanum that he did not help us when he could. If there are disputes among the coloni as to who owned the animals seized by the army that is not really a bad thing. Get these peasants into court, whether as plaintiffs or defendants, and it's surprising what arrears of taxation you can get out of them. And don't complain about the soldiers putting into force the regulations for an emergency. This is the first time it has happened in this Province since I came here. Now in Illyricum they've had it for thirty years.'

Paulinus withdrew, still grumbling, and Felix sat at his desk, thinking idly about the future. He realized, with some surprise, that he was feeling happy and confident, as he had not felt for years. Why was this, he wondered. A threat of invasion had been removed, but that was not a permanent improvement. Presently the Irish would have another King; in any case the small free-lance parties of Scots would be as troublesome as ever. No, it was not a permanent improvement, yet the result of the tempest had cheered him more than the news of a victory by force of arms. Of course, that was it! It was a piece of Luck sent by the Heavenly Power, whether that meant Mars or the Christian God. Twenty years ago the Divine Gratianus had removed from the Senate House the Altar of Victory, which had stood there since Rome was founded; Felix was as shocked by this gratuitous insult to the Unseen as any other old-fashioned Roman, and he had gloomily noticed since then that it was always the Imperial Army which had to fight hard for success, and the barbarians who profited by sudden changes in the weather and all the unforeseen chances of the battlefield. But now the King of the Irish had been destroyed by the Powers of the Air. That absurd Bishop might think his prayers had something to do with it, but every educated man would know that the Luck of the City was helping them again.

He was very sleepy after his late night, and there was not much to do in the office. He drafted a rough copy of the despatch to the Bishop of Rome, explaining the miraculous destruction of the Irish through the prayers of the Bishop of Londinium. He would have it written out fair on the best parchment and sealed with the great seal of the Province; then he would get the deacon to look it over, ostensibly to see it was accurate. He would have the support of the Church next time he annoyed the provincials.

Oh dear, but it was a wearing business running this Province without physical force. He wondered whether he would have been happier as a clerk at Lugdunum, with no responsibility. Then he shook himself and sat up in his chair. He had taken this post to serve the hero Theodosius, and now he was dead there were still the Eternal Empire, and the sons of his old master, to demand his loyalty.

Presently he called for his litter. He could go home and get to bed early, to make up for the excitement of the last few days. But as he passed the inner harbour in the centre of the town, where a small stream from the north flowed into the main river, he saw a strange fishing-boat tied up at the quay. From the crowd of excited loafers who hung round her, and the garlands twined round the rickety mast, she bore good news from the Continent. He ordered the litter to be set down, and sent one of the slaves to inquire. The man came running back.

'Wonderful news, my lord,' he called. 'There was a great battle in Italy, and the Magister Militum wiped out the German invaders.'

'Really,' said Felix, once more the ancient Roman who heard good news and bad with an equal mind. 'Is the news definite? Then why didn't those fishermen inform the Praeses of the Province? Tell the master of the ship to come here at once.'

'I'm sorry, my lord,' the slave replied, 'the master and all the free men of the crew are at the Praetorium. There is no one on board but ignorant barbarian slaves.' The litter-bearer was a verna, born and brought up in the household of his mistress, and he despised new-caught barbarians.

Felix looked at the sun. It was getting late, and he had promised himself an early bed. But this was really intolerable. Important news arrived from over sea and nobody bothered to tell the Praeses. He frowned fiercely, and shouted at the slaves:

'Pick up the shafts. Don't stand there gossiping. Take me

to the Praetorium as quick as you can, and if you don't hurry I'll sell the lot of you to those fishermen.'

By conferring with Constantinus about the defence of the city he had already committed the indiscretion of meeting the military authorities; his reputation would be no worse after another visit.

The sentry at the gate gaped with surprise when the litter was set down at the entrance to the Praetorium. Felix would not send in his name for an interview as though he had come with a petition; the dignity of the civil service forbade. He remained in his chair and sent the best-spoken of his footmen to request the commander to come out. With one of those young officers who aped the manners of a gentleman that would have been asking for a snub; but Constantinus was of the old type, an elderly drill-master with no social pretensions; it would not occur to him that he was compromising the prestige of the Army by waiting on the Praeses.

He appeared almost at once, in a grubby undress tunic and the thick barbarian trousers that even soldiers of Roman blood had taken to wearing in cold weather; set crookedly on his head was an untidy wreath, his eyes were red and out of focus, and he stuttered in his speech. Felix noted that the soldiers must believe the good news; Constantinus was not an habitual drunkard, or he would have heard it from the gossip of the town; but now he was celebrating.

'What news?' he asked, after greetings. 'I saw the ship, and heard a rumour. If you have a despatch from Italy, why didn't you inform the Treasury?'

Constantinus was too happy to take up the challenge, though he would have been within his rights in pointing

out that military despatches should reach the civil authorities through the Praefect of the Gauls, if the Magister
Militum chose to inform his civilian counterpart. Instead he
waved his right arm in an unsteady approximation to the
military salute, and shouted in a thick voice:

'Hurrah for Stilicho, and hurrah for the invincible Army
of the West! They've scuppered Radagaisus and all his
plundering band!'

'That is very good news. But don't you think you should
have let me know? It affects the civil administration, for if
the Army of Italy is to be demobilized we must make
arrangements for the reception of Legio VI Victrix and the
other troops.'

That sobered the veteran in a moment; in any case, like
all soldiers, he was accustomed to standing steady on parade
with a buzzing head. The whole Diocese had long been
awaiting the return of those troops. Every unit in the army
was a hereditary corporation, and Legio VI Victrix was a
British corps.

'Good old Felix,' said the officer, with a belch. 'I mean,
thank you, lord Praeses, for your gracious inquiries. If I'd
had an official despatch I would have passed it on to you for
information. In this little island we must all hang together,
and blow the Imperial regulations! But this isn't official
news. These fishermen heard it in their home port; then
they sailed here as quick as they could, to earn the reward
of the bearer of good news. I've given them a reward, and
I'm convinced they are telling the truth. When I get the
proclamation you shall see it at once. But you may get it
yourself, from the Praefect. And probably the Bishop will
be told to give thanks in his church, if the Christians have a
form for that ceremony. This isn't merely a strategic
success, the sort of thing we have a right to expect. This is
the wiping out of a whole barbarian army, led by a King.

Centuries from now our descendants will remember Stilicho's victory over Radagaisus, and our British troops had a
share in it!'

There was nothing more to be learned, and Constantinus
had been quite helpful when he might have been rude.
Felix was carried back to his house, through streets where
garlanded citizens crowded to the taverns. But he was too
tired to feast after the anxiety of the last few days. He went
straight to bed.

Next day was a Sunday, and the Treasury was closed. Felix
did not think it necessary to attend church; he had given
thanks for deliverance only two days ago, which showed
that the government upheld Christianity. If he made a habit
of church-going the Bishop might start telling him what to
do, as had happened in some Provinces where the Praesides
were devout. Maria went; it was a good thing for women,
and she had done it all her life; besides, she could represent
her husband, and note which of the clerks attended
regularly.

Felix sat lazily at his desk, making notes in his Aeneid
between mouthfuls of honey cake; the furnace was working
well, and the room felt warm; often in this foul climate the
wind blew the heat up the chimney before it had circulated
properly under the floor. The future looked prosperous.
What the Empire needed was a resounding victory over the
barbarians, with plenty of dead and the survivors sold as
slaves. It was worth ten strategic campaigns, such as had
pushed Alaric back to Illyricum; for it showed that raiding
was a dangerous business, and that Germans were better off
in their forests. News travelled quickly in the unknown
world of barbarians that encompassed the Oecumene, and
even the Saxons would think twice before they launched
their keels next spring. If only Britain could have a few

years of peace! Then production would increase, the arrears of tax would be collected, and education would at last get started in accordance with the Imperial decree. It was nearly thirty years since the great disaster at Adrianople in Thrace, and as Felix looked back it seemed to him that the Empire had been living from one crisis to another ever since.

Shortly after noon Maria returned from church, bringing her father. She came into the study for a few minutes, to give a list of civil servants she had seen, and then retired to the company of her slaves in the women's apartments. She was intelligent, and sometimes Felix wondered whether she was bored, cooped up all day with feather-headed tire-women and embroiderers. But there was nothing to be done about it; there were only half a dozen women in Londinium who were socially eligible to be friendly with the wife of the Praeses, and it was the custom of the ancients that ladies of good birth should retire to their own apartments when the men had business to discuss.

Gratianus accepted the victory as true, though the official account had not yet arrived from Gaul. Felix was relieved, for the Senator had his own sources of information. There were mutual congratulations, and the correct tepid acknowledgements of the help of the Christian God. But Gratianus was not as pleased by the news as might have been expected.

'I don't like this story of a bloody decisive battle,' he said, 'though, of course, when we know more we may find it exaggerated. Our army should be able to manoeuvre barbarians into retreat, by cutting off supplies or bribing subordinate chiefs. The Magister Militum was very hard pressed if he had to hazard the safety of Italy on a desperate head-on collision. His is the only army in the West. Just think where we should be now if victory had gone the other way! All sorts of little accidents can lose a battle;

49

Stilicho might have been sick, or a chance arrow might have killed him. I wonder what went wrong with his plans and made him try the equal chance of the sword, as though he were still a war chief of the Vandals?'

To Felix this seemed faint-hearted, and not in accordance with the custom of the ancients. 'It was appropriate to the power and majesty of Rome,' he replied. 'It will have an excellent effect in the whole barbarian world. They know we can usually outmanoeuvre them, or bribe their allies to desert; but since Adrianople they have believed in their hearts that they were bound to win a pitched battle.'

'I don't deny that. I shall make it my business to send a full account of the victory to the new King of the Irish, the only barbarian who otherwise might not hear of it at once. I have an agent buying hides in Ireland at this moment. But it was an unnecessary risk, all the same.'

'Stilicho is the greatest soldier in the world, and he has good reason for everything he does. I wonder how soon he can wind up the campaign, and send the Gallic troops back to the Rhine? We can do with our own men here. I hate relying on barbarian Kings. It's undignified, and none too safe when we really need them. If Cunedda had refused to rescue this city from the Irish the Picts would have raided south to Eburacum, and the Saxons might have joined in. I wish there was some way of making a reliable peace with *one* of our barbarian neighbours, instead of having them all on our backs at once whenever we are in a difficulty.'

'There's never any chance of a barbarian keeping his promise to Rome,' answered Gratianus, who seemed to have made up his mind to be gloomy on this day of rejoicing. 'We don't ravage their homes when war comes; that is the root of our troubles. A German knows he is safe in Germany, even if we drive him out of the Empire. Now Magnus Maximus harried the Picts in their own villages, and they left the Wall alone when he ruled in Britain. King Coroticus thinks of nothing but guarding his flocks, and raiders take their booty past him unmolested.'

'I have nothing to do with military affairs, and I don't understand them,' Felix said firmly. He sometimes wondered whether the Senator grumbled in order to trap him into some treasonable expression of agreement. 'But the decision to withdraw regular troops from the Wall was sound,' he continued. 'I happen to have seen some old statements of revenue from Maxima Caesariensis, and the Province hardly paid for the brushwood on its alarm beacons. There has never been any civilization north of Eburacum, and it was a waste of money to hold those barren moors.'

'Quite so,' his father-in-law agreed. 'There is always a barren zone on every frontier. But when we retire the barren zone moves back with us. Whatever we do, the fields next the Picts will always be uncultivated.'

'Don't be such a pessimist, my dear Senator. We have given the Germans a fright, and that will have its effect all over the world. Perhaps when that Legion returns the Dux will harry the farms of the Niduarian Picts.'

'But Caius, you are not expecting Legio VI Victrix in the near future? Haven't you heard that Alaric is stirring in Illyricum? The Army of Italy must keep the field for some time.'

Gratianus was up to his tricks again, teasing his son-in-law with news that had not yet reached the Treasury. Besides, although they were closely related by marriage, he ought not to address the Praeses of the Province by his praenomen, particularly when Felix always called him Senator. The best way to snub him was to give him a taste of Roman gravitas.

'The Sacred Emperor has confided military affairs to the

Magister Militum, and we must not question his wise dispositions. If our Legion does not return the provincials will be disappointed, but it will make things easier for the Treasury. The army takes too much money as it is. In fact, my clerks will be sending you a request for a loan to tide things over until next harvest. I know a man of your loyalty will advance what is necessary.'

'Of course I shall advance what is necessary, if it is within my means. I hope, lord Praeses, you will make out the papers so that I am repaid as soon as possible. I haven't done badly this year, but I can't afford to lock up my capital indefinitely. Would you make it the first charge on next year's harvest? And while I am asking for favours, there is one that would give me great pleasure, though I do not benefit directly. The Curia of Verulamium have got themselves into an even worse muddle than town councils usually do. They owe generations of arrears, and with the present assessment they can't even keep up the annual interest on the debt. They made me patronus of the city because my family comes from those parts, and I should like to give them a helping hand. Will you appoint a commission to go into their affairs? Then they could start again with a clean sheet.'

Felix felt a certain contempt for his father-in-law. Gratianus was entitled to some reward other than the bare repayment of the money he advanced, and it was more polite to ask a favour for your clients than to demand cash for your own purse. But there were ways of doing these things. It was unmannerly to bargain about the reward before the loan had been paid over. A better system was to leave the Treasury under an obligation until some question arose in the natural course of administration. He thought that by being brutally frank he might shock this huckster into better manners.

'Very well, my dear Senator,' he replied, 'I shall draw up a bond to your satisfaction. In return for a first charge on the harvest of next autumn, and the release of the city of Verulamium from its arrears of tribute, you will advance to the Treasury of Britannia Prima a sum to be agreed, for current expenses. Will that be the security you require?'

'Dear me, Caius, you are too generous.' Gratianus waved a deprecating hand. 'A bond like that would look very odd in the annual accounts, which the Vicarius is entitled to inspect, though I don't suppose the old boy ever bothers. But any document that gets into your archives stays on record for ever, unless you lose it on purpose, like the account of the Bishop's miracle. What you suggest might cost me my head; even you would be dismissed if the clerks at the Praefecture chose to take it seriously.'

Felix was pleased that he had shaken the other's complacency, but Gratianus had scored in his turn by revealing that he knew what fate the Praeses intended for his most private documents. There was no point in continuing to fence with the most eminent citizen in his Province, who was also his father-in-law. He smiled, and rose to end the interview.

'I think we know one another too well to need legal documents,' he said in a friendly voice. 'When you send the money the Treasury will give you a receipt, so that there is no dispute about the actual sum. Rest assured that I shall repay you as soon as possible, for administration is difficult when the government is under an obligation to one of its subjects; and I shall do what I can to ease the burden of Verulamium.'

The Senator put on his formal manners, and took leave as though retiring from the presence of a mighty ruler; he did not actually leave the house, but went to visit his daughter in the women's apartments. Felix sat on in his study, thinking of the future. Would he ever start that Imperial scheme of education? He had been trying for ten years, and always when it came to the point the money was needed for something else. Now he could do nothing for two more years; until next harvest (and this was only September!) the government must economize; when that was gathered the surplus, if the needs of defence left a surplus, must pay off the loan he had just contracted. Another thought worried below the threshold of his mind, until he took it out into the open and examined it. Was Gratianus becoming too powerful for the welfare of the State? Nowadays he did not ask for rewards that would increase his own wealth, which any Praeses accustomed to dealing with the rich would readily grant if it could be done. He had not even asked for interest, which was technically illegal, but which the Treasury was resigned to paying if the money could not be had otherwise. Latterly he had always wanted favours for his clients. He might be building up a faction; and he knew too much about the confidential affairs of the government. Where did he get that information? From Maria? No doubt at this moment he was pumping his daughter for the latest news. Felix deliberately told his wife nothing that her father should not know. But that item he had let fall about the memorandum on the death of the Irish King! Paulinus had arranged that it should be accidentally sent with the contents of the waste-paper basket to light the furnace in the public baths. Maria had not known that, and Paulinus was under orders not to tell any of the free-born clerks. It was a nuisance if his secretary was bribed to pass on what happened in the private office; but on consideration he thought it unlikely. The fellow seemed devoted to his master, he was certainly too discreet to let anything out accidentally, and he was only a freedman. That meant he was a humilioris, with none of the rights in a criminal court enjoyed by an honestioris, a free-born citizen of independent means; if he annoyed the Praeses he might be burned, or beaten to death, after a secret trial. That was one reason he had been chosen as confidential secretary. He decided that Paulinus was not the source of the leakage, partly because it would be so very inconvenient if it turned out that he was.

All that could be inquired into later. He must keep his mind on the question of Gratianus. Perhaps it had been a mistake to marry into that family, though at the time it had seemed a simple and neat way out of a difficult situation. But his father-in-law was beginning to presume on the relationship. A prominent man was wise to employ spies to make sure he stood well with the administration, and to get time to fly with his gold if it was decided to arrest him for the safety of the State. But the system could be carried too far, and the Senator was ripe for a warning.

It must be discreet, Felix reminded himself. If Gratianus made up his mind that he was ruined whatever he did, he could cause a great deal of trouble. There would be a shock to the whole system of credit if his loans were suddenly called in; he seemed to have the Curia of Verulamium as his faithful clients, and he might persuade them to shut the gates of their strong city and hire a band of wandering Scots to defy the government. Even if he fled secretly to Ireland, or the land of the Picts beyond the Wall, the most sensible thing to do if he feared arrest, that would encourage the barbarians when it was important that they should keep quiet. No, the Senator must not be frightened into rash courses.

The obvious way to drop a hint, that would reach him without frightening him unduly, was through his daughter. Felix seldom visited his wife in the day time, though of course they dined together according to the custom of the ancients; he knew that if he sought her out that afternoon she would guess it was because he had something to say, not merely for the pleasure of her company. He sat meditating in his chair for another hour, and then braced himself for the interview.

In theory he had a low opinion of the capacity of women; but secretly he was slightly afraid of his wife. She was young enough to be his daughter, and strikingly handsome; and she had inherited her father's ruthless brain. She could not share his study of Vergil, but in the new and fashionable subject of theology she held her own with the priests. She might laugh at his fears, and tell him he was worrying about nothing; but she could say whether her father's system of alliances was due to fear of disgrace or to ambition.

He set his face into an expression of dignity and determination, until the lines from his nose to the corners of his mouth were as deep and severe as in an ancient bust, straightened his tunic, took a deep breath, and walked firmly upstairs to the women's apartments. A strong door barred this from the public portion of the house, and it was bolted, as it should be. But the eunuch outside recognized his master's step, and opened as he approached. The sight of this eunuch always restored his self-confidence, which faltered when he was about to meet his wife; a eunuch was the most expensive slave that money could buy, for there was a law against inflicting that mutilation; they were very rare in Britain. Felix was reminded, whenever he looked at the grinning beardless face, that the poor clerk in the Treasury of Lugdunum had come a long way. That was because he had been loyal to the Divine Theodosius, and now he was facing an unpleasant interview from loyalty to his son.

Maria sat embroidering a linen altar-cloth, while one of her women read aloud at a standing desk in the corner. Felix listened for a moment, hoping that his wife was learning the classics. But it was only one of those translations from the Christian Scriptures, trashy little works full of unclassical expressions and with every sentence as short and simple as possible. She would not improve her education by hearing that rubbish; the Church should get some educated Christian to make a proper translation into the language of Cicero; he might do it himself if he found time. She stood up respectfully as her husband entered, and dismissed her attendants. When he was settled in the best chair she curled up on a stool by his feet and waited for an explanation of the visit.

Felix was slow in coming to the point. He did not wish to give the impression that he had come charging in to complain that her father's conduct could no longer be borne; but after some talk about the shortcomings of the dressmakers he opened the subject as gently as he could.

'Your father has been very generous to the Treasury, my dear,' he said, in a level neutral voice that caught her attention at once. 'I had to seek a loan, and he immediately offered all the money I needed; he asked no reward for himself, not even interest on his capital. He did beg me to deal gently with the Curia of Verulamium, but of course he gets nothing out of that. It is pure benevolence on his part. He must be very much loved if he goes out of his way to do these favours. In fact, if he were not so closely related to the Praeses the authorities in Gaul might suspect he was too popular for the tranquillity of the Diocese. But there is no danger, for he is informed of all that passes in the Treasury, and the friends who send him these confidential reports would let him know if the Praefect thought ill of him.'

'Dear father,' Maria cooed, looking into her husband's eyes. 'He likes to be popular, and he is very slow to see the appearance of evil while his conscience is clear. He has made all the money he needs, and now he only desires to put his fortune at the service of the Empire. He would never ask interest from the Treasury, when this emergency has increased all expenses. I suppose he thought you might feel uncomfortable if he did not let you do something for him in return, and he hit on the idea of helping Verulamium, the home of our ancestors. I think it shows a very nice nature.'

'Quite so. But an enemy, if such a kind man has enemies, could make it look like seeking popularity for improper reasons.'

'Oh, that's absurd. Imagine Father in politics! Why, he has seen two civil wars, and all he did was to pay his taxes to the ruler of Britain at the moment. He is a far-sighted trader, and he prospers under every government. I wish Magnus Maximus had not given him that title, but naturally he dared not refuse what was offered. A stranger looking up his record might think he was one of the separatist party who hanker after an Emperor for Britain alone. But you know better. Seriously, no civilian gains anything by getting mixed up in a revolt; Eugenius did what Arbogastes told him, and in the end it cost the wretched creature his life. Father has proved his loyalty since we were reunited to the Empire, but the richest man in Britain had to give money when a soldier with a sword demanded it.'

'That is true, and I don't really suspect him of anything. But the government at Mediolanum would like him better if he were not so popular with the provincials.'

Maria opened her big blue eyes, and gazed into the severe face of her husband. Then she laughed light-heartedly. 'You are annoyed because he knows of the trick you played on the Bishop! It's a shame to treat the fussy old man like that! Writing a wonderful story to Rome about his power of raising tempests in defence of his flock, and then losing the office copy so you can deny it later on; no one will ever know for certain whether he does work miracles! I think you were very unkind, though I laughed when Father told me this morning. But he won't tell anyone else, and he admires your strategy. Do you suspect father of bribing your secretary? Shall I tell you how he found out? It was quite simple, really. He pays the furnace-man at the Baths to put aside waste paper from the Treasury; one of his clerks goes through it before it is burnt, and sometimes he finds rough drafts of quite interesting documents. When he found the file copy of the Miracle Letter he nearly sent it back to the office, in case it had been thrown away by mistake; but father saw what you were doing, and it went into the furnace according to plan. Now that isn't a very terrible piece of spying, is it? The labourers at the Baths can't read, but you shouldn't send out anything confidential among the waste paper. I doubt whether you could even prosecute anyone for reading what has been thrown away as useless.'

'So that's how it was. In future our waste paper will be used to heat the Treasury. But the Senator has done nothing wrong.'

'I'm glad I have saved poor Paulinus from suspicion. I like the little man. In fact, Father never bribes people to betray secrets; he says that is tempting them to invent something more exciting than the truth. He knows everything that goes on in Britain, and some of it is supposed to be confidential; but that is because he keeps his ears open, and pays his servants to listen. People talk more than you think. Soldiers boast when they get secret orders, and then there are the barbarians in Ireland and Caledonia. You can come by official secrets quite honestly, just by letting people brag about their work.'

Felix smiled. He liked his wife, especially when she was

working hard to persuade him; she did it very well, and it was a shame to keep her at it any longer. Of course he knew that Gratianus bought secret information by the use of bribes, and she knew that he knew. But family life would run more smoothly if he pretended he had been convinced.

'I am glad your father does not waste his money on secret agents,' he said pleasantly. 'They often invent something startling in the hope of extra reward. Our agentes in rebus do the same. But the government cannot take chances, and a man who is falsely accused usually suffers with the guilty.'

That grim warning closed the subject. He admired his wife's embroidery, advised her to listen in future to something more elegant than a literal translation of Koine Greek, and returned to his study. In his mind he ran over the conversation. Maria did not talk idly. He had issued a rebuke to be passed on to her father; had she conveyed anything important in return?

She had used a phrase he had immediately filed in his mind, to be examined at leisure. How had it gone? 'The separatist party who hanker after an Emperor for Britain alone.' Then some people, somewhere, were beginning to talk about the good old days of Carausius, as they always did when barbarians were unusually troublesome. Perhaps he could narrow it down more than that. If Gratianus had heard from a foreign correspondent he would have warned his son-in-law directly. The discontent must be among Maria's limited circle of acquaintances. He ran through them in his mind. She saw a lot of the clergy, but it could not have anything to do with them; there was a Christian Emperor in Mediolanum, busy writing the tiresome regulations of his religion into the fundamental law of the Empire; and a Church that looked to Italy as its theological centre was bound to be loyal in politics also. There were her friends in society; but the suspicion did not fit them either. Civil war meant a heavy burden on the rich, and those who were not rich were well placed in the government as at present conducted. That left only the shopkeepers, and the middle-class inhabitants of Londinium in general. That was more like it. They often complained that the Emperor thought only of the defence of Italy, and resented their taxes crossing the sea to support the central power.

There had been this tiresome tradition of a separate British Empire since the oldest inhabitant could remember. Britain was a natural unit, with its own barbarian menace from Scots and Saxons; that was a fact of geography which the government could not alter. Unfortunately, the Diocese had once enjoyed great prosperity under a separate Emperor; there were monuments in every city, harbours and walls which had been built by the usurper Carausius. He had been eliminated more than a century ago, but there were would-be imitators in every generation. Yet a separate Britain could only prosper at the expense of the Oecumene; Carausius encouraged the Saxons to raid Gaul, and employed thousands of them in his own navy; the whole discreditable episode had ended in the worst sack Londinium had ever suffered, when the tyrant's defeated mercenaries rioted through the streets while the avenging army from Gaul marched to the rescue. Any further attempt to set up a separate Empire would end in the same way; Constantinus Chlorus had been hailed as 'Redditor Lucis Aeternae'! No sensible merchant, no Roman with the interests of the State at heart, could wish for a repetition of Carausius.

There was nothing a Praeses could do to stop such thoughts; if there was open revolt, or discontent that showed itself in the street, he would strike unsparingly, and the leaders would burn in a slow fire; until then he must wait, collect the taxes, and keep on good terms with Constantinus in case soldiers should be needed to disperse a mob.

He picked up his Aeneid, and forgot his worries as he chanted the verses under his breath. It was a comfort that never failed. Rome had been founded by a brave man who did his duty, and because he did not lose heart under difficulties the Gods helped him and his work endured. If it was true, as the Divine Theodosius had proclaimed, that those particular gods did not exist, Rome yet stood, and it must be this God from Syria Who had founded her to rule the world for all eternity. A faithful servant of Rome was a faithful servant of the human race.

He enjoyed an excellent supper, and Maria took pains to amuse him, describing the congregation in church and the gossip of the city. She was clever at catching his mood, and saw he was satisfied with the state of the Empire.

Monday at the Treasury brought back the worries that never left a Praeses for long. Paulinus brought in a sheaf of demands from the other Provinces of the Diocese, and the harvest actually in the barns had not come up to expectation. Britannia Prima had more arable land than the other Provinces, besides the dues from the busiest port in the island, and the precedent had been established that the Treasury at Londinium should send help where it was needed; now Secunda, Maxima Caesariensis, Flavia Caesariensis and Valentia all clamoured for subsidies at once. It was worse than last year, though there had been no outstanding barbarian raids. When Paulinus showed an application from Flavia for the salary of the Praeses, Felix could contain himself no longer.

'Really!' he said in an angry tone. 'Does the wretched creature collect no taxes at all? For years he did not repair the Wall, then he was let off paying the garrison, then the law court was moved from Deva to Eburacum, all to save expense. I suppose he is popular among his subjects. But this is too much. If he can't collect his own salary he must go without. It's unfair to the traders of Londinium that they should carry the whole Diocese on their shoulders.'

'Lord Praeses,' said Paulinus humbly, but with a suggestion of stubbornness in his voice, 'Rutilianus is entitled to his salary. He has influential relatives in Spain, and some connection with a prominent soldier in Italy. He was appointed to draw a salary. He gambles heavily, and apparently without judgement; in the end his family grew tired of paying his debts. He was sent to Flavia because that is now the land of King Coroticus. The King defends the Wall at no expense to the Empire; but that doesn't mean he pays his men from his private purse. In practice he collects the taxes from the area he occupies. Rutilianus is allowed to occupy his official residence so long as he doesn't interfere with the King. A gentleman of good family would not accept such a post unless he needed the money very badly.'

'Very well. I had forgotten the old dice-player was under powerful protection. Let him have the money for which he has sold his dignity. But what about the other Provinces? Are there any applications we can refuse?'

'There is Valentia, my lord. They had money from us in the past, but that is no reason why we should continue to subsidize them. That Province is the private realm of King Cunedda, as Coroticus rules in Flavia. The only difference is that some hanger-on of the King has been given the title of Praeses, and I am glad to see he is not impudent enough to seek his salary from us. All they want is money to repair their roads.'

'Then strike that out. I won't repair roads for barbarians who march barefoot over the hills. The others we shall have to manage somehow. I have a good mind to write to the Vicarius, and ask him to stop this business of one Province sending its funds to another. In practice it means that Prima runs the whole Diocese.'

But he knew the Vicarius would not reopen a question that would mean a great deal of work, however it was decided; if he was pressed he would refer the matter to Lugdunum, and the Praefect of the Gauls would shy away, as he always did, from making a decision that might annoy someone with influence; he would send the papers to Mediolanum for the personal attention of the Emperor, who never attended to anything; and the regulations, which at present suited four Praesides out of five in the Diocese, would not be altered in this generation. All the elaborate system of centralization built up by the Divine Diocletianus was breaking down through sheer pressure of business, now the government managed every detail of the economic life of its subjects; the rulers of Provinces must make their financial arrangements without help from their nominal superiors. Nor was overwork the only difficulty, though it was the perpetual excuse. The Empire had never been able to discover any better means of regulating the succession than victory in civil war; Honorius was the son of a successful Emperor, and he had inherited the support of the reigning party, the coalition of Christians and native Roman soldiers who had brought Theodosius to power. He had also inherited opposition from the pagan aristocrats and barbarian generals who had fought for Eugenius and Arbogastes. Every government appointment, every administrative decision, was made with the threat of civil war in mind. Felix was loyal, but he had been rewarded for his loyalty; his superiors would not back him if he made himself unpopular with civil servants who might change their allegiance.

He sat alone at his piled desk and tried to make plans for

the winter. He must allow his prosperous and nearly solvent Province to be milked for the support of the rest of the island. Otherwise there would be discontent leading to danger of a revolt. He must raise all the money he could, besides the land-tax that was the principal source of revenue. That meant fines from those who broke the law, stringent collection of arrears, and no investment in education or communications which would cost money now though it might pay a dividend later. He would be unpopular among the citizens, but that did not matter so long as the soldiers were paid and the influential land-owners and business men were not unduly oppressed.

If only they could have a few years of peace! Felix would have prayed to Someone for peace, if he had thought that would do any good; but the Emperor had forbidden sacrifice to idols, as the law now termed the ancient religion that had given Rome the Empire of the World, and if the Praeses grovelled in church the Bishop would become unbearably conceited.

The Empire had defended all its Western dominions, though farther east Illyricum and Achaea had been under Gothic occupation for years; but though troops fought in the Emperor's name on the Caledonian Wall and in Germany beyond the Rhine, the actual taxpaying administered territory diminished year by year. Of the five Provinces of Britain Flavia and Valentia were ruled by foederate Kings, who marched under the Roman standard but sent no taxes to headquarters; in his own Province the Comes Littoris Saxonici per Britannias had gradually come to rule the coast which his cavalry patrolled; he was a genuine Roman soldier, not a barbarian foederate, but the pay of his men was always in arrears, and he seized the harvest as it was reaped. Londinium and the farmlands of the south must pay for the whole administration of Britain. It needed unremitting care from the government, or civilization would vanish from the land. Well, that was what it would get, Felix told himself firmly, as he picked up a list of hereditary licensed butchers who were suspected of working at another trade in their spare time.

During the autumn there was a drive to catch citizens who had deserted their occupations; not many were burned alive, as the letter of the law demanded, for the sale of criminals was a valuable source of revenue. But they did not fetch big prices. Slavery is not profitable without a good system of police, and now the administration had difficulty in recovering runaways; the foederate Kings welcomed new subjects without asking questions, and when a man disappeared it was always possible the pirates had snapped him up. The coloni remained at work, but they were almost in the position of servile tenants; the law forbade their sale apart from the land, they must not be put to any other work than agriculture, and in practice if they paid over the greater part of what they produced their masters did not interfere with their private lives. But a discontented craftsman-slave could easily run away to the barbarians.

By working eight hours a day and keeping his subordinates up to the mark the Praeses could enforce the division of labour that is civilization. Every year things were a little worse, buildings fell down and were not repaired, roads decayed, education declined, and Celtic was more widely spoken in place of Latin. But Felix and his clerks did what they could, by threats of appalling punishment and doubtful promises of reward, to stop the Province sliding into the state of self-sufficient corn-growing and sheep-herding that Julius Caesar had found when he landed in the island.

The law he served was a respecter of persons; a poor

humilioris, even though free and a citizen, did not have the same rights as a well-to-do honestioris. In practice, there were other considerations as well. His wife and his father-in-law had an acknowledged right to get favourable treatment for a reasonable number of their clients; other landowners expected that some of their requests should be granted, roughly in proportion to the taxes they paid. And, of course, the Army, which included the numerous servants of the baggage train, took no heed of civilian enactments. Felix was by no means in untrammelled charge of Britannia Prima. Still, a hard-working honest civil servant could do a great deal for the population under his care, and it was the difficult, exacting, but interesting job for which he had been trained from boyhood. In the beginning of December Felix was tired, but moderately content.

CHAPTER II

GALLIA DEVICTA

The autumn was fine and open; but in December the weather changed. Every night brought frost, and by day the sun was covered. First the little streams that flowed south through Londinium were rimmed with ice, while the ditches in the fields froze solid to the earth beneath; then, as it grew colder, cakes of ice drifted up and down with the tide in the main river. The sun remained behind its curtain of motionless cloud, fog hung round the horizon, and the temperature continued to drop. Normal life in the city was hampered by the cold, and the clerks in the Treasury spent more time blowing on their fingers than writing at their desks. It was not the tradition of the government to allow free play to economic forces, and Felix at once fixed a maximum price for fuel; by rights he should also have bought wood for distribution to the citizens at the official price; but there was no money in the Treasury for unforeseen poor relief, and without calling on the army he could not force the peasants to sell. So the maximum price was disregarded in practice, and the humiliores hung about the public baths instead of getting on with their work.

By the third week in December it was colder than the oldest inhabitant could remember. Dead birds lay under every bush, and wolves were reported from districts where they had not been seen for years. There were no barbarian raids, but the ground was too hard for ploughing. Felix issued his annual proclamation fixing the date of the winter holiday.

This was always a ticklish question. The obvious time for a holiday was the middle of winter, when even in good years there was little to be done in the fields. But he must be careful not to offend religious susceptibilities. Since the Foundation of the City December had been the season of the Saturnalia, a pagan festival when everybody behaved in a very pagan manner indeed; the Christians had persuaded the Emperor to forbid its celebration, but they had a feast of their own about the same time in honour of the birthday of their God; it was important not to cause scandal by giving the ignorant a chance to confuse the two religions. Felix sent his wife to confer with the Bishop, and her good sense found a compromise. God's birthday, towards the end of the month, would be a festival of one day, and the real winter holiday would be put off until the beginning of January, when the Church commemorated His Epiphany; there were many Epiphanies of pagan gods, when a divine being who had appeared in disguise first manifested his divinity, and everyone understood the Greek title; at the same time Janus was a gloomy god, who closed the dead year besides opening the new, and no one would think feasting was decreed in his honour. It was impossible to provide Games; since the city had no Curia the cost would have to come out of government funds, and the Treasury could not afford it. But the decree announced that shops and government offices would be closed for a week, and on the first day the guilds would go in procession to pray for the Emperor in the church outside the walls. It was the best that could be done in this backward Diocese, where only the army, in their remote northern camps, could find beasts for the arena.

*

On the 6th of January Felix sat on a tribunal outside the west door of the church, to watch the procession. He was muffled in a great many extra tunics, for the cold was still intense; but with his official toga unpleated to cover his shoulders and a brazier of charcoal at his feet, he endured the weather with nothing worse than a few sneezes; and he was resigned to these during every winter in Britain. Most of the upper classes sheltered in the warmth of the church, but it was important that the Praeses should be on show to receive the guildsmen in public; for he had discovered that the Epiphany was a feast in some way connected with the giving of presents. He had let it be known that this was a suitable occasion for the guilds to show their gratitude for his labours in the cause of civilization by presenting to the Treasury the gold and incense that played some part in the ceremony.

He could make things unpleasant for the guildsmen if he chose to enforce all the regulations that he or his predecessors had issued. They took the hint, and each hereditary trade had organized a subscription. As they passed into the church a little pile of gold coins grew at his feet, though some of the poorer trades, the wagoners and ferrymen and others that worked with their hands, had evaded the spirit of his request by giving sweet-smelling logs as a substitute for incense. When the last procession, the scavengers, had entered the church he held his hands over the brazier and smiled with pleasure. It was the dream of every Praeses to discover a new tax, something not positively forbidden by Imperial decree which the citizens would pay without open insurrection. He would make this Epiphany an annual event.

Altogether he could look back on the past year with satisfaction. The Empire was in a flourishing condition. The Irish would fight among themselves for years before they agreed on a new King, and though civil war in Ireland meant that the losers would come east as wandering Scots there would be no invasion in force until some warrior had disposed of his rivals; the unusual cold would hamper the Saxons in their ship-building; best of all, the Germans on the Danube, the real menace to the Empire, would be awed by the annihilation of the army of Radagaisus. Italy was safe, and the subjects of the Sacred Honorius could look forward to peace and prosperity. Alaric lay in Illyricum, but that was the responsibility of the Sacred Arcadius at Constantinople; the West had turned an awkward corner, after a few months of real danger. It might look well if the Praeses now entered the Church, to show his gratitude for the Luck of the Empire.

A crowd of women and slaves lined the road from the West Gate to the church door; as he rose from his seat he looked idly down the two broad lines, and saw something odd. A wave of excitement was travelling outward from the city; he could watch it coming towards him, as heads turned first to one side to listen, then the other way to pass it on; and there was more noise than was seemly in the presence of the Emperor's representative. Exciting news had reached the city.

On occasions of public rejoicing Paulinus stayed very near his patron. A confidential clerk at the Treasury must be exceedingly unpopular with the taxpayers, and a freedman should not take precedence of citizens; if he went about on his own his place was among the lower classes, who would murder him if they got the chance. Now he stood beside the tribunal, with three police slaves to protect him. Felix sent him to discover the cause of the excitement, since the people were chattering in Celtic, as they did in moments of stress. Meanwhile he remained on the platform, trying to make out from the faces of the crowd whether the news was good or bad; but all he could see was that it was very exciting.

Presently Paulinus pushed his way back, his Germans banging the bystanders with their spear-butts; his eyes were wide with amazement as he related the astonishing rumour: 'They say a courier has ridden in with a despatch for the Praetorium. The despatch is secret, but the messenger drank in a tavern by the Bridge, and told the innkeeper the Germans had overrun Gaul. The humiliores believe it, though it can't be true. Shall I send to the Praetorium to inquire?'

This was so absurd that Felix sighed with relief. He had feared tidings of a revolt at Eburacum, the only thing that would normally excite a crowd of citizens to that extent. But even wild rumours usually had some foundation in fact; perhaps there had been a barbarian raid on some part of the Rhine frontier. He was about to enter the church, where he would find Gratianus. The Senator always knew what was happening; he would inquire if he had heard anything, though this weather made regular campaigning impossible.

The church was crowded, and the choir sang very loudly. Felix stood at the back and sent a footman to find the Senator. The news was already being whispered about the congregation, and Gratianus had heard it; but he made it clear that he had no private information. The rumour was all he knew, and he thought it absurd.

'I suppose they have been holding a jolly Saturnalia in Gaul,' he said, shouting above the noise like a true Roman who was not to be bothered by priests. 'The courier picked up a story that began as a hoax; now he tells it as the truth. All the same, someone has sent a courier to the Comes Britanniarum, with an open message for all the military authorities *en route*. Would you like me to find out what it is, or do you think Constantinus will tell you?'

In either case the Praeses would have to rely on someone else to learn what was going on; Felix thought it more dignified to ask the soldiers than to rely on the spies of Gratianus. He sent word to Maria that her father would take her home when the service was finished, and set off for the Praetorium.

There was excitement in the streets; but the crowd was subdued, talking quietly at street-corners or waiting for news in the forum; the taverns were on the whole emptier than was to be expected on a holiday, and Felix saw with relief that there was no threat of disorder. Once inside the Praetorium there was no one to see his behaviour except the military, and they held such a low opinion of all civilians that he need not stand on his dignity. He asked straight out if Flavius Constantinus could spare a moment to see Sempronius Felix; that put the matter on an unofficial basis and if he received a snub he must swallow it without complaint.

But he was shown at once into the private room of the officer commanding, where he found Constantinus, with his son Constans and a uniformed clerk who stood at a tall desk copying a paper; the others were in undress, obviously called from dinner; they made him welcome.

'Come here, lord Praeses, and look at this amazing despatch. (I suppose you can read it while the clerk is making his copy.) It is an urgent message from the Comes Littoris Saxonici per Gallias, addressed to all the military authorities in Britain. That is most irregular. At a pinch the anti-pirate patrols in Gaul may communicate direct with their opposite numbers in Britain, though they incur suspicion of plotting if they do it too often. But ordinarily if a Comes in Gaul has something to say to a Comes in Britain he should write through the Magister Militum in Italy. This has not come through the usual channels, and that impresses me even more than the astonishing news it contains.'

Felix read the message over the clerk's shoulder. The Army used a strange handwriting, but it did not take him long to puzzle it out. The Comes at Gessoriacum in Gaul wrote to say there had been a sudden and unexpected invasion; the Rhine had frozen from bank to bank, and on the last night of December an army of Sueves and Vandals crossed on the ice; there was no news from Augusta Treverorum, the headquarters of the Army of the Rhine, or from Colonia Agrippina, the other great fortress on the frontier; it was believed that both were closely besieged, if they had not already fallen. Meanwhile he, the Comes, was without instructions; therefore if the Comes Britanniarum would come at once, or at least send his Dux with the heavy cavalry, the troops on the Gallic coast would put themselves under his orders.

No wonder Constantinus was excited by this message, and delayed it while he took a copy. Felix had been a civil servant all his life, and he was always on his guard lest some official in another department should try to give him orders; notoriously, the Army was even more touchy about these things, and yet here was an officer in Gaul, who ought to have been delighted that the chance of war had cut him off from headquarters and made him a commander-in-chief, offering to put himself under the orders of a neighbour. He must be scared out of his wits. Perhaps he was a notorious coward.

'Do you know anything about this Comes?' Felix inquired.

'I've never met him, of course,' answered Constantinus. 'I serve in Britain and he serves in Gaul. But he has risen to be Comes, so Stilicho trusts him. We must take it that he is telling the truth as he sees it. This is serious. So serious, in fact, that I have put the courier under arrest for babbling in that tavern, and now the copy is finished I shall send my son to Eburacum with the original. He will speak unofficially to Marcus Naso, that young officer who came south last autumn, and find out what they think at headquarters. Now look here: this is a serious disaster to Roman arms. I think of the safety of Britain, which is my home; and you are a loyal Theodosian. We should stand together. Will you let me come to a conference when we have more reliable news? Truly I am as loyal to the Emperor as you are.'

Felix was impressed by the genuine sincerity of the proposal. It would look bad in an agent's report, and might bring them under suspicion of treason; but in risking his career for the safety of the Empire he would not be outdone by a crude and bloody soldier.

'You will be welcome whenever you choose to visit me,' he answered. 'Come to the Treasury, if you wish, though we should be more private in my house. Would you like me to invite the Senator? He knows a great deal about the state of the country.'

This was to show that the Praeses also was indifferent to suspicion. Civil and military authorities might confer if desperate remedies were called for, but to bring in a wealthy and influential citizen made matters ten times worse.

But Constantinus was so impressed by his own heroism that he merely gave an indifferent assent. Wine was brought, and they toasted young Constans before he set out on his long ride; then Felix went home through thronged but silent streets.

That first cry of despair was followed by a distressing absence of definite news. The first duty of the Comes

75

Littoris Saxonici per Gallias was to guard the coast entrusted
to his care, and he could not spare troops to patrol to the
eastward. The authorities in Londinium learned more from
refugees who crossed the Channel than from military
sources.

Gratianus had his unofficial newsgatherers in Gaul, as he
had them all over the West. Felix suspected that he
sometimes guessed rather than admit ignorance; but on the
whole he knew more about what passed on the Continent
than anyone else in Britain, and it was he who took the
initiative in summoning the first conference of all the
authorities in Londinium.

It was in the beginning of February, after four weeks of
alarming rumours and wild, soon-contradicted reports of
miraculous Roman victories, that he asked his son-in-law
and Maria to come to supper. Felix would have preferred to
go alone; his wife would be the only lady present, which
was always embarrassing, and she might lay herself open to
the inevitable suspicion of treason; though perhaps that did
not matter, for when an official was executed the government usually made a clean sweep of his family. But he could
not keep her away from her father's house, and he
reluctantly brought her in the family litter.

The great frost had at last broken in floods of rain and
heavy gales from the south-west; the streets were deserted,
and as they passed the harbour in the middle of the town he
saw that no ships had arrived. Presumably the Senator had
pieced together various reports from his correspondents,
but no news had come to-day from over sea.

Gratianus was proud of his supper parties, though Felix
privately thought they showed too much wealth and not
enough refinement; at least one could be sure of the best
food and drink in Britain, and the company of the leading
citizens of Londinium, such as they were. It was unusual to

find a prosperous private house in a city at all; most of the better families on the Continent lived entirely on their country estates; but this island was in many ways behind the times.

Felix felt slightly annoyed that his host did not meet him at the front door, for he was accustomed to being the most important person in any gathering. But a Senator was of higher rank than a civil servant, if he chose to stand on his rights. However, it would be wrong for the conference to begin on a note of dissatisfaction; he entered the dining-room with a smile, and there was a slight contest of politeness before the Senator took the highest couch, with the Praeses in second place. The other guests were Constantinus and his son, the Bishop, and L. Flavius Philo, a prominent shipowner and partner of Gratianus. Maria had a chair at the foot of the first table, where she could enjoy her food without taking part in the discussion.

This was a supper party, and it was assumed that everyone had eaten his main meal at dinner. There were native oysters, sardines and Spanish anchovies as a first course; then came roast sucking-pig; and when that was cleared the slaves withdrew and the guests could talk business over their wine. There had not been much conversation while the food was on the table; anchovies and sardines both came from over sea; they were rare treats nowadays, with all these pirates about. Felix was used to sitting still and looking dignified, which is an important branch of a judge's duty, and he made no effort to break the ice; he was disturbed to see young Constans whisper several times to Maria, with a silly smirk on his face; it was a nuisance that these young soldiers treated any pretty woman like a waitress in a tavern.

When the servants had left, Gratianus drew a packet of papers from the breast of his tunic. Finding it awkward to read lying down, he sat on the end of his couch and put his elbows on the table; the Bishop and the other guests followed his example, and Felix reluctantly did the same, not to be conspicuous. It was the custom of the ancients to recline on a couch, and it was always right to follow the custom of the ancients; but one must make allowances for provincial manners.

Gratianus coughed for silence. 'Well, gentlemen,' he began, 'I have here a summary of various reports from my agents in the cities of southern Gaul, and from the barbarian villages to the north of Gallia Belgica, where I arrange ransom for citizens taken by the pirates and export to Germany such goods as are not on the prohibited list.' Felix listened keenly. It was forbidden to sell to the barbarians any metal or clothing, or anything that might be useful in warfare; in fact, about the only commodity that could be exported was wine, which was not produced in Britain. Gratianus was going dangerously near to boasting that he habitually broke the law.

'Putting together these reports from both sides,' the Senator continued, 'we get a picture of the state of Gaul at this moment. I do not claim that normally I get better information than the government; but there have been no official reports from Gaul, either military or civil, since the end of December. The Comes Littoris Saxonici per Gallias wrote to various soldiers in Britain; but that is the very opposite to an official report, for he had no business to communicate with them at all. Now this is what they say in the Saxon villages by the North Sea. In December the Rhine froze from bank to bank. A warband of Sueves and Vandals, who were plundering on the right bank, seized their chance and crossed the river. They met with no resistance, and pushed on to attack certain walled towns (these barbarians never know the names of the cities they besiege). The moats of these fortresses were frozen, and they got right up to the walls. They stormed city after city, and now they are deep in Gaul, marching south-west.'

'That is a considerable feat of arms for a band who set out to plunder in the frontier regions beyond the Rhine,' said Felix, who was listening intently, as he listened to a doubtful witness in court.

'Yes, of course,' answered Gratianus, 'that is the story as it reached the Saxons. Barbarians boast, and each petty nation pretends it has done all the fighting. Now let us see what they think in Burdigala, where my wine-ships are loaded. They say it was a plot by the coloni of German race who live in north-eastern Gaul. On the darkest and coldest night of the winter they treacherously attacked the walled cities of the frontier, and massacred the sleeping soldiers. But they agree that a great army of Germans is now in the heart of Gaul, and they fear their arrival on the coast of Aquitania.'

'Obviously both sides tell part of the truth,' put in Constantinus. 'The plunderers won a local success, and then the coloni joined them. I suppose every barbarian in Germany is now hurrying to the gap in the frontier.'

'That explains what has happened,' said Felix. 'Now what news have you of the Roman army that is gathering to expel them.'

'There is no army in Gaul,' answered Constantinus, 'except the limitanei in the cities. You don't think the Magister Militum would have fetched troops all the way from Britain before he had mobilized every comitensis in Gaul who could march? Either the limitanei are shut up in their fortresses or they have already surrendered. An army to liberate the country must come from beyond the Alps.'

'That is so,' Gratianus agreed. 'My informant in Burdigala makes it clear that the barbarians march where they will.

We have no army in the field, and he believes, without definite proof, that Augusta Treverorum has fallen already.'

'Then Stilicho will send an army from Italy, if that is where our soldiers are,' said Felix. 'But we in this Diocese must do our share. The Treasury is short of money, but I will see what I can raise, by borrowing, and even by selling Imperial domain. Do you know when the Comes intends to march south, and what force he will bring with him?'

Constans spoke from the other table. 'I took the first message to Eburacum, and I saw the Comes myself. General officers don't tell their plans to junior tribunes, but my impression was that he intended to take no action until he heard from the Magister Militum. There were no preparations before I left.'

'But this is intolerable,' Felix burst out. 'The barbarians march at will through the richest lands of the Empire, and the Comes Britanniarum, one of the highest officers in the service, does nothing because he has no orders! If he isn't a fool he must realize that orders will take a long time to reach him. Let me see, how would you get from Mediolanum to Britain without going through Gaul? By sea to Spain, I suppose, and then by sea again from Burdigala. But even urgent despatches will not come by sea in the depths of winter. We are cut off from Italy until next summer. I suppose, Senator, you called this meeting to put pressure on the Comes, since he is not already preparing to march?'

'Why borrow trouble?' muttered Constantinus, and his son shrugged his shoulders. Gratianus raised his hand for silence.

'Gaul is in distress,' he said, 'because the Gallic army was sent to Italy. Remember that Britain is lightly garrisoned. I did not assemble this company of civilians to tell the Comes what action he should take. We shall be arrested for sedition if we do that. I thought you would like to know the situation in Gaul, purely for your own satisfaction, and I trust the Praeses will acquit me of any intention of putting pressure on the military authorities.'

Flavius Philo uttered a preliminary cough, and launched into a speech. He was known to the Praeses as a wealthy and punctual taxpayer, though it was rumoured that in most of his dealings he was merely an agent for the Senator. Presumably he had been put up to say what Gratianus thought in his heart, but was ashamed to pronounce in public.

'Let us look on the bright side,' he began. 'The defence of Gaul is not the responsibility of Britain. Our Comes cannot leave his own command without orders. He is here to defend us from Saxons and Scots. But all the unoccupied barbarians of the West will now hasten to the plunder of Gaul, and that should mean fewer pirates on our coast. Perhaps the Dux can at last march north to harry the Caledonians. We shall enjoy a peaceful summer. In civil affairs also this setback may bring advantage to Britain. Augusta Treverorum is lost, and no messenger can get through to Lugdunum; we cannot send money over sea. Either the taxes will be lower or at least our silver will be spent in the Diocese.'

This was what many taxpayers would be thinking privately, though it was an astonishingly bold speech to make in the presence of the Praeses. Felix felt greatly annoyed, but he kept his face unmoved and remained silent. In normal times he would have arrested Philo at once; he could be burned for what he had said, and his property confiscated. But this whole conference could be made to look treasonable; Gratianus, with his talk of pooling information and consulting together for the welfare of the State, had drawn them all into a position that would not bear investigation.

Everyone at table was now acutely conscious of danger. Constantinus looked sharply at the Bishop; there were no regulations forbidding him to associate with servants of the government, and churchmen were always trusted; he could delate them without fear of suffering himself. Constans caught his father's eye, and clenched his fist as though holding a sword. Felix saw the gesture, and guessed its meaning; these ridiculous junior officers had taken fright, and were planning murder. He had no love for the Bishop, and murder was a risk run by every prominent man who listened to seditious speeches without making clear his own position. But the one thing they must avoid was an open scandal; the murder of a Bishop could not be hushed up.

He rose formally to his feet, and raised one arm, as he had been taught in the schools of rhetoric. He was an educated man, the only educated man present, and nine-tenths of education taught the technique of persuading a critical audience; he was confident that he could make these boors forget their fright.

He began quietly, as one man of the world to another. He thanked the Senator for his zeal for the public service which had led him to call this conference, and praised the loyalty of the soldiers who had disregarded convention to attend; but he pointed out that the regulations which frowned on meetings between civil and military authorities had not been devised without justification; if officials met to make plans they were bound to discuss hypothetical cases, and from that it was only a step to criticizing the conduct of their superiors. He regretted that he himself, in his ignorance of military affairs, had presumed to express an opinion on the action to be taken by the Comes Britannia- rum; that showed how careful they should be. He begged all present to forget any criticisms he had made, as he would forget everything spoken this evening. Now he must leave, since the hour was late, but before going he begged them to have confidence in the high command of the Army, and especially in Stilicho, the conqueror of Radagaisus.

When he sat down the atmosphere of the conference had changed. It had begun as an informal exchange of views, frankly expressed in very plain language; by making a speech in rhetorical form Felix had turned it into a public meeting, and reminded his hearers of the behaviour that was expected from them. He did not actually leave at once; he drank more wine and chatted with the Bishop. When he finally said good-bye he offered the old man a seat in his litter, though it meant leaving Maria behind; such an open demonstration of friendship should prevent young Constans from doing anything rash.

Next day, at his desk in the Treasury, Felix vowed that never again would he attend such a conference; even when they did not set out to be treasonable everyone present was at the mercy of an informer. The signals between Constantinus and his son had been a shock. These soldiers were so easily frightened! And, what was even worse, they were poor judges of character. The Bishop was not the man to inform on his fellow-guests at a supper party. That was a thing all honourable men despised; Felix himself would try to frighten a plotter into better courses, or argue with him, before he denounced him to the torturers; the real danger to reckless grumblers was some money-grubber who wanted a reward, and the Bishop was not avaricious. The most likely informer last night had been the merchant Philo, who would probably do anything for money; once he had come out as an advocate of a separate Britain there was no danger from anyone else.

So many revolts came to a head not because people felt rebellious, but because they had burnt their boats and were already regarded as traitors. If young Constans had cut the Bishop's throat, and that had been in his mind at one stage of the evening, he must then have led the garrison of Londinium in open insurrection. It would have been a silly, hopeless, pointless tumult, easily suppressed by troops from Eburacum; but while it lasted every official in Prima would be in danger. Either Felix must pretend to approve while sending secret information of his real loyalty, a very tricky business without efficient secret messengers arranged in advance; or he would have been compelled to flee the city, leaving the records of the Treasury at the mercy of illiterate and frightened soldiers.

That particular danger was past. Would it be wise to send a message to the Comes, pointing out that Constantinus had been stationed in Londinium for a long time, and was beginning to think of himself as an independent commander? Felix considered the matter, and decided against it. Soldiers did not take kindly to advice from civilian governors, they thought themselves the best judges of the loyalty of their subordinates, and at Eburacum they would suppose he was delating a personal enemy in the course of some dispute with the local troops.

Meanwhile the government of Britannia Prima needed all his attention. The barbarians in Gaul seemed to have turned to the south-west, and the Channel coast was not in immediate danger. The Comes Littoris Saxonici per Gallias reported all quiet in his territory, but no reliable news came from farther inland. Stilicho was said to be manoeuvring against Alaric on the borders of Illyricum, so there would be no campaign of reconquest until the Goths had been dealt with; this year there would be no trade across the Channel. That meant a thorough reorganization of domestic policy. The Province fed itself, with a small surplus of corn in good years; but they relied on Gaul for wine, and the better-class metalwork came overland from Italy. He must negotiate with the authorities in Spain to open up new channels of trade; the Spaniards had wine to spare, and would be glad of extra corn; but they had a regular market for their exports, and would not want to upset it for a temporary arrangement. A lot of tiresome correspondence must be despatched when the sailing season opened in the spring; if the Spaniards realized that Britain faced a crisis matters could be arranged in time for the harvest and vintage; but if they chose to act through the usual channels, referring everything to Mediolanum, the business might take years.

Most of the Treasury clerks assumed that since no money could go to Italy the Province would have revenue to spare; in spite of all he could do the eternal harrying of defaulters and the relentless collection of arrears was slackly pursued. But Felix knew the army would need every penny that could be raised in ready cash; in the south-east the coastal fortresses must be repaired and enlarged, and the Dux Britanniarum, who commanded the mobile field force, clamoured for a new road to Belerium in the far south-west; no one had ever bothered about that district before, but now it might be invaded from Aquitania, if the barbarians got hold of shipping. All this would cost money, and when disaffection was already muttering the government must press its subjects harder than ever.

In May the time had come for the Comes to move, and Felix was delighted to hear that Marcus Naso had been sent from Eburacum to consult with the officers of the southern commands. Maria suggested inviting him to supper; there had already been so much intercourse between soldiers and civilians that the old convention must be regarded as obsolete, and it would look rude to take no notice of the

trusted emissary of the Comes Britanniarum. Felix agreed
that he must be polite to the young man, though he did not
expect to enjoy the function. Soldiers at a party usually ate
and drank heavily without contributing to the conversation. He had made up his mind never to give Constantinus
another chance to get drunk in his presence, but he
arranged a small party of well-to-do citizens, including the
Senator and the Bishop. Married guests were asked with
their wives, since Maria did not like to be the only lady
present. This was not the normal way to entertain; usually a
wife supped with the ladies in a separate room while the
husband drank with the men; but it was in accordance with
the custom of the ancients, if you chose to regard the
Claudian Emperors as ancient; they had flourished three
hundred years ago, but Felix privately considered that
modern.

In the end they were a party of twelve, including Maria
and two other ladies; these sat on chairs on the service side
of each table. It was an ingenious arrangement; the men
could talk to the ladies, but they could not paw them like
dancing girls if they got drunk. Since each table had room
for three couches, three tables were placed end to end, to
solve the problem of precedence. Felix, the Senator, and the
Bishop, each took the head of one table, and Marcus was on
the right of his host, in the second place, which was quite
good enough for a soldier.

The supper began well, for the guests were congenial,
and most of them were flattered to have been invited.
Naturally Maria sat opposite her husband, and Felix was a
little annoyed when she began to talk to Marcus like an old
friend. She only inquired if he had had a comfortable
journey, but she ought not to have spoken until addressed;
these unsettling events over sea had made the most

respectable people forward and loquacious. The other ladies ate correctly in silence.

When the servants had left the room the Bishop, who had very little tact, asked point-blank what plans the army had made for the summer. This was what everyone wanted to know, but it was not good manners to inquire directly, in case Marcus had to confess that the Comes Britanniarum was powerless to do anything. One of the basic policies of the government was never to admit openly that nothing could be done. However, Marcus answered politely and cheerfully: 'The Comes Britanniarum cannot himself leave the island committed to his care, but we are preparing a field force under the Dux. It will be a chance for the old boy. If he can win a battle he will be due for promotion, and he is very keen to try.'

'I suppose the troops will march when the time comes?' said Gratianus, bluntly asking what was in everyone's mind.

'Why not? Gaul is now hostile country, and they can plunder as though they were beyond the Empire. I think you civilians underestimate the spirit of the army. For generations we have been bred to the sword, a campaign against unarmoured barbarians is not too dangerous, and everyone is bored with forced marches after pirates who won't stand and fight. A big battle means promotion for the officers and booty for the men.'

'That is comforting,' said Felix politely. But the Bishop wanted to get to the bottom of the subject. 'Suppose you are beaten?' he asked. 'What will then become of Britain?'

There were murmurs of shocked disagreement, but Marcus kept his temper. 'Oh, our comitenses can face any number of barbarians,' he said easily. 'You only see limitanei in the south, but you must not judge the army by them. If we find ourselves so heavily outnumbered that

87

there is no chance of success we can retreat to the forts on the coast. But I don't think that will happen. Our armoured cavalry can ride down any German foot, and barbarian horse always scatter to plunder when they should concentrate for battle.'

'Yet Gaul is now ravaged by barbarians,' said Felix. He was angry to hear a soldier boast of the army while a great Praefecture lay defenceless.

'There were no comitenses in Gaul,' answered Marcus. 'When the invasion came unexpectedly the limitanei did not hold their defences; that was bad, but limitanei are nothing to be proud of. Perhaps it was an error of judgement to take so many good soldiers from the Prefecture of the Gauls, but they were needed to beat Radagaisus; and remember they did beat him.'

'You mean the comitenses are invincible, but there are not enough of them,' Maria said brightly.

'Quite right, dear lady. We need more well-equipped, well-mounted, well-paid lancers, fit to ride with the Emperor himself. That is what we mean by comitenses. If you want to sleep safe in your bed just make your husband give us more money.'

'All those in favour of paying more taxes raise their right hands,' said Gratianus ironically. 'There is always room for another stake in the palisade, and another soldier in the ranks, as the saying goes. Come now, lord Praeses, have we spent money on anything except soldiers since you governed this Province?'

There was a moment's silence. The conversation was becoming too earnest for a supper party. But a merchant at another table happened to ask if the amphitheatre at Eburacum was still in use, and that began a discussion of the chance of holding Games in Londinium. The Bishop was enjoying himself, and he liked to be thought a man of the world; he pointed out that the Church did not oppose Games, as some people thought; that was the influence of the Greeks, who had never enjoyed bloodshed even when they were pagan; if criminals had been rightly condemned to death, why not kill them in public and make a holiday of it? Everyone applauded his breadth of mind, but Felix was not interested. For a variety of historical reasons there never had been an amphitheatre in Londinium. In any case there were no ferocious beasts in southern Britain, and the few criminals he condemned were burned at the stake, a smelly death and not very amusing to watch. But the lack of Games was an old subject of controversy, everyone who would not have to pay for them had ideas about how they should be run, and the party grew animated.

Then Gratianus mentioned as a curiosity that his native city of Verulamium had a genuine theatre for stage plays, probably unique in the Diocese; though it had been a rubbish dump for many years, and no one could recognize it unless he knew it was there. 'It would be amusing to find out who built it and why,' he continued. 'In the old days when we could afford it our Curia was most enlightened, but it was a strange waste of money. No one has ever produced a play in Britain. My grandfather told me they used it for cock-fights and bear-baiting, though the spectators could only watch from one side, and it damaged the carving on the front of the scene.'

'I hope you are not thinking of producing a play, Senator,' said the Bishop, smiling at the absurdity of the idea. 'That is something the Church definitely forbids. It is right to kill wicked men and to hunt dangerous beasts; there can be no harm if citizens on holiday watch what is lawful in itself, as we would all peer into the street if the police were fighting a robber. But actors are infamous creatures, and their lascivious goings-on would lead to widespread immorality if the public were allowed to watch them.'

'Yet we all read plays, and make our children learn grammar from them,' put in a corn dealer who wanted to show what a good education he gave his sons.

The general conversation was now safely switched to literature, as it should be towards the end of a party. Felix lay back on his couch and sipped slowly at the one cup of Greek wine that he could afford now the sea was closed to traffic. He had been honest with his guests, and shared equally; the provincials put it down in one gulp and were now filling up with raw Gallic liquor. He resolved that in future he would keep the best wine for his own use while his guests drank what was good enough for them; it was a custom he thought rather low, but Greek wine was going to be scarce in future.

He stared at the coffered ceiling, the best feature of this rather commonplace official residence, remembering the solemn feasts at Constantinople and Mediolanum he had attended in the train of the Divine Theodosius; he was then a junior clerk in the Sacra Largitio, but specially appointed for outstanding loyalty to the Emperor, and there had been a humble place for him at all Imperial feasts. Now he was host, and the most important man in the island, but the parties were not so amusing.

Anyone with a classical education fell easily into that sort of sentimental reverie; but a familiar voice brought him back to the present. Maria was talking steadily, and appeared to be leading the conversation. He sat up, and saw that she was engaged in animated discussion with Marcus; the young soldier had swung himself upright on his couch, with military lack of breeding, and gazed into her face as he listened. This must be stopped; Felix abruptly broke in to ask what troops the Dux would take to Gaul, and whether he would leave a sufficient garrison to maintain order.

Marcus turned round in surprise, and put his legs decorously back on the couch. Maria dropped her eyes, but not before she had exchanged a friendly smile with the handsome young man. Felix had spoken more loudly than he had intended, and the other tables waited in silence for the answer.

Marcus replied in a military voice, as though rendering a report to a superior; it was his way of showing that he did not like the interruption, but must fall in with the wishes of his host.

'The Dux commands five alae of cavalry, companions of the general who follow him always,' he began. 'I suppose there are about three thousand of them all told. Their absence should make no difference as regards keeping order, because they are normally held in reserve to deal with an invasion in force. What other formations will go with him I don't know, but it would be natural to take infantry to garrison fortresses, and guard communications with Britain. Would it matter to you if the Barcarii Tigridenses were removed from this city? The forts on the coast would still be held against the Saxons.'

A merchant at another table put the unofficial point of view. These citizens always complained that garrisons were a burden, but objected when their protection was withdrawn. 'The Celtic-speaking coloni are quiet and orderly at present; they stay on the land and pay their rent, or as much of it as they can. But whenever they come into town to sell a cabbage they see the sentry at the Praetorium. If there were no soldiers some of them might turn Bagauda, as they do in Gaul.'

That started another hare, and Felix was pleased that it was a topic on which ladies could say nothing. It was rather astonishing that there were no Bagaudae in Britain, although the taxes were as high as in other Dioceses where bands of desperate broken peasants plundered outlying farms. Gratianus pointed out that incessant raids by Saxon pirates kept the coloni in sympathy with the Imperial government which protected them; luckily Saxons were more barbarous than the Germans on the Rhine; they killed everyone they met, and discontented taxpayers could not join them as allies. But in other parts of the island there was a different danger, as a travelling cattle dealer said from the Bishop's table. If Londinium managed without a garrison things would remain quiet whilst the coast was held; but if they called in foederati, as the government had done in the north and west, the coloni might take service under the allied Kings. Then you got no taxes from them, and no rent for the landlord.

All the guests agreed that foederati were really no better than hostile barbarians; they might fight for the Roman cause, but under their rule the rights of property were invaded, and they took the taxes for themselves. Felix and Marcus kept silent; neither was willing to admit that there were not enough regular soldiers to hold the outlying Provinces of the Diocese. When the Bishop gave the signal for the guests to leave they had thoroughly enjoyed themselves, grumbling at the government in the presence of the Praeses and a distinguished officer from Eburacum, and working off some of the resentment they felt at the enormous taxes they paid.

Next morning, as Felix sat in the public basilica, listening to a civil action, his mind went back to the talk at table last night. The case was of no interest to the administration, a dispute between two honestiores about a mortgage; but from the standing of the parties it had to be heard in public.

He did not listen carefully; both sides relied on perjured testimony, the legal aspect was not clear, and he had decided at the outset to give judgement for the defendant, who had a blameless record, while the plaintiff's father had supported Magnus Maximus. All the same, he must allow both sides a fair hearing, after the expense they had incurred in hiring witnesses; let their advocates bellow and declaim, while the Praeses turned his mind to serious affairs.

The Comes Britanniarum was sending the Dux to help the Roman cause in Gaul, as was his duty. That meant that by next autumn, when the harvest was reaped and the country most tempting to raiders, Britain would be very lightly defended. Should he start some military formation among the citizens of Londinium? In normal times that was the sort of thing that frightened Mediolanum out of its wits; a Praeses who raised bands of armed citizens on his own responsibility would be dismissed, and probably executed. But the times were not normal; it was five months since he had received a despatch from Italy, and even if the forthcoming campaign was successful he would not hear anything definite this summer. He was left to his own resources, unable to communicate even with his Vicarius.

It seemed only right in this isolated position to concentrate all the energies of the State on defence. Londinium was a large city, with a population of more than thirty thousand; he might raise a force of three or four thousand men, to hold the coastal forts and free regular troops for other duties. Although he would incur suspicion, if he had armed men at his command when communications with Italy were restored the Praetorium Praefect would hesitate to dismiss him; that was how a number of quite loyal servants of the Emperor had first risen in the world.

But would armed citizens obey his orders? Last night several of the most influential honestiores had been at his table, and they did not talk like loyal subjects of the Emperor. They grumbled incessantly, about the taxes, about the high-handed dealings of the foederati with the private property of law-abiding Romans, about the slackness of the regular army. He realized with a disturbing sense of guilt that a year ago he would not have allowed such disloyal and defeatist chatter at his table. But a year ago the position of affairs was very different; every two or three days messengers took his reports across the Channel to the Praefect of the Gauls, and he constantly received orders and advice on every subject of government. Now there was no Praefecture, unless it lurked, cut off from its subjects, in some besieged city; even he, Sempronius Felix, promoted for outstanding loyalty to the Divine Theodosius, had begun to feel dangerously independent.

The lawyer for the defence was finishing his speech; Felix pulled himself together and delivered the judgement that had been in his mind since the beginning of the case. That would confirm the loyalty of an influential landowner, though another would be so disappointed that henceforth he must be watched. He rose from his chair of state and retired to his private office; Paulinus awaited him with the usual bundle of papers, but he told the freedman to stay by the entrance to the courtroom, where the successful defendant, if he had good manners, would bring a suitable present in gratitude for the decision in his favour. The Praeses wished to think undisturbed.

He had allowed himself to dream of independent power, with armed men under his sole orders. He, a civil servant who despised the uneducated soldiery, had looked forward to bargaining with the central government, bartering his support for secure tenure of his office. It had been an idle daydream, occupying his mind while he was bored by a tiresome lawsuit; but if he had felt these stirrings of ambition, surely every officer in the army must be undergoing the same temptation. The comitenses were now concentrating at Eburacum, and this would be a favourable moment for them to proclaim a new Emperor. It was a danger that must be faced; what could he do to hinder it?

There was always this danger that each self-contained army would set up its candidate for the throne. The wise Diocletianus had foreseen it, and the high command had been arranged to make it as difficult as possible. The Comes Britanniarum had been chosen for his loyalty; he was a strict disciplinarian, careful of government money, and unpopular with the troops. Besides, the Comes Littoris Saxonici was jealous of him; the limits of their respective commands had been laid down so that there must always be friction between them. Then there was the Dux Britanniarum; he liked to call himself second-in-command of all the forces in the island, but he had no say in the disposition of the limitanei; those second-line infantry resented the higher pay and greater prestige of the mounted comitenses, and of course every Roman soldier hated the barbarian mercenaries and foederati, with their lack of discipline and disgusting habits. On the whole, there was no reason to fear a revolt by a united Army of Britain, unless they found some dashing young officer with enough money to buy support; and young officers never had any money.

What about the civil population? There was this tiresome tradition that things had gone very well under the separate Empire of Carausius. In a sense that was true; the island had its own problems, and an Emperor who did not have to defend the Rhine and the Danube could give them undivided attention. Yet no ruler of Italy and Gaul would recognize an independent tyrant in Britain; there might be insincere negotiations, and periods of truce in face of another enemy, but in the end Rome always reconquered the island. Only once had the Emperor proclaimed at Eburacum died in his bed after a successful reign; that Emperor was Constantinus the Great, and he had conquered Rome from Britain, instead of Rome conquering him. But it came to the same thing in the end; Constantinus had not reigned in an independent British Empire, and he had won the civil war, against great odds, because he was supported in quite an unprecedented way by the Heavenly Powers.

This longing for a separate Empire was bad statecraft, for the thing could not be done; but to Felix it seemed even worse, it seemed immoral. The Empire was a unity; by forced labour, and the taxes which forced labour produced, it maintained civilization, assailed by barbarians on every side. To leave it was to shirk a duty. The taxes of Britain were needed to support the necessary splendour of the Imperial Sacred Palace, which had such a good effect on barbarian chieftains, and for the defence of Italy, that there should be a constant supply of honest, educated civil servants (like himself) to compel bakers to bake and miners to delve for the comfort of the taxpayer.

The heavy cavalry of the comitenses, the disciplined troopers who could ride down any turbulent throng of barbarians, concentrated at Eburacum in May. The Dux Britanniarum reviewed them in preparation for the expedition which was to liberate Gaul. But then came a long pause.

The official reason for delay was lack of transport and supplies. Orders came to Londinium to send wagons north and arrange depots of provisions along the intended line of march. Constantinus informed the Praeses, and civil and military authorities planned together to impound the oxen of the coloni, though it hampered work in the fields at a vital season of the year. Wagons could be provided, but two months before harvest there was little corn to be seized; the coloni hid what they had and ran away to the woods, until

Felix stopped the collection for fear the new harvest would never be reaped. The army must wait until it was gathered, and so lose most of the campaigning season.

That was a disappointment, with the barbarians ravaging unchecked in Gaul. But perhaps things were worse than was officially admitted. The rumour spread that the reason for delay was not shortage of supplies but the unwillingness of the troops to leave their native island. In normal times every regiment remained in the same station for generations and centuries; the two remaining Legions had been in Britain for more than three hundred years, though those slow-moving formations of heavy-armed foot were no longer regarded as troops of the first class. But even the new alae, cavalry regiments less than a hundred years old, had become attached to their permanent barracks; some of them had been reluctant to march as far as Eburacum; they had insisted on bringing their families, which needed a great many wagons, and clamoured that their homes would be burned by raiding Scots if they stayed away any longer. Unofficial travellers from the north told Gratianus, who passed it on to his son-in-law, that the Dux dared not give the order to march, because he was not sure it would be obeyed.

On the evening of the first Sunday in July Felix sat at home in his private study. He had not looked at his Vergil for months; he was too busy, and it was disheartening to read of the miraculous foundation of Rome when so many Provinces were in barbarian hands. It seemed that the Heavenly Powers were no longer on the side of the pious Aeneas; it had been a mistake to remove that Altar of Victory. On the table lay the usual estimate of the harvest that always came in about that time, but he was not interested; whatever course he adopted the usual very large proportion of the crops would go to the Treasury; the coloni were the most docile part of the population. But the townsmen were another story. He must deal gently with them while the army was away. His tired brain was running through complicated sums when a footman came in to say the Senator Gratianus was at the door, and wished to see the Praeses at once on urgent and confidential business.

This was queer and disturbing. His father-in-law must have news that had not yet reached the government; but it could not be good news, which never came secretly in the middle of the night, but was proclaimed by laurelled couriers in the public forum. Either there had been a great reverse to Roman arms in Gaul or the barbarians had landed in some distant part of the island. When Gratianus was shown in Felix had braced himself to hear a tale of disaster with unmoved dignity, in accordance with the custom of the ancients.

But the Senator's first words were a surprise. After a perfunctory greeting he began to babble about the weather. 'Amazingly clear afternoon for the time of year. No haze in spite of the heat. But the woods are dry, and we must beware of fire. I walked on the wall towards sunset, and saw a column of smoke in the north. It looked like a signal fire, but when I asked the sentry by the North Gate he said the Army had no beacon on that hill-top. What do you think of that, my boy?'

Gratianus was about the same age as the Praeses, but because Felix had married his daughter it amused him to treat the other as a young man; it was a rude and detestable habit, but Felix fell in with his mood. He answered gravely:

'I suppose you mean it was a private signal of yours. But isn't it rather daring to run a signal service of your own? Mediolanum would consider it proof of treason, and remember that in a year or two we shall be under their rule again.'

'Well, son-in-law, you may call it proof of treason. At least it is proof that treason has been committed. I had word that something very important might happen in Eburacum, and I wanted to be the first in Londinium to know definitely.'

'Good Heavens, has the Comes seized the Purple? I trusted the old man, after all these years.' Felix's mind was racing. A commander at the head of a body of comitenses was always a public danger; but the elderly Comes had been content with his status for more than ten years, he was in poor health and due to retire shortly, and had already made plans to settle in the East on his pension. 'I suppose the soldiers hailed him against his will, and he had to comply or be murdered. We must send a message to Italy at once, through Spain. Do you know of a ship sailing?'

'Not so fast, Caius. You are the husband of my daughter, and I don't want you to run into danger. You can't go against the soldiers. Let me tell you what has happened, and then we can make plans.'

Felix pulled himself together. He sat upright in his chair, his face set in lines of Roman gravitas, and motioned to Gratianus with the gesture that gave permission to a lawyer to open his case. But the Senator was not impressed; he was determined to keep the interview on the footing of a private chat between old friends, and he talked as though he were relating a funny story, not describing a political crisis that must end in civil war.

'This isn't a tumult got up by ignorant soldiers who sacrifice a loyal officer to their whims,' he began. 'This is a carefully planned revival of the good old days of Carausius. And you haven't guessed the name of the new Emperor, in spite of ten years in office and the memory of two civil wars. Tut tut, Caius, I expected better from you. Our new ruler is, of course, Marcus Julius Naso, who has taken great pains to prepare the ground. Let me explain. The soldiers don't want a long campaign in Gaul, which will take them away from their homes and benefit no one except Stilicho the Vandal. And the citizens don't see the point of paying more taxes to defend a parcel of Gauls when those Gauls won't defend themselves, and even welcomed the Germans. When we first heard the frontier was broken I consulted with my friends concerning the welfare of Britain. I left you out because you were loyal to the House of Theodosius; now I give you the chance to come in with us. Our party had money, but we lacked an inspiring candidate for the Purple. The two Comites and the Dux are loyal old veterans, unpopular with the army and afraid to take the plunge. But when Marcus came south in February he hinted that the time was ripe for a change, and I saw he was the very man we wanted. He is a good soldier, though that is not important since there will be no fighting; he is popular with the men, he will make a handsome figure riding through the streets, and he will be guided by the wisdom and experience of the merchants of Londinium. We made a compact, and when he went north he took enough of my money for the donative that marks a new reign. He also has support in the south. Constantinus is in this, and the guilds of the city; that gives him Londinium. The Curia of Verulamium will do as I tell them, which gives him control of the road to the north. The only doubtful factor is the Comes Littoris Saxonici; we dared not let him know in advance, and he may try to hold the coast against us. But why should he? He is loyal to Mediolanum, but he can't fight all the rest of Britain. We shall advance on Rutupiae very gently, leaving him time to put his wealth on a ship for Spain; that is what he will do if he is sensible. So now you know the position of affairs. I give you warning because you are the husband of Maria. You can come in with us now, and let the public think you were one of the conspirators from the beginning, or you have a day and a night to get out of Londinium before the new Emperor is proclaimed.'

Felix had listened in silence, without betraying his feelings. His mind was in a whirl; his first impulse was to arrest the Senator, but he guessed his father-in-law had not visited this official residence without taking precautions. The garrison of Londinium would obey their commanding officer, as soldiers always did at the opening of a civil war (though it might be possible to buy them for the right side later on). The wise course was to join the winning party, at once.

'You know I have always been a loyal subject of the Divine Theodosius, and of his sons. I can remember the founder of the family, Theodosius the Magister Militum,' he began, in a reminiscent voice, as though settling down for a chat about past politics. 'I once saw him ride in triumph through the streets of Lugdunum. But young Honorius is no help to Britain at the moment, and a change might not be a bad thing. However, I should like a little more information. You saw a beacon, which you were expecting. But a beacon is only a general alarm that something has happened. Do you know for a fact that Marcus now rules in Eburacum, or only that he has begun his attempt to seize power?'

'Well done, Caius. I was afraid you might rant about your duty. I see you are a sensible man, eager to join the stronger side, so long as you know it really is stronger.'

'I can't promise anything. I didn't see your column of smoke, and I wouldn't know what it meant anyway. You understand, I am trusting you. I have only your word for it that there is a plot at all. If you were not a friend and a relative this would be an easy way to trap me into declaring against the Emperor while an agent waited outside to arrest me. The Vicarius of Moesia was caught like that just before the war against Eugenius.'

'Now that is unkind,' Gratianus said with a frown. Apart from the advantage of getting an important official to join his faction he enjoyed the thrill of telling exciting news to someone who ought to have known it first; his pleasure would be spoiled if Felix did not believe him. So he began to explain in great detail, which was what the Praeses had hoped for.

'I am a member of your family, and my prosperity is bound up with yours. I don't want your appointment myself, and there is no one among my friends who is after it either. Why should I trap you into a bogus rebellion? I will tell you the whole thing, and you can judge for yourself whether we shall succeed. Now first about that beacon. It is not a very informative signal, but I took that into consideration. I had fires laid in groups of three, all the way from Eburacum to the heights above Londinium. Three fires together meant failure, and I would have fled over sea before the agents in Londinium knew there had been a plot. Two fires meant the revolt had begun, and met opposition; while the fighting continued I could have found out whether anything was known against me, and perhaps bought my way out of trouble. That is one degree better than flying to the ends of the earth. One fire alone means success. The troops followed Marcus when he called on them, and the Comes Britanniarum is dead. You can take that for a fact.'

'You know the Comes is dead? Just from that one signal? Surely he might have joined the revolt; though he was a man of honour, and loyal to his Emperor.'

'Watch your tongue, Caius. A phrase like that is

dangerous. The Comes was blind to the needs of the Diocese, and notoriously attached to the tyrant Honorius. I know he is dead, because we decided not to give him the chance to change sides. Now we have an opportunity to reward some soldier who helped us; one must promote the officers who risk their lives in these tumults. Besides, the troops are now committed; Stilicho cannot forgive this murder, and they must stick to our side even if it looks the weaker.'

'Thank you. I understand. You mean that if I wait until the courier arrives from Eburacum it will be too late for me to adhere to the new government. But I must have time to consider. When will the messenger arrive? Do you mind if I give my decision in the morning?'

'The Emperor was proclaimed this morning, two hundred miles away. The courier cannot arrive until the day after to-morrow, but you must join us before that if you want to keep your office. I can give you until the morning. Otherwise you should leave the city to-night. The sentries will let you go, but after that you must make your own arrangements. I don't want Spain to know immediately, before we are settled in our rule of the Diocese; so I dare not lend you the ship I had ready in case of failure.'

There was no more to be said, and Felix wanted to consider his plans alone. After an extremely formal leave-taking, for to-morrow they might be enemies hunting one another implacably to the death, he showed the Senator to his litter. Then he sat down at his desk, and tried to think straight.

It was more than thirty years since he had seen Theodosius the Magister Militum riding through Lugdunum. Since then he had served the son and the grandson of his hero; in the civil war he had run an enormous risk for love of the unproved son of the great soldier, and for that he had been well rewarded. He had been right to follow the younger Theodosius, who had turned out an exceptionally good Emperor. But now it was time to think of the welfare of the Oecumene, without being sentimental about a particular family. Was it for the good of the State that Honorius should continue to rule? He was not notably debauched, the usual failing of a civilian Emperor. Though gossip said he was lazy, yet the high officers of State who ruled during his childhood had managed things very well.

They had chosen the best soldier in the world for Magister Militum, and the beauty of it was that a Vandal did not know how to rule Romans, so Stilicho could not seize the Purple. The laws had been enforced, Britain had been defended and its population compelled to behave like civilized beings, and Radagaisus had been defeated in a decisive battle. All that stood to the credit of the government in Mediolanum.

On the other hand, whispered the tempter, the principle of hereditary succession was alien to Rome. The Emperor was a military commander chosen to rule in a crisis, a crisis that had now endured for more than four hundred years; and military skill was not a hereditary quality. The barbarians lived under hereditary rulers, and look what a mess they made of everything they undertook. Felix tried to remember a civilized State that had been well governed by hereditary Kings; there were the Spartans, perhaps; but the Ephors had actually governed, and in any case independence had been lost long ago. He concluded that although Theodosius the Magister Militum had been one of the glories of Roman arms, and his son the great Emperor had reunited the Oecumene, these eminent ancestors were no reason why a patriotic Roman imbued with the traditions of the Gens Sempronia should serve Honorius.

Very well. The Empire might be better off under a new
dynasty. He thought he could trace a rule running through
the civil wars of the last two hundred years. A competent
general attained the Purple by successful rebellion; in the
nature of things he was elderly, or he would not have
reached high command; that meant his eldest son had been
educated as a private individual. So it had been with
Constantius Chlorus and his son, the Divine Constantinus; if
you went back into history so it had been with Vespasianus
and Titus. But the trouble came in the third generation,
after two good Emperors. The grandson would be born in
the Purple, and no one could endure absolute power from
childhood without becoming slightly mad, or at least very
wicked; the fratricidal sons of the Divine Constantinus were
proof of that. It was lucky for Rome that Honorius was no
more than lazy, and unusually childish for his age. But he
would never be a good ruler, for he thought of the
sovereign power as naturally his, and so would not guard it
with the incessant detailed devotion to duty that was
necessary if an Emperor were to die in his bed. A Praeses
who remained obstinately loyal to an outworn dynasty was
not doing his best for civilization.

On these lines Felix persuaded himself that he was not
bound in honour to die for the House of Theodosius. But it
did not follow that Marcus Julius Naso was the ideal
successor. He knew nothing of the young man except that
soldiers liked him, and that Gratianus and his party thought
he would put the prosperity of Britain before the welfare of
the Empire as a whole. That was wrong in principle, but
possibly the Senator was mistaken. After all, the men who
proclaimed Constantinus the Christian had expected him to
set up a separate Empire in Britain; but he had at once led
forth his army to unite the Oecumene under his sway.
Marcus had fairly good manners, for a soldier, though he

talked too much to other men's wives; he might be sound at heart; he would need advice from gentlemen trained in government service. His present backers were gross middle-class merchants, unskilled in rhetoric and thinking more of their wealth than of the prosperity of the civilized world; it should be possible for a trained speaker to argue them down. In fact, Felix might find himself the real ruler of Britain, if he was courteous and kept his temper. The great thing was to teach his new chief that one Diocese could not contract out of the trials that beset the Empire, and that it was the duty of all brave soldiers to rescue the whole Oecumene from barbarian attack.

It was midnight when he had come to a decision, and strenuous thinking had left him very sleepy. He was tempted to go to bed, and send word of his resolve to Gratianus in the morning. But news of the proclamation of an Emperor sometimes travelled unexpectedly fast; it would be a pity if he gave in his adhesion just too late to save his head. He sent the night porter to rouse his litter-bearers; the household would be astonished when he went out in the middle of the night, but he was about to behave unconventionally in other ways.

It was a fine July night, and he enjoyed the passage through sleeping streets; there was no one about save the watch, who challenged at a street corner, but were satisfied by the official liveries. No slave, and in practice no poor man, was allowed to wander in the streets after bedtime, and even the rich were supposed to give a reason for being out late; but officials never obeyed their own regulations.

The mansion of Gratianus was darkened, but the porter was awake; as Felix entered he heard a hum of conversation from the private rooms at the back. Naturally the conspirators could not pass the night in sleep, when their dangerous undertaking hung in the balance, and the obvious place to wait for news was the home of the leading citizen of Londinium, with his notorious private service of spies. Felix was pleased at this evidence that the plotters were nervous; it would make his support more welcome; but they were breaking one of the elementary rules of conspiracy, which was to do nothing out of the ordinary. He had behaved exactly as usual up to the night when he robbed the Treasury of Lugdunum, all those years ago.

Two German slaves met him in the hall; one led him to a lobby off the entrance and remained to keep an eye on him, while the other informed Gratianus. That was not the way to welcome a Praeses; it would have aroused his suspicion if he had been an enemy. It was wrong to trust slaves with a secret; these Germans were loyal, but they did not know when to stop boasting, and the agents were skilled in torture; even the bravest suspect told all he knew on the second day of questioning. He began to wonder if the plot was already known to the agents of Honorius; they might be letting it come to a head, to enrich the Treasury with confiscations. But they had left it too late, for now an order of arrest would be resisted. Nothing could stop the proclamation of Marcus in Londinium, and then the conspirators might fly if they dared not fight.

Within a few minutes the steward came with two foot-men to greet the Praeses in correct form. He was conducted through the entrance hall, past the bogus ancestors in their niche and the little shrine where was displayed the diptych of appointment to the Senate (the last one, issued by the Divine Theodosius, for the original of the tyrant Magnus Maximus had been quietly destroyed) to the dining-room at the back of the house. The room was crowded, and the company wandered about in small groups; there were no couches, though little tables were set with wine and light refreshments. Many of the guests were unknown to Felix, but he recognized Constantinus, in linen cuirass and military boots, attended by his son Constans in full armour. Then Gratianus came up with a smile, and each bowed to the other's superior rank, in the way they had worked out for getting over the difficulties of etiquette when a Senator met a Praeses.

'Thank you for making your decision so quickly, my lord Praeses. These are the supporters of the new government. You see, we have on our side both the army and the merchants, which is unusual; you don't often find tax-payers and soldiers in the same ranks, but I think Britain is unanimous for our new Emperor. Now you have brought over the civil service taxes can be collected, and lawsuits decided, without a break. That is very important at the start of a new reign. Our Emperor will not forget it.'

'My dear Senator, I shall do all in my power to assist you. One cannot be neutral in civil war. You are a man of the world, and you know that at one time I favoured Honorius. But I am not a hero, to perish leading a forlorn hope, and this Diocese needs above all strong government. Have you any orders for me?'

'Orders, Caius? Nothing of the kind. We welcome you, and would be glad of your advice, but we will not begin the new reign by giving orders to such a distinguished servant of the State.'

So the position was laid down, without fear of misunder-standing. Felix was not merely to serve the new Emperor as an expert in administration; he must give advice, and commit himself to the conspiracy without hope of changing sides in future. Very well; if he must plot treason, it would be successful treason. He looked round the room.

'Are you in touch with the troops on the Littus? I don't see any strange soldiers. I know you decided not to tell the

Comes, but you ought to make sure the soldiers don't attempt resistance. Once fighting starts you never know where it will stop, and people change sides again. It is most important that the new government should be welcomed unanimously.'

'No, we dared not risk it. But I have arranged to keep the defences occupied. I know an exile from Gaul who has settled among the Frisians. Through him I got word to a pirate chief that this would be good time for a cruise. All the cavalry on the coast are now engaged in a fierce little pursuit, and can't be bothered with civil war. Don't think I brought barbarians treacherously into Britain. The pirates believe a civil war broke out last month, and they will get a shock when the Comes meets them with all his force. It needed careful timing, but I think I have brought it off. The Comes will be busy, the pirates will be beaten, and it costs nothing except that the Saxons won't trust me in future.'

'It was brave of your agent to deceive the barbarians, since he lives among them.'

'Oh, he thought he was telling the truth. I'm afraid he will have a painful end. But he was a fugitive from justice, and any Roman is entitled to compass his death.'

That eliminated the danger from the garrison of the south coast, though Felix noted for future reference that Gratianus must be a convincing liar.

The Senator presently wandered away to console a nervous trader, and Felix looked carefully round the room; it was important to know who was in this conspiracy, and in certain circumstances his fellow-guests might deny that they had been present. Young Constans, whose armoured back faced him squarely, was talking to someone with an elaborate coiffure of piled curls. There was a law against boy-friends, though it was not enforced against officers in the army; but it would be interesting to know who the boy was. Felix shifted his position to get a view, and was amazed to recognize his wife.

It was past midnight, there were no other ladies present, and she had not asked permission before leaving his roof. For such an escapade he could divorce her. What dismayed him more than the light behaviour of Maria, whom he privately considered capable of any outrage, was the discovery that he could not trust his domestic staff; the chief lady's maid, in particular, had orders to report privately on the movements of her mistress; that girl would spend the rest of her life grinding corn on a remote hill-top; but the porter must have known as well, and probably every slave in the house. The trouble was that they feared their mistress, who flogged them frequently, more than their remote master. He boiled with rage as he strode up to his wife, but checked himself when he remembered that his host was her father. He must postpone his reproaches until he had the wanton safely at home.

She greeted him calmly, with an artificial society smile. 'Hallo, Caius darling. How nice to see you here. Poor Father needs my help in this tricky state of affairs, and of course he could not give such a big party without his daughter to look after the servants.'

'We will discuss your conduct later, in private,' Felix answered grimly. 'I shall make some changes among your attendants. But why did you creep out secretly? If you ask to go to your father's house I always give my consent.'

All this time that young boor Constans was listening with his ears pricked; but Felix was too angry to be discreet.

'My darling,' Maria answered impudently, 'if I had known you were coming I would have come with you. But, don't you see, that was just what I didn't know. Father was afraid you might flee from the city, to help that little mollycoddle in Mediolanum. You would have taken me with you, and then poor Father would have lost the support of his only child. Thank God we are all on the same side now.'

Constans guffawed at this plain speaking, and slapped Maria on the shoulder as though she were a man and a comrade. Felix stepped between his wife and the young man; the important thing was to get her away from this excited party of nervous plotters, who had been drinking heavily to keep up their courage. 'Perhaps you were right to come, my dear,' he said, with an unconvincing attempt at a smile. 'Your father's house is a good refuge in time of revolution, if you fear to remain with your husband. But you are the only lady in this room. I suppose you have been too occupied to notice it. Now run along to the women's apartments, and go to bed. I shall take you home in the morning.'

She dropped a curtsey to her husband, and left the room without another word; but the effect of this unquestioning obedience was spoiled by the grin she exchanged with Constans as she turned to go.

Felix walked over to a table and gulped down a cup of unmixed wine; he was angry and flustered, at a time when his life depended on clear thinking, though a gentleman educated in philosophy should control his emotions in any circumstances. He tried to think as a Stoic; no misfortune should ruffle a good conscience. That applied to loss of money, and to danger of death, but it was not so easy to face unmoved the menace of a flighty wife. A man who wore the horns with calm dignity was no less a laughing-stock than one who made a fuss about it. Not that he feared Maria was carrying on a real intrigue with young Constans; the fellow was nothing more than a beefy stand for polished armour, and could not amuse an intelligent woman. Yet even Socrates had looked foolish when he could not control

Xantippe. He filled his cup a second time, and concentrated on the political problem; family affairs must wait until he was sure he would survive this revolution.

He had committed the worst mistake of an official; he had miscalculated the loyalty of the population. This coup was not even a military revolution, arranged by a few soldiers whose secrets he could not be expected to discover. Looking round the room he saw many well-to-do merchants, the natural object of suspicion to every sensible government; the taxes took most of their income, and they always thought, poor fools, that a change of rulers would lighten the burden. Of course, what had made this scheme more successful than the usual desperate struggle of bankrupt taxpayers was the great wealth of the Senator. But that was no excuse; a competent Praeses should make sure that every rich man was a supporter of the Emperor, or confiscate his property on a charge of disaffection.

He saw that his only possible course was to join the revolt. Even if he loyally upheld the legitimate Emperor, and finally, after a struggle, kept his Province faithful to the central power, the ministers at Mediolanum would dismiss him for incompetence. How blind he had been! But also, how ungrateful were the citizens of Londinium! He worked long hours at his desk, and what was even more boring, sat for long hours in the law court, to keep civilization in being. But for him, these rebels would have had no bakers or skilled metalworkers, possibly no slaves at all unless they kept them permanently locked up; and because all this necessary and paternal care cost more money than they could conveniently afford they were about to change the whole foundation of society without consulting their governor.

The wine was making him angry. He took a handful of olives to settle it, and began to consider his position under the new regime. It was no good merely to be carried along by events, giving support to whichever government the soldiers put in power; some hanger-on of the Emperor Marcus would want the salary and official residence of the Praeses, though he might not find it necessary to do the work. He must make certain of keeping his office.

He found Gratianus sitting on a stool against the wall; the Senator was sober and wide awake; he had seen other revolutions, and was old enough to stop drinking when he had had enough. Felix came to the point at once. 'Look here, my head is as much at stake as yours, though I was not brought into the scheme until a few hours ago. But no one has given me a firm promise that if I co-operate I will continue to rule this Province. Scribble something, in a note-book if you like. We are near the door, and your porter would not stop the Praeses; if I don't get a promise from you I shall leave the house now, and proclaim myself Emperor at daybreak. The German police will hold the city for me. There will be enough fighting to sack Londinium and ruin you, even though I am beaten in the end. Now send for a note-book without leaving this corner.' He moved his foot quietly to trap the Senator's toes, so that neither could move without an unseemly struggle.

Gratianus looked hard at his son-in-law, and grinned. The general public thought of the Praeses as a hard-working bureaucrat, who sat at his desk all the daylight hours and spent the evenings alone with his Vergil. They forgot that he had run desperate risks in his youth, and seen civil war at the side of the Divine Theodosius. But he knew very well the first rule of the bloody game; an eminent man must exploit his nuisance-value; unquestioning fidelity earned nothing. Gratianus was also a veteran of politics. He answered cheerfully:

'It is kind of you to be content with a note-book, whose

writing can be melted off in a moment. But I have something better for you. Maria is now sleeping on a properly engrossed parchment, appointing you Praeses under the new Emperor. It is sealed by the new Vicarius, myself, and countersigned by Marcus. That is not a document I care to leave lying about, but it has been in existence for some weeks. If you don't believe me (and why should you?) go to the women's apartments and read it.'

Felix moved his foot to release his host.

'I suppose if I hadn't asked I wouldn't have got it,' he said pleasantly. 'Then you could have promoted a more businesslike supporter. But I will take your word for it. I was half-asleep when you saw me a few hours ago, and these years of peace made me forget how to look after myself in time of revolution. So you are to be Vicarius? Well, the one in Gaul has been caught by the barbarians, unless he fled to Spain. But I hope you will allow me as free a hand as he did.'

'My dear Caius, I am not trained in administration, and you govern this Province very well. All I want is the seal of the Vicariate, to get my goods through the ports without interference. I have supplied the donative Marcus must give the soldiers at Eburacum, and I don't suppose he will pay me back. But if I can excuse myself the thousand and one useful and commendable regulations that govern trading with the barbarians I shall not be the loser.'

'Then I remain ruler of Britannia Prima, if I leave your business alone? Well, I have winked at a good deal for my father-in-law, and so I shall for the new Vicarius. But if the soldiers see you making money they will take it away for their bottomless pay-chest. Are you certain you can manage the new Emperor?'

The Senator smirked and put one finger to his nose; he was a very vulgar man. 'Money talks, my dear son-in-law,' he said, 'and I am the only man in Britain who can buy a mutiny in the army.'

'But you will not be able to buy one until you have got your money back by trading with the barbarians, which I suppose means buying cheap the plunder they steal in Gaul. This summer will be dangerous, as you must know without being told. That brings me to another point. As I understand the scheme, we in Londinium do nothing until we hear from Eburacum. We merely follow the lead of the soldiers, and your advance information is wasted; incidentally, you have invited so many foolish people, and given them so much to drink, that the secret will be all over the city by midday. Let me proclaim the new Emperor from the steps of the Treasury at once. Then Marcus will owe us the rich city of Londinium, and we shall carry more weight in his councils than if we tamely follow Eburacum.'

'Please, Caius, don't be too dashing. I know you have taken a leading part in civil war, while I am only an amateur who obeys each government in turn. We discussed the idea of a proclamation, and Constantinus was against it. The troops on the Littus might think it was an isolated revolt, and attack us; and we haven't the money to bribe the Barcarii Tigridenses. They are not loyal to Honorius, but they might proclaim someone else, and then there would be fighting in the city.'

'Yes, Senator. Naturally Constantinus wants to be the moving spirit in the whole business; it will increase his influence with the new Emperor. But why should we give way to him? Don't you see? Proclaim Marcus when the citizens are going to work in the morning, and my bet is that not a dog will bark. We show our independence of the army, snub Constantinus, and prove that the merchants of Londinium, and the civil service, are an important factor in politics.'

He spoke earnestly, to convince this poor-spirited money-grubber that in a civil war it was fatal to sit back and let things happen to you; every prominent man must himself influence events, or someone who had taken a really active part would be given his office as a reward. But Gratianus was not to be moved. The revolt had been planned in detail, and he dared not suddenly alter the part he had sketched for himself. If they set the example of extemporary departures from the course laid down someone else might be inspired to proclaim a different Emperor. Let the civilians provide the necessary funds, while the soldiers took the lead in public.

In the end Felix gave way. It was not worth antagonizing his father-in-law, and the chief architect of the revolt, merely to bring himself prominently into the public eye. There were sound arguments for keeping in the background. Gratianus had his commission as Vicarius, Felix was to continue as Praeses; those were the highest civilian posts in the Diocese, and it was difficult to see what more could be done to reward them if they alone invested Marcus with the Purple. As for their influence over the new government, the public might think the soldiers had imposed their will on the merchants and civil service, but Marcus would know where the money had come from that made the new reign possible. Gratianus was fond of power, but indifferent to position; he only wanted the Vicariate because it would bring profit, and what he really liked was giving advice when he felt like giving it, not governing the country when he had other things to attend to. It was an outlook that had kept him safe in earlier civil wars.

The party remained in full swing until the early daylight of July. No one was eager to go home, for all felt safer while they were together. There was still a faint chance that some zealous adherent of Honorius might come with armed watchmen at his back to arrest the conspirators, and they clung to the protection of Constantinus and the soldiery. As a point of revolutionary practice it was not the right way to behave, for the officers had not brought a guard. Felix toyed with the idea of collecting the German police and making prisoner all the heads of the new government in one swoop. It could be done, and it would leave him master of Londinium. If there had been any trace of a party in favour of Honorius it would have been rather amusing; for the weaker side must offer greater reward to its followers. But with the army at Eburacum solid for Marcus he could not remain in power, and he reminded himself that he was already at the top of the tree. He would follow quietly where his father-in-law led.

But the government must be carried on, and the Treasury was due to open two hours after sunrise. Felix sent word to Maria that he would take her home before he began the day's work. He was carried back through peaceful busy streets to breakfast and a bath, which must do instead of sleep.

Maria was silent in the litter. She seemed frightened and ashamed. So she ought to be, but they would continue to see a good deal of one another in the future, and life would be more pleasant if they remained friends. Felix chatted about the behaviour of the guests as though they were leaving an ordinary supper; she saw that her escapade was to be glossed over, and responded to his mood. For the first time for several years they breakfasted together.

Afterwards Felix sat for half an hour in the hot room of the bath, to drive away his fatigue. This was a suitable time to deal with household affairs, and he summoned the steward. He gave orders to sell the lady's maid to a dye works immediately; he would lose money by it, for she was a skilled hairdresser and would only fetch the price of an untrained hand; but it would make the other servants more reliable in future. The slaves in a dye works soon turned a very odd colour, then they broke out into sores, and in a year or two they died; it was a worse punishment even than the corn-mill.

The night porter was not so much to blame. Seeing the lady of the house dressed for the street, even at a late hour, he might suppose her husband knew where she was going. But he had guessed wrong, and a porter who guessed wrong might one day cause a great deal of trouble. In future he would stoke the bath, live in the cellar, and be locked up at night, instead of sitting about and seeing the world as guardian of the door.

The eunuch also had been lax, but he could not be replaced. In any case, he was rather a sign of luxury and good breeding than a sentry; for it was a regrettable fact that the cheapest complete slaves made fun of eunuchs and paid no attention to their orders. It was enough to give him a flogging, and remind him that he must allow no one to leave the women's apartments after dark, except by definite orders from his master.

When he had made these arrangements Felix left for the Treasury at once, so that Maria could not make a fuss about the change of her personal attendants. Not that she was foolishly attached to the servants she saw every day, like some badly brought-up wives; she was naturally talkative, and chattered in an undignified manner to whoever was in the room with her; but in matters of discipline she was a severe mistress, who flogged for very slight offences. Felix was worried about the right course to take with his wife. She had behaved very badly, and some husbands would have locked her up in the country until age brought discretion. But she was the daughter of Gratianus the

Senator, who was powerful now and would be more powerful under the new Emperor. He had married her to win the friendship of her father, and to put her away would be to lose it. When it came to the point he dared not punish her.

CHAPTER III

MARCUS IMPERATOR
SEMPER AUGUSTUS

For the next thirty-six hours Londinium was full of rumours. But on the evening of the second day a courier rode up to the Praetorium, and everything passed off as the conspirators had planned. There was no donative for the Barcarii Tigridenses, though in the old days a pretender to Empire gave extra pay to every man in his army; but a soldier would be more generous to his troops than a hereditary prince in the civilian atmosphere of Mediolanum, and the garrison cheered with a will when Constantinus gave the word. No one shouted another name, though Marcus was almost unknown to them. They were only limitanei; they knew themselves to be second-class troops, unfit to dispute with comitenses the rule of Britain.

Constantinus led the procession to the forum, where Felix and Gratianus awaited him at the head of the civil service. The square was filled with citizens, who cheered, with occasional cat-calls, as they would have cheered for an execution or any public show. After all present had sworn fidelity to Marcus the Senator was inducted as Vicarius, and Felix was confirmed in his office. The government could not afford much in the way of rejoicing, but next day was declared a holiday, and a little free wine was provided at the expense of the tavern-keepers. The curfew was suspended for one night, and bonfires blazed in the streets.

It was late when Felix sat down alone to supper. For a long time he remained at table, considering the new situation and his own prospects in it. There had been no trouble at all, and Marcus was undisputed ruler of Londinium; if the Comes Littoris Saxonici remained loyal to Honorius he must quickly see that resistance was impossible; then he would presumably emigrate. There was no danger of serious fighting in Britain.

He considered the personality of Marcus, or what little he knew of it. The Emperor intended to march south almost at once, to settle the affairs of the richest city in his dominions; would he have the sense to remember that he owed his elevation to the merchants of Londinium, or would flattery and the thrill of untrammelled power have already turned his head? Yet perhaps this was looking too much on the dark side. There had been wise and humane Emperors, or the State could not have endured for more than four hundred years. Theodosius had been absolute, and there was flattery at his court, yet he had reigned wisely. To be a savage tyrant needed energy and application. There were three main types of Emperor, the good, the wicked, and the lazy; if the good were rare, so were the really wicked, and for the lazy there were competent ministers.

Whatever the future might hold Gratianus was at present the most powerful man in Londinium, and the nominal superior of the Praeses. It was foolish to continue on bad terms with his only child. Felix drank a cup of wine, to give himself courage for what might be an unpleasant interview, and went to call on his wife. Maria was sitting over her embroidery, while a maid stumbled through a passage of the Iliad, though she could barely read the Greek letters. He was touched at this evidence that his wife was improving her mind as he had so often advised her; she knew a little Greek, chiefly the fashionable terms used in theology and dressmaking, but the archaic polysyllables of Homer must be quite incomprehensible to her. She was not looking so attractive as usual, and that was partly his fault. He had bought her a new maid as soon as the other was sold, for no lady could be expected to arrange her own hair; but the only girl available had been trained in a straitlaced household, and though she could arrange hair she knew nothing of make-up. Like most husbands, Felix abhorred rouge in theory, but he missed it when it was absent.

He dismissed his wife's attendants, and came straight to the point: 'My dear, our new Emperor will date his reign from to-day. That makes your father the most powerful civilian in the State. But I am powerful also, and we can live prosperously if the family holds together. Now you married me in obedience to your father's command, and I have no right to expect your love. If there is someone else you really want to marry I shall not stand in your way; I can divorce you to-morrow if you wish it. But if you are not deeply in love with anyone you cannot do better than remain my wife. Will you preserve outward decorum, obey me as your husband, and behave as you should? I will not submit to the role of a cuckold, but I shall not demand much of you. As mistress of this house you will be the most important lady in Britain.'

Maria listened to this speech with a businesslike expression. Since her husband did not expect her to pretend a devotion she did not feel she was prepared to discuss her future as one politician to another. She smiled, but it was the friendly smile of a colleague, not the humble simper of a dutiful wife.

'Dear Caius,' she answered, 'of course I will do everything a wife should. There is no one I like better than you, except my father. Let me remain in your household. I am sorry I was too forward with Constans, and before that with our new Emperor. It was to help Father with his plan, and we could not tell you until we knew you were on our side. But all that is finished; Britain is safely under a ruler who will put this Diocese first instead of worrying about Italy. Henceforth you will find me as retiring as a well-bred wife should be. Anyone who wants a favour must send a lady to ask for it, for I shall have no dealings with men.'

Felix was satisfied. It was a pity that his wife was so unwomanly as to hold an opinion about the government of Britain; ladies did not understand these things. He saw also that if ever he was compelled to break with Gratianus Maria would side with her father; but at present they agreed in politics. He retired to his own bedroom in a contented frame of mind.

He had come to a sensible arrangement with his wife, which ought to ensure continued support from the new Vicarius. He knew that she would be happy in receiving the courtship of every citizen who wished for favours or promotion; it was not quite a suitable occupation for a lady, concerning whom the ancients had wisely said that the highest reputation was to remain completely unknown, but it was a great deal better than making gay conversation with young officers. He need pay no more attention to the affairs of his household, and could settle down to economic planning. Perhaps there was some sense in the popular idea that Britain would be better off with no taxes going over sea.

At the end of the month the Imperial Court moved to Londinium. There was some discussion in the city as to the location of the Sacred Palace. To remove the Praeses from his official residence would cause great inconvenience, though it was the most comfortable dwelling that was already government property; luckily the Emperor sent word that he wished to live as a soldier, and would lodge in the Praetorium until he had made up his mind whether to build a new Palace for himself. Since the Praetorium contained no large rooms for official ceremonies the Basilica of the Treasury was set aside as a throne-room and banqueting hall. That was not really a disadvantage; the Basilica was only used for the few lawsuits that were held in public; Felix much preferred to try all cases in private, and now he had a good excuse. If some honestioris stood out for his right to a public hearing he might have it with the Emperor himself as judge; no one would want that, for it meant appalling delay, and the Emperor, untrained in jurisprudence, would be extremely erratic in his verdicts.

The Comes Littoris Saxonici had loaded a ship with the pay-chest of his troops and everything else of value at his headquarters, as soon as the garrison of Eburacum marched out; rumour said he had escaped the pirates of the Channel and arrived in Spain. His troops offered their submission in return for immediate pay, and the merchants of the south raised the necessary loan with alacrity. It would have been a serious setback if the garrisons on the coast started to plunder for a living, but luckily they were so accustomed to defending the countryside from raiders that they did not turn easily to raiding themselves.

One morning at the beginning of August Felix took his place at the North Gate to welcome the Sacred Emperor. Gratianus had gone as far as his native Verulamium to meet the expedition, and the Praeses was the senior official present. There had been some trouble with the Bishop, who put forward the view that since Londinium had no Curia he should represent the populace of the city; that would have been awkward, for according to the official table of precedence a Bishop ranked with a Praeses; but they had persuaded the old man to wait at his church outside the West Gate, where he could receive a special Imperial visit all to himself. The Emperor was believed to be a Christian, or at least a catechumen if he had never been baptized; no one knew for certain, but if he had been a militant pagan, like Eugenius of evil memory, his supporters would have heard of it.

It was about midday when the expedition appeared over the northern hills. In advance was an ala of light cavalry, small men riding ponies of native breed. Felix looked on them with contempt, for he remembered the magnificent troops of the Divine Theodosius; but they were more dashing than the dingy limitanei who garrisoned the south, and the crowd gave them a cheer. Then came the two Legions left in the island; they made a fine show as they swaggered along in brazen armour, swinging the metal strips about their loins. These slow-marching swordsmen were little use in the field, now that the enemies of Rome no longer fought in the phalanx of heavy hoplites; they could not catch light-armed raiders, and Gothic lancers had been known to ride them down; but they were the traditional embodiment of the majesty and dominion of Rome, and Felix felt his eyes water as they passed with measured tread; for ceremonial occasions infantry, who can keep step and hold their bodies immovable, are more impressive than cavalry, who must control their jigging horses when they should be steady on parade. The Legions were a moving spectacle, eloquent reminders of Zama and Actium, but like many other parts of the military machine they were more impressive than useful.

Then came the first ala of the comitenses, and Felix looked carefully, for these were the real striking-force of the army, the companions of the Emperor. They were heavily armoured lancers mounted on tall horses of the Lycian breed; the riders had their feet in iron stirrups, and the crowd pointed at these and exclaimed with awe. They were the very latest invention of the military art, and this was the only ala in Britain so equipped. Behind the lancers came an ala of mounted archers. But though they carried bows in imitation of the Huns they also wore strong armour and long swords for hand-to-hand fighting; they rode in the correct Roman manner, without stirrups, feet behind the knees and toes down. Barbarian inventions might be all very well for heavy lancers, themselves a novel branch of the service, but the old-fashioned cavalry, whose equipment had been devised by the Divine Septimius Severus, would not learn new methods of riding at the whim of Stilicho the Vandal.

In the middle of the procession rode the Sacred Marcus, on a showy white stallion. Of course he sat without stirrups, following the custom of the ancients; he was bareheaded, save for a wreath, and he wore a gilded linen cuirass moulded to give him the figure of an Apollo. He had even bared his legs, though that must be uncomfortable on horseback; his thighs gleamed white above bronze greaves, in contrast to the coarse barbarian trousers worn by every other soldier on parade. He looked from side to side at the cheering crowd, and smiled on his subjects; it was customary for the Emperor to appear impassive and godlike in public, and Felix did not wholly approve of such levity; but perhaps it was excusable on this joyous occasion.

A handsome young clerk declaimed a panegyric which Felix had composed with enjoyment; it was pleasant to be sure of an audience, even though the poem was written to order. But he had thought it undignified to declaim in the open air amid the murmurs of a crowd and the trampling of horses, and the clerk had a good loud voice.

Behind the Emperor came the rest of the army; altogether there were ten alae of horse in the northern parts of the Diocese, and the Emperor had brought them all. With the Legions and a small body of engineers and light infantry they made up an army of more than twelve thousand men, a very large force of purely Roman troops, without barbarian foederati. It was doubtful if Stilicho had as many genuine Romans in the great Army of Italy. Felix inspected them keenly as they passed through the gate. They were not up to the standard of the Divine Theodosius, but they were still a formidable force; the ministers of Honorius might recognize this new Emperor, at least until Alaric was beaten back across the Danube.

Behind the army came the litters of a few prominent citizens, and Felix called up his bearers to join them. Most of the troops continued right through Londinium, over the Bridge, to bivouac in open ground beyond the southern suburb; but the Emperor dismounted in front of the Basilica, where the senior officers and civilian officials joined him for the State Banquet.

In the good old days a new Emperor formally began his reign by receiving from a duly qualified augur the auspices, the right to sacrifice and examine entrails on behalf of the whole Roman People. But now the sacrifice of oxen had been forbidden, and there was a distressing lack of ceremonial to mark the handing over of supreme power. The obvious substitute would have been a service in the Christian church; but Felix had discovered, when he went into the matter, that the Bishop laid claim to some kind of supernatural power that had been given once for all by a laying-on of hands, and that in any Christian service the priests would perform functions that an Emperor could not. Of course that made the whole thing impossible. The Emperor was omnicompetent, in every field, and could not

begin his reign by taking second place at a religious service.
Since there could be no inauguration, and no service in the
church, all that remained was the Banquet which in the old
days had followed the sacrifice.

Every middle-aged man could remember the tyrant
Magnus Maximus; but Felix was the only official who had
seen the court of the Divine Theodosius, and he had
instructed the guilds in the etiquette to be followed.
Naturally he had insisted on forms that no provincial
merchant would have thought of, to show that he knew
better. For example, there were no couches, only benches
for the guests and a chair for the Emperor; this was because
the Sacred Marcus wore military dress, and must dine as
though in the field. It was also convenient, for benches did
not take up much room, and all the guests could be placed
at one long table. The citizens wore their richest tunics and
mantles, with the badge of the guild; but the Vicarius and
the Praeses were tightly wrapped in their pleated official
togas. (The toga had long been obsolete for everyday wear,
but high civil servants suffered its clinging embrace on very
solemn occasions.) Felix noted with pleasure that Gratianus,
walking up the steps of the Basilica before him, was already
sweating from a very red neck; he himself wore full dress in
the law court, and his valet had worked out a way of
pinning the folds that allowed him some comfort.

This Banquet was an important omen for the new reign.
The Sacred Marcus would be conscious of absolute power,
as he sat in this great public building with his richest
subjects hanging on his words and his army encamped
outside the city. There would be strong wine and unlimited
flattery. If the Emperor could refrain from some freakish
display of his new authority it would show that the
business men of Londinium had chosen wisely. Felix was
near the throne, though below the chief officers of the

army, and he could see and hear all that went on; it was more nerve-racking than the Imperial feasts of his youth, for now he was important enough to be a target for the wrath of a capricious despot. But by the evening he ought to know a good deal about the prospects of this new Empire.

As the excellent meal progressed the Sacred Marcus behaved like the ideal of a Stoic Emperor. His cup was never empty, and he pledged his guests in turn, so that all might drink freely; but he himself took only small sips, and remained sober. Gratianus had coached him to recognize the chief men of the city; he made some appropriate remark to the head of each guild, without saying anything that mattered. Presently it was the turn of the Praeses, and the Sacred Emperor raised his cup. Smiling, he called down the table: 'Good health and long life, Sempronius Felix. Tell the lady Maria I have not forgotten how pleasant she made my first visits to this fine city. I have business to discuss with you, but I shall not begin in the middle of a banquet. This afternoon I visit the church, but I shall see you privately in the evening. Come to my office after supper.'

Felix murmured his reply in a trembling and awestruck voice. It was correct to be overcome with emotion when the Sacred Emperor deigned to speak to you in public, and it pleased him to overdo things a little, to remind his fellow-guests that he had learned his manners in Constantinople. The Emperor had been affable, and his mention of Maria was a signal mark of distinction; although it was embarrassing to hear her name spoken at a public feast.

The meal went smoothly to its end; provincials were more accustomed to sitting up in chairs than to reclining like gentlemen on couches, and no one lolled, or got drunk enough to be disrespectful. Presently it was announced that the guard was ready to escort the Emperor for his formal call on the Christian God. It would be a mistake to keep troopers hanging about on such a day; they would be drunk to-night, and if they were in a bad temper they might sack the taverns. So the guests were permitted to withdraw. Felix did not know whether to be amused or ashamed when he saw their prostrations; in spite of his toga he sank down gracefully, bent his forehead swiftly to the floor, then rose and walked backwards to the entrance; but some fat merchants fairly wallowed on the ground, and had to be assisted to their feet. Ceremonial functions in the presence of the Sacred Emperor were always a strain, for he was at the same time the representative of Heaven on earth and a busy executive who must listen to advice and take important decisions; they were more embarrassing when the courtiers were incompetent, so occupied in putting their bodies through the appropriate motions that they had no time to assist in graver matters.

Marcus had the makings of a good Emperor. At least he was still sane, able to hear flattery without taking it literally. He went out of his way to be polite to his supporters, and had not forgotten that the merchants of Londinium had raised him to the Purple. Perhaps Britain would prosper under his rule. Anyway, they were all finally committed to his service.

Back in his private office Felix went through the dossiers of the leading merchants. While the army was in the south the government would need gold and silver, fresh every month, or the soldiers would plunder for their pay. There were a few silversmiths and jewellers in the city, and of course the wine-sellers must hand over their cash as soon as they got it, so that the troops drew the same coins next pay-day; but in this planned economy of forced labour and direction of industry a great deal of business was done by barter. The tax-gatherers could collect corn and wool and meat, but it was not easy to turn them into the money the soldier demanded. The only mines of precious metal were in Valentia; but King Cunedda was protecting Valentia from the Scots, and he took the profit from its gold-mines. In the old days there had been a mint in Londinium, until it was closed as a matter of policy; because an island with its own army, its own industries, *and* its own currency, was too much temptation to any officer of spirit. Now the Sacred Marcus would wish to strike coins bearing his titles; they must refound the mint, and perhaps make a small profit by issuing coins a little lighter and a little baser than those of the tyrant Honorius. Felix took from his purse a treasured gold solidus of the Divine Constantinus, one of several good coins of full weight that he carried in these exciting times in case he had to fly suddenly to save his life. The actual manufacture did not look very difficult; he knew more than one silversmith who could turn out embossed fragments of metal as good as some provincial coins. The great thing was to give the soldiers something every pay-day, to prove that the government was doing its best; presumably Stilicho's troops were as badly in arrears as any other Roman army, and the grumblers could be reminded of that.

Felix ate a light supper in his office, with his papers still spread before him. When it was time to set out for his interview with the Emperor he had the whole financial situation of his Province on one sheet of paper; he could promise food and clothing for the army, and workshops for weapons; there would be a shortage of bullion, and especially a shortage of coins until the mint was started; but if the soldiers were fed and equipped they would be better off than some armies. He had not attempted to plan beyond the harvest; it was a waste of time to look too far ahead.

Someone had attempted to decorate the Praetorium in what he imagined to be the style of a Sacred Palace. The square wooden pillars of the porch had been covered with plaster to give the effect of stone columns, and there were coloured cloths and swags of greenery along the brick front. It still looked what it was, the squalid headquarters of an unimportant garrison, but you could see that it was for the moment the dwelling of a commander-in-chief. The numerous sentries were Legionaries in gleaming armour, and a groom ran round with a shovel, cleaning up behind the tethered horses of the couriers. But the private office of the Emperor was the same mean little room where Constantinus had told the terrible news from Gaul.

The Sacred Marcus, in undress tunic and comfortable trousers, sat at a desk by the window; Felix knelt when he entered the room, but the Emperor stopped him before he could get his forehead to the ground. 'No prostrations in here, my friend,' he said heartily. 'This is where I work, and I can't consult you while you stand on your head. Now sit down on that stool. Never mind the etiquette. I was a junior officer the last time we met, and if I am now commander-in-chief it is partly because you helped my cause.'

Felix felt his conscience at rest for the first time since he had abandoned the son of his old leader. This little provincial captain of horse would make a good Emperor, and he had done right to support him. It was exactly the note to strike; to impress the vulgar an Emperor must submit to a good deal of ceremonial in public, but he would never get through his business if he expected the same salutes in the office that were his due in the Basilica. Yet he had not offered the Praeses a chair; the stool was a humble one, in a corner of the room. That was right, for even when all formalities were laid aside they were still ruler and subject, and it was easier to bear it in mind if the subject crouched in a corner. A foolish Emperor sometimes insisted on being treated as one of the boys; then someone went too far, and his boon companions faced the sword, if not the fire.

'I shall tell you my plans first,' continued the Sacred Marcus. 'Then we can fit your resources to my expenditure. I know it should be the other way round, but there are things I must do, whether my dominions can afford them or not. The army will remain concentrated round Londinium for the winter. I shall not invade Gaul until I have come to some arrangement with my colleague at Mediolanum; there is no point in fighting all the Germans of the West and Stilicho as well. If I can't make terms with Mediolanum I shall look for some barbarian in Gaul who will serve me as a foederate King. I dare not cross the Channel until I can rely on a friendly power over sea. Yet I can't lead the army back north until I am recognized on the Continent. At present this is the most exposed frontier of Britain, and King Coroticus must repel the Picts without my help. Is that clear? Now these men are a long way from home, and we must keep them happy. Their families will be here before long, and they must be housed. Any sort of weather-proof hut will do; they don't expect tiled floors, and some of them have rather barbarous habits in the home. Get carpenters to run up huts outside the North Gate; I won't let my soldiers live in the city, where you can never get them on parade in a sudden emergency. You can requisition timber without spending money; but you will have to pay the workmen. Can you?'

Felix explained the shortage of coined money; he could feed the workmen, but wages would be difficult. Marcus agreed that food was enough to give them.

'But mind you feed them properly, and their families also.

There must be no starvation among the poor while the army is in the city. It makes the soldiers discontented. This will be an easy time for your Province. We used to screw out of you everything we could, and let the northerners off lightly; now the position is reversed. Of course you must provide for the bare needs of the soldiers.'

Felix sighed, for he knew that the bare needs of an army covered more than the wealthiest Province could produce. He thought it time to say something, before this untried Emperor got the impression that he could administer his dominions without civilian help.

'I understand what Your Sacred Majesty has in mind,' he said smoothly. 'We can take corn and wool from the coloni if we leave them just enough to keep alive until next harvest. Otherwise they run away to the woods, and the land is untilled. I shall be gentle to the humiliores near the city, and the soldiers will hear no complaints. But, as I said before, the difficulty is coined money. We must start a mint. I have here a list of wealthy citizens, with a rough estimate of the plate in their possession. I would like guidance on one point. Will Your Sacred Majesty inform me which of these citizens deserve special consideration, in return for their efforts for the better government of the Diocese?'

The Emperor smiled. 'Very delicately put, my dear Praeses. I want the Vicarius to get his money back, because he really helped me. The others only wanted a revival of the Empire of Carausius, and they cannot complain if it is expensive. Be guided by the Vicarius, but argue with him if he is too generous. The rich must not flaunt their wealth while there are arrears of pay owing to the soldiers.'

'I shall repeat to the Vicarius the very words of Your Sacred Majesty. They describe the situation in a masterly manner.'

The Emperor saw that Felix was disappointed; he

reminded him that there were advantages in having the army in the south.

'Every coin that you take will be spent here in Britannia Prima. Nothing will go to Eburacum, and of course nothing will go over sea. The limitanei in the north will be given land instead of pay, and I shall not attempt to administer the regions defended by foederate Kings. Also we shall save the salary of some military commands. While I remain in the Diocese there is no need for a Comes Britanniarum, or a Dux; though I must appoint a Comes Littoris Saxonici to watch that dangerous frontier. That will be Constantinus of the Barcarii Tigridenses. He is only a limitaneus, but I can put his son, young Constans, in command of the two alae of horse. They both deserve reward. No money at all is to be spent on roads or public services, even in this Province. By stopping civil expenditure for a year I hope to pay the army without increasing the taxes.'

'As Your Sacred Majesty pleases,' answered Felix, setting his face into the expression of Roman gravitas with which he heard bad news. The Emperor ended the interview with a few gracious words:

'Naturally, my dear Praeses, you will draw on the Treasury for your own salary, and the pay of your clerks. I regard you as my friend, and I shall not examine your accounts too closely. Hand over everything else to my paymaster, and consult with the Vicarius before you take from any honestioris the whole of his possessions. That settles financial affairs for this year, and you must be as sleepy as I am. I shall receive you in private audience any time you wish to see me, but don't bother me with petty details. Good night, and don't prostrate yourself.'

The Praeses did in fact make a graceful prostration, for all rulers like to receive the proper marks of respect if their courtiers can give them neatly, without apparent effort. He did not like the plans he had heard for the future of Britain, but his own position in the government seemed secure.

He was carried home in his litter, through streets that were already beginning to be noisy with drunken soldiers; but the troops had been compelled to leave their swords in the camp, and would not attack private houses.

He recognized the litter of Gratianus outside his door, and was told that the Vicarius was in the women's apartments. It was late, but there would. be no sleep to-night, while the soldiers explored the taverns of their new cantonment; and it would please his wife if he discussed affairs of State in her presence. Instead of asking the Vicarius to join him in the study he went himself to Maria's sitting-room.

Father and child were quietly playing backgammon, but he was a little annoyed to see the new lady's maid also in the room. He guessed that Gratianus had already bribed her to send him any news she picked up. His father-in-law's passion for spies could be a bore. But he greeted his family cheerfully, and sent down for a jar of the best wine.

'Well, Caius,' said the Vicarius, in that hearty vulgar manner which always rasped the nerves of his well-educated son-in-law. 'What plans have you made with the Sacred Marcus, for the fleecing of the unfortunate citizens? And what do you think of his capacity as Emperor?'

The maid had left the room, and Felix answered frankly.

'The Sacred Marcus is an intelligent young soldier, and the great thing in his favour is that so far he manages to distinguish between his own will and that of Jupiter. But I can see trouble coming. He has thought out a coherent policy, and unfortunately it's all wrong.'

'How sad. But isn't that a little sweeping? Surely in one interview he can't have suggested anything very absurd.

Perhaps I can have a little talk with him, if you were too tactful to disagree. Or if it is a matter of delicate persuasion we might get Maria to ask him nicely, after a good dinner,' answered Gratianus in an indulgent tone, as though admitting that boys would be boys.

'My wife has had enough of society for the present,' Felix said firmly. 'She prefers to remain in her own apartments. Don't you, my dear?'

'Of course, Caius. Running the house keeps me busy, and it would be wrong if my name were spoken frequently,' Maria answered meekly.

Gratianus frowned; he loved his daughter, and did not like to be reminded that she was now under the authority of this pompous and correct husband from Africa. But the frown only lasted a moment, just long enough for Maria to note that he would support her if she chose to defy her lord; then he continued with a smile:

'Well, what exactly is wrong? At present the Sacred Marcus remembers I supplied his donative, and he is willing to oblige me. But gratitude wears out, and I ought to give my advice before he persuades himself that he achieved the Purple single-handed.'

'It isn't any one particular thing, lord Vicarius,' Felix explained. 'It is the whole cast of our Emperor's mind that seems to me unfortunate. You wanted a ruler to look after Britain, without bothering about the rest of the Oecumene; but the Sacred Marcus is not interested in the welfare of the Diocese, he thinks only of paying his troops. He plans to remain here until next summer, while he negotiates for allies in Gaul, or even for recognition from Mediolanum (which he won't get). He has withdrawn the comitenses from Eburacum, and handed over the north and west to foederate Kings. He will spend nothing on building, education, or even roads. You know my politics. I was a

Theodosian, not out of the ridiculous loyalty that makes barbarians die for their hereditary Kings, but because I thought Theodosius was the best man to rule the world. I serve Rome and Civilization, not this Emperor or that. Now the Sacred Marcus, who is a better soldier than the tyrant Honorius, and whom I serve for that reason, proposes to abandon more than half his territory to the barbarians.'

'He will not abandon one foot of his dominions,' Gratianus said sharply. 'The foederate Kings are loyal, and the lands they administer are part of the Empire. It is sensible to husband the resources of Britannia Prima, instead of spending money on bridges in Flavia and Maxima. We pay the army, whether it is stationed in Eburacum or here, and now the comitenses have come south the pirates will leave us alone. Londinium should prosper.'

'Oh yes, Londinium will prosper,' Felix answered bitterly. 'Unless the tax-gatherers take everything. But the north and the west will go downhill. Cunedda and his Otadini march and fight under the Labarum, and so does Coroticus on the Wall. But Roman law is not enforced in their territories, and civilization as we know it does not exist. If King Cunedda wants to set up an inscription, or build a tomb, he has to fetch workmen from this Province. Soon Eburacum will be in the same condition. I know how things were in the past. Less than a hundred years ago there were thriving cities right up to the Wall, and all the Brigantians spoke Latin. Forty years ago Theodosius the Magister Militum handed over the Wall to the foederati, and soon everything beyond Eburacum was barbarous. Then the Otadini were sent to expel the Irish from the west, and Valentia was made a Province under their protection. Now the Sacred Marcus proposes to turn over Eburacum to King Coroticus, and the frontier of civilization will be withdrawn to the middle of the island. It breaks my heart to

see Roman rule withdrawn from such a large proportion of
the Diocese, not through the attack of some barbarous foe,
but merely because the Emperor feels safer with his army in
the south.'

'Come, come,' Gratianus said soothingly, 'you should not
be upset by these temporary withdrawals of the regular
forces. The Empire is not diminished while the foederate
Kings obey their orders; and they will obey the more
willingly while the army is concentrated. In my opinion our
gallant Emperor is afraid to invade Gaul. Soon he will make
a treaty with whoever rules across the Channel, and
disperse his forces to occupy the whole of this Diocese. The
Irish are fighting to decide who shall be their next King,
and we can turn all our attention to the Saxons. I foresee a
very bright future for the subjects of the Sacred Marcus.'

Maria now joined in the discussion. She forgot that it is
the duty of a good wife never to ask questions.

'Please tell me, Caius,' she began, 'why are all these laws
necessary to civilization? Why don't people weave cloth
and bake bread of their own accord, in return for payment?
The new girl has been reading to me in Tacitus, and it seems
that in his day a free man could do any work he pleased,
and if the Emperor interfered with trade the historian calls
it tyranny.'

Felix answered politely; he was glad his wife wished to
talk, for if she sulked in the presence of her father it might
drive a wedge between Praeses and Vicarius.

'It is the duty of the government to provide the
necessities of life at a price the poor can afford; once you
start doing that you have to fix the price of a good many
other things as well, and compel people to work at the
unpopular trades that lose money. That is the explanation, I
suppose. Do you agree, Vicarius?'

'Quite right, my boy,' answered Gratianus. 'Although I

sometimes think we would be better off with a little more freedom. I wonder what would happen if you abolished hereditary restrictions on labour, and allowed every man to choose his calling?'

'Come, lord Vicarius,' Felix said quickly, 'there is no need to wonder, when you can see the system in action. In the Province of Valentia anyone can do what work he likes, and all have chosen one of two trades; the brave and idle hang about the Court as badly trained swordsmen, not a match for real soldiers; the diligent cultivate the soil, not very well, because when their implements break there are no competent smiths to repair them. So far I have not heard of anyone painting himself blue, but otherwise they live like their ancestors before this island was civilized.'

'That is true,' Gratianus admitted. 'Although that district was never very cultured at the best of times. They always bought their luxuries in Londinium.'

'Perhaps Valentia is no great loss. As you say, it was always rather barbarous. What I complain of is that the Sacred Marcus is willing to see the other Provinces of Britain, except Prima, relapse into the same state. I wish you would advise him to reoccupy the north before that loyal foederate Coroticus has ruined it. If you won't, I shall try myself, but he is more likely to listen to you.'

'Very well. I shall remind him of his duty to Rome and Civilization. But he must keep the army here until he has found allies or colleagues or subjects in Gaul. Then it will be late in the season. Next spring will be time enough to go north.'

Until dawn they continued to discuss the affairs of the new Empire. Gratianus was confident he could persuade the Emperor to follow the right course. But he could not abruptly give him orders, and persuasion would take time. For the winter they must put up with the presence of the army, and hope that when spring came the foederate Kings could be induced to withdraw peaceably from the Provinces they occupied.

The night was noisy, but they heard no fighting and could see no fires. The soldiers were content to go home when they had spent their money, and did not try to get more by plundering the city. At sunrise the watchmen of the guilds and the German police appeared rather timidly in the streets, and order reigned once more. The Vicarius went home in his litter, and Felix retired to bed. The new rule had been inaugurated without incident, and there should be a quantity of good coined silver in the strong-boxes of the tavern-keepers; the next business was to get that money back to the Treasury, but the Praeses could think of it after his rest. Meanwhile he was satisfied with his private affairs. Maria had been friendly and helpful; the way to keep her happy was to let her see plenty of interesting visitors at home. She was not flighty in the sense that she wanted a lover, merely bored with the company of foolish servants.

During the next week Londinium grew accustomed to the presence of the army. The soldiers were a nuisance, but they might have been much worse. Only the Emperor's own lifeguard was quartered in the Praetorium; the other troops bivouacked north of the city, where they could see all the builders and carpenters of Britannia Prima busily erecting huts for their families. There were sentries on each gate, and no one was allowed to carry arms in the city. Of course the soldiers were big men, used to violence; with their bare fists, or a bit of stick, they could rob elderly shopkeepers; but when caught they were punished, and it was obvious the Emperor wished to enforce discipline in his army.

The Sacred Marcus worked hard to fulfil the duties of his rank. Everything done by any branch of the government was in theory done by express command of the Emperor; he could fill a long working day merely by reading all the documents that must bear his monogram. In practice he might do as much or as little as he chose, for it was the custom to cut the Imperial monogram on a seal and get clerks to stamp the papers. If the Emperor was a child, or a notorious idler like the tyrant Honorius, civil servants made their own decisions, and all worked smoothly; but now fear that the ruler might query something done in his name paralysed the whole administration. The Emperor was doing the work of the Comes Britanniarum and the Dux, whose offices had been suppressed; that meant a lot of detail about postings and promotions in the army, but at least as a regular soldier he understood the business; in civil affairs he was unpredictable, torn between solicitude for the revenue and a desire to please his subjects, and the administration lurched from side to side under his untrained guidance.

Felix had worked at Imperial headquarters in the past. But in those days he was a subordinate who did not make decisions, and his ruler had been trained in administration as commander of a large army. The Sacred Marcus had risen in one day from junior tribune to commander-in-chief, and he did not know how to delegate authority.

At the end of a week the unfortunate Praeses begged his father-in-law to use his influence with the Emperor, that the affairs of the Diocese might be administered by the competent authorities without constant interference from the Sacred Palace. Gratianus was sympathetic and understanding, himself a little worried by the Emperor's activity.

'It was I who decided this Diocese needed an Emperor of its own,' he admitted ruefully, 'and out of a great many possible candidates I chose young Marcus Julius Naso. I wanted a popular and unassuming young officer, who understood the defence of the island, and could keep his sanity under the temptation of supreme power. But I chose a ruler who is really too good for the job. Of course his chief trouble is too much youthful energy, and time will cure that. But meanwhile we must try to fill his day, and particularly his nights, with something more amusing than affairs of State. Leave it to me. I shall arrange a little supper for His Sacred Majesty. I can put my hand on a troupe of Spanish dancers; they are wanted by the authorities of Burdigala for a list of offences as long as your arm, and they must do as I tell them. Yes, that is the best plan. The Sacred Marcus is strong and energetic, and too conscientious to drink himself into a stupor, the only amusement of remote Eburacum. I shall teach him how to enjoy life; intimate little parties, nothing coarse or brutal; but he will sleep late next morning, and find the headache interferes with business. Then we can rule the Diocese as it should be ruled, while our Emperor confines himself to military affairs.'

'Please, lord Vicarius,' begged Felix, 'don't do anything of the sort. If you encourage him to drink with those vile Spanish dancers he is bound to feel out of temper in the mornings. His reign began without executions; let him learn the habit of killing, and no one will sleep safe. We must think of something else to keep him occupied.'

'There is truth in that. Under a drunken tyrant it is his closest companions who suffer first. Yet we must find him some amusement.'

'Will he lead his army into battle, either in Gaul or against the Picts? He may prove a good general.'

'Not this year, at any rate, though he talks of winning Gaul in the spring. In my opinion he likes to see this fine army gathered round his person, and when the time comes he will be reluctant to expose it to the hazard of war.'

'Then the army will not keep him busy; and I insist that if we encourage him in debauchery we shall endanger our heads. What else can we find to amuse him? He is not interested in theology, and there are not enough Bishops here to hold a Council, though the Divine Theodosius spent a lot of his time arguing with Christians in Constantinople.'

'What else is there?' said the Vicarius, half to himself. 'Literature? He can barely read. Building? We can't afford it. Hunting?'

'I have thought of something,' Felix broke in excitedly. 'Do you remember how pleased he was, as plain Julius Naso, to come to my supper party? He is a soldier, of military stock. In his youth he was probably snubbed by civilians of good birth, even in military Eburacum. I am sure he is still nervous of the gentry, and afraid of making mistakes at a polite party. He won't know that the parties in Britain never are polite. I suggest that you, Vicarius, invite him to a grand dinner; but don't have low dancers and the strongest wine in the city. Make it very formal, be very much the Senator, and invite learned men to meet him. Later on we can ask him to other good houses, and show him there is a higher way of life than that of a bloody soldier. He will be impressed with his own ignorance, and will recognize that the country should be governed by trained civil servants, without interference from the commander-in-chief.'

'That's a good idea, though it won't be easy to make up a party of educated men in Londinium. But, as you say, it is never safe to encourage an absolute ruler to drink. One other thing. He remembered my daughter. We shall revive the old custom of ladies dining in public. They used to, before all this Christianity came in, as you can read in the history books.'

They made their plan, and settled whom to invite. The clerks of the Treasury came from decent families of hereditary servants of the State. Because higher education was neglected in the Diocese they had not the polish of Constantinople or Mediolanum, and as juniors they were poorly paid; all the same, the lowest free-born administrator felt himself superior to any soldier, and though they would be excited at meeting the Emperor, who might promote them out of turn, they could all be trusted to make him feel his ignorance. After a few such parties the Sacred Marcus should understand that the civil service could administer the country without his help. It was a plan that would have been useless with a tough and brutal fighting man risen from the ranks; in the old days the tyrant Maximinus killed any educated gentleman who made him feel his inferiority; but Marcus had begun as an officer, and he was sufficiently civilized to recognize a higher way of life when it was brought to his attention.

Londinium was ransacked to provide delicacies for the feast, though Gratianus followed the advice of his son-in-law, and concentrated rather on rare dishes, snails and pheasants and dried tunny-fish, than on wine. There would be very little drinking. In the manner of the ancients they would appoint a tricliniarch, to see the wine was watered and to regulate the toasts. The Divine Gratianus, with his subversive love of German customs, had encouraged his guests to drink individually, and for the last twenty years that bad example had been the fashion; but any educated man must admit that the remote past was more worthy of respect than the previous generation, since our grandfathers were better men than our fathers. They would go right back to the time of Lucullus.

The couches would be nine, the number of the Muses consecrated by tradition; but it was impossible to find nine ladies worthy to sit opposite them. The Emperor had picked up two or three concubines among the lower orders, to replace those he had left at Eburacum, but of course they did not appear in public; he would come alone, and so would the widowed Vicarius. Felix and the six clerks who made up the company would bring their wives, but that made only seven ladies; Maria must have the place of honour, facing the Emperor.

That made Felix regret the plan, but there was no going back on it now; he realized that he had been jockeyed into it, although Maria's besetting fault was that she behaved too frivolously at mixed parties. He had been eager to squash the idea of leading the Sacred Marcus into debauchery, and had not paused to consider whether this alternative would make things difficult for his wife. He had a quick brain, and elaborate schemes took possession of it suddenly, before he had time to think of possible objections. Gratianus must have noted the possibility that his daughter would become friendly with the new ruler; probably he was willing that such a friendship should arise, and he had not thought it necessary to point out the risk to her husband; he might even have made his first dangerous proposal so that Felix should amend it, for the Vicarius loved intricacy for its own sake. It was all very worrying, and not for the first time the Praeses felt that unseen but very practised hands were gently pushing him into a position that he would not have chosen of his own accord.

He warned Maria that he would be sitting at the left hand of the Emperor, where he could see all that went on. But of course he could not protest if the Sacred Marcus made love to his wife; the story was well known that hundreds of years ago the Divine Tiberius had led Roman matrons from the dinner table to his bedroom, and then back to their husbands, as though Empire made him the colleague of every married man in the State. It was a pity that these stories about Imperial tyrants were to be found in every history book; they put ideas into the head of a dull ruler, who might have reigned justly, but was tempted to prove himself as all-powerful and unconventional as Heliogabalus or Caligula. Maria promised she would behave with discretion, and after all the whole idea of the party was that the Emperor should be awed into recognizing his own unfitness for civil administration; it was unlikely that a man who was being dazzled by the erudite conversation of learned civil servants should interrupt a discussion of the relative merits of Claudianus and Vergil by making indecent proposals to the wife of a senior official.

The new reign had lasted three weeks, and the soldiers were sufficiently accustomed to their new quarters to go to bed quietly at lights-out, when the great dinner took place. In the early hours of the next morning Felix undressed with a light heart. He was still perfectly sober, although the party had continued for ten hours in the manner of the ancients, and that showed everything had gone according to plan. They had lain down about three in the afternoon, and by five the excellent food and a sufficient but not excessive quantity of wine had driven away the awe of the sacred ruler which at first made the junior clerks awkward and tongue-tied. When the tables were cleared each in turn had recited at least one long poem; even the Emperor had given a reading from a panegyric by Claudianus, which was known in the army because it gave a graphic account of the destruction wrought on invading Picts. Apart from the modern Claudianus, who could be quoted in any company because he wrote very accurately in the antique mode, all the poets discussed had flourished in the time of the Flavian Emperors or earlier; and in the end Felix himself had been emboldened to read part of his epitome of the Aeneid. Finally it had been agreed that, although Vergil was supreme, in theory it should be possible to surpass him; for the rules of taste were better understood nowadays than they had been in the time of Maecenas.

Throughout the evening the Emperor had been interested and alert. He was not a fool, although his education had been purely military; it was natural that he should enjoy the most fascinating amusement open to a gentleman of culture, when he was gently introduced to it by well-mannered and charming young men of wide reading. He might develop into a discriminating patron of letters, eager to start that long-neglected scheme of higher education; and he must realize that the clerks of the civil service were capable of managing the affairs of Britannia Prima without constant interference from the Sacred Palace.

As for the danger that he might be attracted by Maria, or that she would attempt to capture his desire, all that was past; Felix could congratulate himself that his wife had behaved with perfect decorum. The other ladies were desperately shy, and the conversation had been over their heads; she was self-possessed, and during the meal had talked freely about the military processions and ceremonies that now marked Londinium as the seat of Empire; but she could not discuss Vergil intelligently, and the presence of blushing and stammering ladies on either side reminded her of the behaviour appropriate to her sex. It was always easier for a woman to behave like a man in exclusively male company.

In this new reign the five Provinces of Britain should prosper. It was becoming obvious that the Sacred Marcus had no intention of invading Gaul, either as an ally of Mediolanum or to win territory for himself; in the spring he would probably make a tour of the island, and the foederate Kings would be reduced to obedience. The Provinces in foederate hands might even contribute to the central funds of the Vicariate, as they had not done for years past. But the change of government had introduced a new worry; it was more than three weeks since the last payment to the soldiers, and the Treasury must have enough in hand, in hard cash not too grossly debased, to pay them again on the due date. There would be very serious trouble if the money was not forthcoming. When the army was in Eburacum it was possible to delay, and make up arrears after the harvest; the soldiers did not like it, but there was nothing they could do; there was no money in Eburacum except what came from the south, and they would not plunder the homes of their cousins, the local coloni. But the comitenses regarded Londinium as a foreign country, and, moreover, this foreign country of the south was notoriously rich. If the Treasury defaulted they would sack the city.

The citizens realized their danger. Provided the army intended to march in the spring they would keep it paid up to date during the winter, though it was an effort that could not be kept up indefinitely. The tavern-keepers handed over their cash, in return for receipts which cancelled future taxes, and citizens with silver plate in their vaults brought it to the new mint on the same terms. On the appropriate day the troops were paid in full.

Then Felix held a private conference with Paulinus and various civil servants, for another pay-day was due in four weeks. Ever since he had served the State there had always been some rapidly approaching date when an insolvent Treasury must raise a large sum of money or face complete disaster, and he was used to a condition of affairs that in theory should have caused a nervous breakdown. There were the tavern-keepers to borrow from again, although now that the families of the comitenses were beginning to arrive in their new quarters the soldiers showed a regretta-ble tendency to save their money. The ordinary merchants of the city could pay no more without complete ruin, but a few of them might be ruined, and agents produced a list of those who merited the displeasure of the government. Something would turn up at the last minute, as it always had in the past; the pirates were beginning to raid the Littus again, and perhaps Constantinus would catch a band of them after they had gathered valuable booty. As a last resort, there were the military lands in the north; now that the soldiers' families had come south these might be sold, if a buyer could be found; the trouble was that followers of the foederate Kings were in the habit of squatting on vacant land, and brandishing their swords when a citizen arrived with the title-deeds. Only very daring speculators would bid for government land on the borders of the Picts.

The menace of the third pay-day was still a fortnight distant, and Felix was sitting in private, to interrogate a party of fishermen who had been caught trying to escape to the barbarians in Gaul, when the chief doorkeeper told him that the eunuch of his household was waiting in the lobby with an urgent message. It must be very urgent indeed for his wife to have sent Eros, who normally did nothing but stand with dignity at the entrance to the women's apartments; he hated going out in the street, where the lower classes made fun of him, and he had a slow and ungainly walk; but he was a well-chosen messenger all the same, for he impressed the ushers of the Treasury as a whole man would not have done. Felix cut short the whining defence about the remarkable gale that had driven the boat out of its course, and condemned the culprits to the fire; the government had been very lenient recently, and now that the Sueves had reached the coast they exercised a dangerous attraction on insolvent coloni; besides, he must read this message from Maria in private, and it was the quickest way to end the trial.

When the shrieking criminals had been removed the eunuch entered. His message was written on a large sheet of the best army paper, folded and tied with a thread that bore fragments of purple Imperial wax. The address showed that it was to be given into the hand of the lady Maria, and a wavering and ill-drawn M proved that the courier had done his duty, and asked her to sign as though he were delivering a despatch. Below her initial Maria had added a single line of writing. 'Read this', it said, 'and then come at once. I have sent for Father.'

Felix dismissed his attendants, and opened the letter when he was alone. He had already speculated about its contents, for he dared not open it in the presence of his subordinates. The only explanation he could think of was that he had incurred Imperial displeasure, and that out of regard for his father-in-law the Emperor would graciously permit him to commit suicide and transmit his property to his heirs. He had long ago made up his mind that a prominent servant of the State like himself was unlikely to die in his bed, and the thought of a dignified suicide in the manner of the ancients was never very far from his mind; it had come at last, and he opened the letter with a firm hand.

But the shock of what he found made him sit down suddenly, gasping for breath. For the Sacred Marcus expressed himself crudely. It was an invitation to Maria to come to the Sacred Palace that very night, and stay there as long as she pleased: 'we can decide later what to do with that boring old pedant of a Praeses,' it ended.

When the porter announced that his litter was waiting Felix had got over the first shock, and could walk past the petitioners at the entrance with a firm step; then he drew the curtains of the litter, and sat in the half-dark planning what to say to his wife.

A great many foolish women would have jumped at the

chance of becoming one of the mistresses of the Sacred Emperor; that Maria had sent the letter to him showed that she was fundamentally honest, and level-headed also: unless it meant nothing more than that she feared she would be unable to get out of the house without his consent, since he had punished those who were responsible for her last escapade. No, she had also sent for her father, and that could only be because she wanted to find a way out; although there was no way out when the Emperor sent an invitation; a patrol of Legionaries would be the answer to a refusal.

He found Gratianus already in the women's apartments, talking excitedly to his daughter; they were so deep in discussion that they continued without noticing him. 'It's not good enough,' Gratianus was saying. 'If he offered to make you his Empress, or even to instal you as sole mistress, you should jump into his bed as quick as you can. But as one of a dozen concubines you would be less important than you are now.'

'Do you mind if I join you?' Felix asked, with anger in his voice; his marriage had been arranged without love on either side, solely to give the lady Maria a position in keeping with her father's wealth, but that was no reason why he should let her go without a struggle.

'Of course, my dear fellow,' said the Vicarius absent-mindedly. 'If you can think of an excuse we shall be glad to hear it. But there isn't one. Little Maria can say she is unwell, and keep the young stallion waiting for a few days; but we can't refuse the Sacred Emperor.'

'You will have to divorce me, Caius, and apply for another Province, somewhere up north where Marcus is not likely to meet you. He will feel jealous if he sees you every day, and then you will die, no matter how willingly you give me up.' Maria spoke kindly; they had lived together for nine years, and habit and propinquity made them friends even though they had never been lovers.

'I shall not be safe, even in the far north,' Felix answered. 'By the custom of the ancients it is your duty to defend your chastity with your life. The Emperor will not imagine that you might refuse his desire, and we can get away to the coast now, this afternoon. Will you fly with me, to some part of Gaul beyond the new limits of the barbarians? We shall be very poor, but I am a trained civil servant. I ought to get employment in Italy or the East.'

'I will not allow my daughter to fly penniless to some distant land, where my family has no influence,' Gratianus said firmly. 'Besides, man, consider your position. It's too late for you to serve Honorius, or Arcadius either. When the Sacred Marcus was proclaimed you jumped in with both feet to welcome him to Londinium. The Theodosians would take your head as soon as you landed.'

'If there is nothing to be done,' said Felix bitterly, 'I can't think why you bothered to tell me in advance. Maria should have crept out of my house in the night, as she did before; that would have given me twelve more hours of happiness, before I begin to sharpen the dagger for my heart. I shall not be the first Sempronius to make that protest at the wickedness of a degenerate age. To-night you will go to the tyrant a widow.'

'The trouble with you, Caius, is too much education and not enough knowledge of the world,' Gratianus said roughly. 'If you kill yourself now you will make the Sacred Marcus uncomfortable. His conscience will bother him every time he plays with Maria, and he will discard her very quickly. Can't you go away, like a sensible man? I agree that you mustn't live in Londinium, because your own clerks would despise you; but you should demand handsome compensation for your wounded honour, and retire with your books to some secluded estate. The Emperor would gladly give you an Imperial domain near the Wall, and you could devote yourself to civilizing the Court of King Coroticus. But Lucretia has been dead a long time, and we are not living in the days of the Tarquinii. Pull yourself together, don't whine, and see what you can make out of this regrettable affair.'

'Of course, there is one way out,' said Maria. 'I must go to the Emperor. But he will receive me alone. If I take a good knife I can kill him without a sound, and walk out of the Palace saying he wishes to sleep undisturbed. The body will not be discovered until morning, and by then Father will have sent me into hiding with some of his disreputable friends.'

Both men looked up, appalled. They had been thinking of her as a valuable object, which the Emperor desired and they were reluctant to give; it took them a few moments to adjust themselves to the idea that she could influence her own fate. Maria continued, in a voice that was persuasive but not at all excited:

'We all thought it would be a good thing to have an Emperor of our own, to save us from the troubles that afflict Gaul. But now we are discovering the disadvantages. Taxes are as high as ever, and they have to be paid even more punctually. We would be better off as part of the world-wide Oecumene. Now forget about me personally, and sit down to think out what you would do if Marcus was killed by a thunderbolt, and you had to carry on the government.'

Gratianus was the first to consider calmly this amazing proposal. 'I have a very intelligent and spirited daughter,' he said, 'and there is something to be said for her plan. Things have not worked out as I expected, and I agree that we were better off with a distant Emperor. The soldiers' families are in the south; it will be difficult to move them north again, so Londinium will be protected whoever bears sway in Britain. But there are two questions to consider. What will the soldiers do when they find their leader murdered? And will the authorities in Mediolanum forgive us our part in the original revolt? What do you think, Caius?'

Felix considered before he spoke. One part of his brain was still shocked at the idea that a woman should propose such a desperate bloody way out of their predicament; but another part was already racing along the familiar channels of intrigue. There was a plot to remove an Emperor, and these provincials needed the advice of a skilled politician, trained under the Divine Theodosius.

'We must have everything arranged before the troops know Marcus is dead,' he said. 'There must be a proclamation at dawn. Can you win over the senior officers this afternoon, or must we rely on the prestige of the civil government?'

'Can you really plan a change of Emperors in six hours?' cooed Maria, with admiration in her voice.

'It's got to be done in the time, and if anyone can do it I can,' Felix answered proudly. 'Now we want a return to the undivided Empire of the West, under the Sacred Honorius. I suppose, Vicarius, there is no chance of raising money for a donative? I have nothing in the Treasury, and the soldiers won't be interested in land from the Imperial domain. Could you produce a sack of silver, at once? Enough to bribe one or two regimental officers, as an earnest of what the rest will get? And we must sound the leaders of the guilds, and send messages to neighbouring cities. The great thing on these occasions is the *appearance* of confidence. Let the soldiers think this change was planned long ago, and that they are the last to hear of it.'

'You are going very fast,' said Gratianus doubtfully. 'Why not remove the Emperor, and leave the choice of his successor to the army? Wouldn't that be cheaper than trying to buy their allegiance?'

'No, it wouldn't. That is asking for the sack of Londinium. Masterless soldiers can do a great deal of damage; they must find another ruler over them the minute Marcus is dead, and as we have no time to make plans that ruler can only be the Sacred Honorius.'

'There is one soldier in Britain with an independent command,' said Gratianus. 'Constantinus was in the last revolution, and it paid him well. I suppose the troops of the Littus would obey him, though he is still a stranger to them. We must send a message to Rutupiae at once, though we cannot expect an answer before we are committed.'

'An excellent idea. If he is friendly we can escape to the coast, if things go wrong here. Make him an offer. Although we propose to return to the government of Mediolanum, we are in fact cut off by the barbarians in Gaul; there must be some sort of provisional administration until communications are reopened, and meanwhile there are offices vacant. Promise to make Constantinus Comes Britanniarum, and let him keep the Littus as well. Then he will be supreme over every soldier in the Diocese. Tell him what is in fact the truth: that Stilicho has more pressing worries than the affairs of Britain, and that he will probably let our appointments stand.'

'I shall write to Rutupiae as soon as I get home. I have one sack of money in my cellar, and the silversmiths will let me have another. That will be just enough to give something to the senior officers; we must promise a good donative in the name of the Sacred Honorius, to be paid after harvest. Are you sure the Treasury can't help? This emergency is important to you personally; if there is a final reserve anywhere under your control now is the time to use it.'

'Any silver we take in the Treasury must be kept for next pay-day. Even then it will be a struggle, and I doubt if we pay the troops in full. But some officers might accept a reward in kind. We breed good horses on the Imperial lands, and I can condemn debtors to slavery and give them away as grooms. The law says a farmworker must always stay on the land, even if he changes owners; but we are breaking more than the rules of government economy.'

'There you are,' said the Vicarius triumphantly. 'There is always something in the Treasury if you look hard enough. I shall approach the officers to-night, and promise them practically anything that is or can become the property of the State; there will be confiscations if the supporters of Marcus are slow in changing sides. Leave these negotiations to me; I know how to bargain, and I have a pretty good idea of the Imperial domain in this Diocese.'

The professional politicians were so absorbed in planning this scheme to win the allegiance of a doubtful army without money, and at six hours' notice, that they had almost forgotten the desperate expedient on which the whole plot turned. Maria broke in to remind them.

'You are taking a great deal for granted,' she said sharply. 'The Sacred Emperor is so overcome by my remarkable beauty that he offers me a life of luxury as chief of his concubines; and when I propose to defend my honour like some heroine of old, you merely discuss what you will do after I have destroyed your most dangerous enemy. I have never had occasion to stab anyone to death while I kissed him, and when it comes to the point I may miss, or prick him in the backside. Suppose I change my mind, and decide for wealth and power as mistress of the Emperor? Eventually Marcus will tire of me, but it will be fun while it lasts.'

Felix at once began to protest; but Gratianus, that practical man, cut him short.

'We have gone into that before, my dear,' he said casually. 'You would not really enjoy yourself. You could not feast on account of your figure, and as for power, you have that already. When Marcus casts you off you would not be allowed to live peacefully on the price of your shame; your successor will want your head. No, your best course is to kill the tyrant. But if you will find it difficult you ought to have a rehearsal now.'

'Very well. Who shall I practise on? Eros the eunuch?' Maria answered with a laugh. She spoke flippantly, to keep up her courage, but her father answered seriously.

'Caius,' he said, 'she ought to find out how much force is needed to reach the heart of a strong man. Suppose she tries and fails? Then we all face the torture. This is no time for scruples. Is there an able-bodied man under arrest, who could be brought here for interrogation?'

Felix looked at his wife with disgust. Her dilated nostrils and bright eyes showed that she would enjoy the demonstration; her father was utterly unprincipled, and she was equally merciless at heart. But it was the custom of the ancients to treat slaves and criminals as things, without rights, and he should not feel upset; this modern solicitude for the lower classes was the product of Christianity, which had removed the Altar of Victory; he answered as casually as he could:

'Unfortunately I cleared up my only criminal case when I got your note. Those fishermen will have burned by now.'

'Then we must use a servant,' Maria said firmly. 'I will not attempt this murder unless I can first find out how much killing a man needs before he is dead. Let me see, Eros is too valuable. My ridiculous new maid would be quite as much use dead as alive, but she is a puny little thing, and the wrong shape. It should be a man, and a strong one. Which do you suggest?'

It was exciting to discuss the death of a slave in this carefree manner, as though they were living in the good old days. The present code was more tender to slaves than to taxpayers, and to kill one without cause was murder. The law was definite on that point; and that was what the two highest legal authorities in the Diocese were going to do. Felix felt pleasurably thrilled as he made his godlike decision of life or death.

'I think it would be appropriate,' he said, 'if we sacrificed Heraclion, who used to guard the door. He was responsible for letting you out, my dear, in the days when you concealed your private affairs from your husband. Now that you are a worthy matron, preferring any risk to dishonour, every reminder of that past should be removed.'

'The man who was your doorkeeper, eh?' put in Gratianus. 'That is a wise choice. I expect there is a secret agent here, and he will not be surprised if you interrogate your porter more strenuously than the law allows. It won't look like politics, but rather as though you suspect a love affair among the women. Fetch the man up at once.'

There were arrangements to be made before Maria could begin her experiment; it must be done without the assistance of the Germans who normally tied up a servant who had earned a flogging; but the stout bars across the window of the sitting-room had been fixed to stand firm against burglars or adventurous lovers, and they would serve as anchor for the bonds. Felix collected several lengths of chain from the kitchen spits; he also chose two or three sharp skewers, which would be easier to conceal than broad-bladed carving knives. The cooks were extremely puzzled, and next day it would be all over the town that something very queer was going on in the official residence

of the Praeses; but the advantage of plotting against time
was that warning would not reach the Emperor until too
late.

The stoker submitted to his chains without resistance and
came meekly to the women's apartments; he thought he was
to receive a few strokes of the rod for allowing the bath to
grow cold, and if he must be beaten it was better to suffer at
the hands of his unathletic master than at those of the
strongest litter-bearer in the establishment. Maria's attendants were sent to the ground floor, where they could not
hear what went on, and Eros stood outside the barred door.
There was a struggle when it came to tying the man up, for
he realized, when told to put his back to the window, that
he was to be tortured, not flogged; but the two officials
managed it, while Maria gave directions. When he was
safely tied by the elbows, in the attitude of a lover holding
out his arms to his beloved, Gratianus calmly sat down to
compose his letter to Constantinus, Comes Littoris Saxonici
per Britannias. But Felix could not tear his eyes away from
the blood-curdling, fascinating sight of his wife committing
premeditated murder.

Maria enjoyed every minute of it. She acted convincingly
the part of a woman eager to embrace her lover; several
times she came up to her victim and laid her face on his
shoulder, seeking with her right hand the throb of his heart
below the shoulder-blade. Then she tried a few light digs, to
see if it was easy to hit the right spot; it was a full hour
before she drove the skewer home and the body hung in its
chains, too limp for further experiment. Felix had enough
knowledge of the world to see that Maria had discovered a
pleasure greater than any she had known in the past.

The evening wore on, and the conspirators began to suffer
from anticipatory fears. That hacked and untidy corpse

hanging in the window was a vivid reminder that their own lives were at stake, and its presence entailed practical inconvenience. They had not eaten since breakfast, but they dared not allow a servant to enter. Gratianus was still businesslike, even when on edge; he sent the eunuch to fetch wine and cold meat, and took the tray from him at the door, pretending that the interrogation still continued and that secrecy must be preserved. They longed to drown their troubles in wine, but that would be fatal; they must force down great slices of cold pork before they touched the comfort of alcohol. The Vicarius went to and fro between the desk and the tray, altering a phrase in the letter to Constantinus, and making notes of what he would say to the officers when the assassination became known. Felix had always thought he could compose a proclamation in the normal style of the civil service, no matter how worried his mind; but he found he could not put two coherent words together, and even had difficulty in remembering how to spell. In despair, he sealed with his private signet several blank sheets of paper, and told his father-in-law to write anything suitable that he could think of, if only it would facilitate a peaceful change of government. They were both in this affair together, and he could trust Gratianus.

Then it was time for Maria to be arrayed in her most attractive gown. They dared not call the maids, since there was still time for a warning to reach the Emperor; her husband and father did their best to fasten her bracelets and arrange the folds of her skirt. Luckily she had a handsome girdle of gold wire, in the fashionable Celtic style; this would do admirably to conceal the skewer, which had been washed clean of blood and whetted against the marble door-jamb. The difficulty was her hair; no lady could cope with the multitude of little curls piled high on her head that she must wear on formal occasions, and of course the two men were equally helpless. After great searchings of heart Felix at length called in the new lady's maid. The eunuch naturally thought she had been implicated in the interrogation, and no suspicion was aroused in the servants' quarters. When she had finished her hairdressing Maria wished to stab her also, but Felix was firm; she was tied up, gagged, under the bed, to be released in the morning.

It would look odd when the lady of the house went out alone, while the women's apartments remained barred against its usual occupants. The maids must spend the night downstairs, and next spring half of them would have to be excused their duties while they bore unwanted infants of unknown parentage. But if an agent reported these goings-on there was a natural explanation. The husband of the latest Imperial concubine could not be expected to behave as though nothing had happened.

At last Maria sent for the litter. She was looking more beautiful than Felix had ever seen her, but she was not the young girl he had married. She was now a person in her own right, with the wary concentrated eye of a politician in a crisis. As she left the room with a firm step, her hands steady, he felt that she could be relied on to carry out her mission; the trouble would come afterwards, when he had to control a wife who had changed the succession of the Empire. Perhaps it would be a good thing to divorce her, pleasantly and without recrimination; he would be too frightened in future to sleep in her arms until he had counted the skewers in the kitchen.

Gratianus left at the same time, to send his message to the Littus and call on the regimental officers. All night he would go from house to house, in a series of secret visits that needed very careful timing; he must hint that the rule of Marcus would end in the near future, and that there would be rewards for all officers who supported the rightful

Emperor; he must get enough of an answer to know who could be relied on, and he must do it without wasting time; but he must not allow them to guess that Marcus was doomed to-night, or an informer might betray him. The nerve-racking uncertainty would continue until day-break, or whatever time the Emperor was usually aroused (he was a professional soldier, and they were an early rising class). Meanwhile there was nothing whatever that Felix could do to influence events; he must spend the night alone, on guard over the bloody remains of Maria's experiment.

There was no reason why he should not get drunk; nothing now depended on his intelligence, or even on the steadiness of his hands. He drank a cup of wine without water, but he could not force himself to continue. For one thing, the wine was very nasty; now that the barbarians had reached the coast of Gaul good drink was scarce, and his cellar was nearly empty. In the second place, he had been abstemious for more than fifty years, and even his fears could not overcome the habits of a lifetime.

What did it feel like to be chained to a post, while you watched the executioner lighting the brushwood at your feet? A lot depended on the weather; sometimes the victim was suffocated by smoke, sometimes he died quickly in a roaring blaze; but very often, if the wood was damp and there was no wind, he writhed, scorched and screaming, for a long time. And it would not even begin until he had been tortured for several days. But abject terror wears itself out by its very intensity, and presently he found himself standing in the middle of the room, sweating and shaking, but with his mind longing for some occupation.

There were no books in the women's apartments except Christian theology, and the Iliad that Maria occasionally listened to for the improvement of her mind. Every educated man should be able to read Homer, no matter what the state of his nerves; but Felix could not. The letters blurred before his eyes, and he found himself repeating the same verse over again. It occurred to him that this might be an omen, but even in that he was disappointed; he had begun in the Catalogue of the Ships, and there was no augury to be drawn from a list of the Achaeans who had sailed for Troy. That was a pity, when the poem contained so many passages dealing with death by violence, or escape from it, which would have been easy to interpret. He put the book down, and began to pace his wife's bedroom, stopping occasionally to fiddle with the pots on her dressing-table. What a lot of ingredients of unknown use went to the upkeep of Maria's beauty! By a natural transition, how little he knew of her mind, as little as he knew about what she put on her face!

When he had managed to break a little jar in the shape of a Cupid riding on a dove, a snort from the end of the room reminded him that he was not alone. The lady's maid under the bed seemed to be choking in her gag. After a moment's reflection, he decided not to remove it, for if the girl shouted that the Emperor's life was in danger there was still time for the eunuch to betray his master; but it was foolish to allow an expensive servant to suffocate before his eyes. He pulled her from under the bed, and stood helplessly looking down at her struggles for breath. Then he had an inspiration and got out his handkerchief. Like every other slave in Britain, the girl had a cold in the head, and her nostrils were blocked. When he had blown her nose she breathed more easily, and lay without struggling.

He continued to gaze down at her; he could put her on the bed and untie her legs, without removing the gag; it would be a way of passing this endless night. But in the end he decided against it. Maria would certainly find out, and it was contrary to his habits. A householder who used ordinary servants as concubines endangered his dignity, and might be giggled at when he gave them orders about their regular work; he had always treated them purely as animated tools, following the definition of the great Aristotle, and he would not be so light-minded as to play with one at this crisis. He blew the maid's nose again, then rolled her back under the bed and covered her with a rug. It was ridiculous to count her as a person, and practically he was still alone with his thoughts and fears.

It must be about midnight. The sky through the uncurtained window was clouded, and he could not tell the time. There was a water-clock in his study, but he had never bothered to instal such an expensive machine in the women's apartments, where normally the outer door was barred from sunset to sunrise. The window faced north, and at that time of year the dawn showed a little north of true east; but it was not pleasant to go right up and peer out of the window sideways, with that corpse beginning to stiffen and change colour as it hung from the bars. Presently he went through to the room at the end where the female servants usually slept. The room had the clinging unpleasant odour of female sweat that he associated with busy housemaids, but in his present mood he preferred that to the perfume of his wife's dressing-table. He sat down on a pallet, and forced his mind to be calm until day should end this ghastly situation.

Philosophy was the obvious consolation; in the teaching of all reputable philosophers the virtuous man could not be unhappy, and if he felt miserable he must have done wrong; he would examine his conscience. He was disturbed to note how wicked he had been during the past summer. All his troubles arose from his betrayal of the rightful Emperor; he was a civil servant, a member of the noblest calling in the world, and it was his duty to control the inhabitants of the

Oecumene that they might lead the good life, in spite of the temptation to wealth and idleness that lay before them if they could escape the regulations of the government. His whole time should have been occupied in seeing that skilled tradesmen continued in their hereditary callings, and that the revenue was collected promptly and handed over to the appropriate military authorities; the personality of the Emperor hardly mattered, so long as the civil service functioned. The really important thing was the solvency of the Sacra Largitio, for that was the one weapon which Rome possessed and her enemies did not. Barbarians were hired as mercenaries; one nation was bribed to attack another; subordinate chiefs were encouraged to rebel against their Kings in the middle of a campaign; as a last resort a host of plunderers could be paid to go away, though that was an expedient that must not be used too often. All this depended on a solvent Treasury, and that was filled by the devoted work of civilian officials, not only ruthless collection of taxes, but also compulsion on the humiliores to do the definite tasks laid down for them; there would be no surplus to corrupt barbarian armies if each man grew his own corn and made his own tools, and that was how the coloni would live if the rule of the civil service were withdrawn.

He had been right to assist the Divine Theodosius; the Empire had been stronger under the rule of one man, and that man a great soldier. But his adhesion to Marcus had been an unmitigated evil. Civil war weakened the revenue, since donatives must be given to the army and prominent supporters must be forgiven their debts; but civil war leading to a separate Empire of Britain was worse, for it struck a blow at the Sacra Largitio in Italy, on which hung the safety of the world.

There was one consolation. He had learned his duty, and

to-morrow Britain would be back under the Sacred Honorius. But it was unseemly that he should be sitting in the servants' quarters, long after bed time, leaving everything in the hands of his wife. Gratianus had led him astray, and now he was making all the arrangements for the return of the Diocese to the undivided Empire; that so-called Senator and irregular Vicarius had been responsible for the whole affair, and it looked as though in future he would be more powerful than ever. Yet Mediolanum could be trusted to see that such power was too much for a private individual; one day Gratianus would find an agent at his door, and all those connected with him would be in serious danger. It was time for a loyal Praeses to break with this over-mighty subject. He had been wrong to support Marcus, but now he would be on the right side; the mere resolution pacified his well-trained conscience, and he lay down, half-asleep, on the dirty pallet, dreaming of a life in which Maria would have no part.

He must divorce this bloodthirsty woman before her father's disgrace; he need not mention a political reason, it would be enough that she had left his roof by night without asking permission. Then he would marry some gentle young girl, poor but of good family, and perhaps beget children; he could afford them now, and he would choose a wife whose honesty could be trusted. It had been a mistake to ally himself with Gratianus; but the old rogue would soon be crushed, and then the Praeses would be supreme in Britain.

He fell into a light doze, though he was too frightened to relax into complete unconsciousness. He was roused by a sound of knocking, and jumped to his feet with his heart pounding and his face running with sweat. Beyond the window lay a bank of white mist, the usual accompaniment of an autumn dawn. A servant would not bang on the door in that peremptory way; it must be an agent, come to lead him to the fire. He took a deep breath, straightened his back, and walked to meet his fate like a Roman and a Sempronius.

He unbarred the door, and his heart missed a beat when Eros beckoned forward a Legionary in armour. At least he was to be spared torture and the fire, but death was at hand; he stretched out his neck, in silence, hoping that the man carried a sharp sword and would get it over quickly. The soldier stared for a moment, and then chuckled disrespectfully.

'Please, sir, compose yourself,' he said with a smile. 'I have not come to take your excellency into custody. See, my sword is in its scabbard. The Sacred Gratianus sent me to escort you to the Palace.'

Felix was so surprised he sat down on the nearest chair. 'The Sacred Gratianus?' he gasped. 'Is there a new Emperor? Things happen so suddenly, and no one tells me beforehand.' Then he pulled himself together; a Legionary should never see the Praeses of Britannia Prima gasping like a new-caught fish, just because politics had taken an unexpected turn.

'I must bathe and be shaved before I wait on the Sacred Emperor,' he said with conscious dignity. 'The eunuch will look after you until I am ready.' Then an idea came to him. 'Legionary, will you do me a favour? A veteran like you must be familiar with wounds and blood. In the window lies the body of a slave who was killed in a brawl. Kindly take it downstairs and put it outside the back door for the scavengers to remove. My servants would be upset if they had to remove it. Eros, Heraclion has gone, and no one may discuss what has become of him.'

The soldier walked over to the window, his face expressing no emotion. He pulled the corpse by the shoulder, and saw it was still attached to the window-bars; without a word he whipped out his sword, and cut through the arms in two clean strokes; then he pulled the severed limbs free of their chains, and tucked them neatly into the corpse's loincloth. As he hoisted it to his shoulder he permitted himself one remark. 'Lord Praeses, you should take off their bonds before they are killed in a brawl.'

At last Felix could leave this horrible prison, the women's apartments. He tottered wearily to the bath. The terror he felt when he unbarred the door to an armed soldier had drained away the last of his energy; he lay back in a comfortable chair, with a wet towel over his eyes, too exhausted even to speculate on the latest change in the government of Britain. Gratianus had deceived him, but that could wait. At least he was married to the daughter of the new Emperor. When he felt a little stronger he would find out how these changes had come about.

CHAPTER IV

GRATIANUS IMPERATOR
SEMPER AUGUSTUS

After two hours Felix felt better. The bath calmed his nerves as it always did, and no matter how wearing a sleepless night is nearly everyone automatically feels fresher after sunrise. His household was disorganized, but the steward had guessed that Heraclion would not be fit to stoke the furnace after his interrogation, and had detailed a hefty footman to keep the fire going; Maria was away, and she had the key of the store cupboard, but there was wine and cold pork to supply a more substantial breakfast than usual. The maids were told to return and clean their quarters; the lady's maid could have the day off and spend it in the slaves' bath. She knew everything, and the tale of Maria's desperate resolve and bloody preparation would be all over the city in a few hours; he hoped that would please her.

It was the middle of the morning when eventually Felix set out to obey the summons of the new Emperor. He had asked no questions of the soldier, partly because it was difficult to frame inquiries about a transfer of the Purple in such a way as to demonstrate unbounded loyalty to the new sovereign, partly because he could not bring himself to admit that he had not the slightest idea of how it had come about; but the man must have guessed, from his undignified behaviour when he opened the door, that he was ignorant of the latest developments. It was a humiliating position for a Praeses, but there was no way to repair the damage. However, soldiers had such a contempt for civil servants that the man probably would not bother to make a funny story of it. The small one-man litter moved slowly, while the solitary escort marched beside it with the haughty swagger of a soldier whose duties are rather ceremonial than military.

When he reached the Praetorium everything looked normal. The gate was open, and the gleaming sentries were obviously there for show, since they held themselves so rigid that they could see nothing but the sky. As he descended from his litter he was relieved to notice a dismounted trooper of the Bodyguard just within the open door of the Praetorium proper; it was the first sign that any body of troops more warlike than the impressive but obsolete Legions were willing to serve the new Emperor. The Bodyguard had been chosen for their alleged devotion to Marcus; if they made no effort to avenge his death the army must be willing to accept the accomplished fact.

Physically Felix was limp and exhausted, but his brain was noting everything he saw and drawing the appropriate deductions, while his self-confidence rapidly returned. This was his first audience with a new Emperor, and that was rather a frightening business; but the new Emperor was his father-in-law, whom he had known for many years as a private citizen; what was even more encouraging, he was not secure in his office. He would need the help of the civil service, and must reward his followers generously.

As Felix prostrated himself in the private office he had a feeling that time stood still. Of course, it was only seven weeks since he had touched his forehead to the ground, in this very room, at his first interview with the tyrant

Marcus. What seemed quite uncanny was that as he bent down a quiet voice called: 'No prostrations in here, my friend.'

But when he straightened up Gratianus grinned back at him very much as usual. The new Emperor wore none of the insignia of his rank; he was dressed in a shabby brown tunic and indoor slippers; his face bore the rather malicious smile with which he usually greeted his son-in-law, as though there was something comic about civil servants, and he did not even seem especially tired.

'Well, young Caius,' he said, 'you manage your prostration so gracefully that you may do it as often as you please, even when I tell you not to. But I want your advice on a good many things, so you had better sit down on that stool. Why do you stare as though you had seen a ghost? Don't tell me, I think I can guess. This interview is exactly like another you had in this room? Well, why not? Marcus was quite sensible until he tried to seduce my daughter without offering me compensation for the dishonour; he had the same troubles that face me, and he depended on your advice as I do. But before we discuss our plans I suppose you want to know why you find yourself a subject of the Sacred Gratianus, and not of the tyrant Honorius?'

'As Your Sacred Majesty pleases,' muttered Felix, who was afraid of showing the surprise he felt; it was not complimentary to a new ruler to be stricken with amazement because he had attained the Purple.

'Yes, my faithful son-in-law,' said Gratianus, in the gloating voice of one who knows his audience must listen for as long as he cares to talk. 'I concealed my intentions very well. I would not tell my own daughter, in case she has no secrets from her husband. You see, Caius, in matters of high politics I trust no one. Bear that in mind, and remember that even you are not entirely in my confidence.

It will make you a more faithful subject. For you are my subject now, not the mighty Praeses who grants or withholds permission for a merchant to trade with barbarians.'

This was no simple soldier, anxious to do the right thing when he was for the first time brought into contact with men of good education; Gratianus would be served by trembling subordinates.

'It was quite simple,' he went on, in a satisfied tone. 'Maria did the dirty work, for which she is eminently fitted. Your wife is a competent assassin, but she needs the control of a calm intelligence. All that remained was to buy the allegiance of the officers, who had no candidate of their own. You made it easier by giving me those sealed drafts on the Treasury, because you were not man enough to do business with a murdered corpse hanging in the window. Since there is precious little hard cash in the pay-chest I promised estates from the Imperial domain. I may have to honour those promises in the end, but we can cross that bridge when we come to it. The officers in Londinium are on my side, and they are now explaining matters to their men. The comitenses will be disappointed not to receive a donative, but times are hard and it's not so long since they had the last. No one else in the Diocese has any ready money, so they cannot be bought for another candidate. Marcus was a fool to concentrate his troops in a strange city; it made it easier to buy them than if I had had to send untrustworthy messengers with compromising documents from one end of the island to the other. There is one doubtful factor, an amusing instance of history repeating itself. So far I have no news from the Littus; Constantinus may take a line of his own. He has an independent command, and his troops would follow him against a civilian. Soldiers always resent being ruled by a business

man. But he is short of money, and my cavalry outnumbers
his five to one, if they fight for me. He is worth buying, and
I shall buy him honestly for a generous price. In any case,
he can't retire over sea, like his predecessor; if he dodged
the barbarians Stilicho would want his head, since he was so
prominent in the first revolt. I have summoned him to
Londinium; if he sends an answer at once by a fresh horse
we shall know this evening whether he is on my side. Now
you know the position of affairs. The soldiers won't die for
me on the battlefield, but there is no other candidate who
can offer a donative. I must rule sternly for the first year,
but after that my knowledge of finance will tell, and when I
reduce the taxes I shall become very popular indeed. Now
how do we carry on over the winter, with no cash in the
Treasury, and every senior officer holding a sealed promise
for a bribe that isn't there?'

In the course of this long speech the Emperor's manner
had changed; at the beginning he had threatened all the
ghastly tortures of the agentes in rebus, but towards the
end he was discussing his difficulties with a trusted
colleague. Felix had passed through moments of desolating
fear; in theory the son-in-law of a new Emperor should be
in a good position; but Maria did not love him, and
Gratianus might want his daughter a widow, to be promised
in marriage to a powerful supporter. As the atmosphere
changed his courage revived. A civilian ruler could only
keep his army loyal by punctual and lavish payment, and if
his father-in-law was going to depend on a well-filled
Treasury he would need expert advice. He shut his eyes,
and made a strong effort of will; he imagined he was an
unimportant junior official reporting to the Divine Theodosius, who never lost his temper. When he heard his own
voice he realized he was striking exactly the right note,
deferential but not obsequious.

'The only way Your Sacred Majesty can fill the Treasury is by confiscation. The late tyrant must have relatives in the north, since he was a Brigantian by birth; they had only two months to get rich in, but I expect some Imperial domain has been alienated. I know nothing of military affairs, and I would not presume to advise on the movements of the army; but I suggest that a body of comitenses be sent to Eburacum at once, to scour Brigantia for properties unjustly taken from your Fisc. There may be citizens round Londinium who still have a little ready money, or plate that can be melted, but that will be needed for the monthly pay of the troops. Could the officers be rewarded with Imperial domain in the lands administered by the foederate Kings? The usual trouble about that is that the Kings won't recognize Imperial title-deeds; but a senior officer will get possession, if he brings troops with him.'

'A sensible idea, Caius. The citizens of Prima think northern title-deeds are worthless. If we can show a few examples of Romans getting their land from the Kings without any bother, we might sell more before the fools find out that only soldiers can evict the squatters. Now to raise money for the ordinary monthly pay . . . '

They settled down to discuss that everlasting problem in a friendly fashion. Felix knew more about the revenue of Britannia Prima than anyone except the freedman Paulinus, and Gratianus was an expert at raising money for doubtful enterprises. They could talk in a quick shorthand, without putting into words the unpleasant methods they might have to adopt; each filled in the gaps in the other's outline. Felix grew so interested that he forgot he was talking to the Emperor; it was like the old days, when he used to ask unofficial advice from his vulgar father-in-law. Several times he absent-mindedly addressed Gratianus as Senator, and was not corrected.

The Indiction would begin on the 24th of September, in a fortnight's time, and by then the first of the contributions in kind should be in the barns of the Treasury. By midday they had worked out a plan for the winter. Regretfully they decided not to recognize the debts incurred by the tyrants Honorius and Marcus, unless the creditors were men of influence who might cause trouble; the resulting bankruptcies would hinder production, and the administration would face very reluctant lenders, but there was no other way of creating even an illusion of solvency in the Treasury. It was interesting and delicate work deciding who should be ruined and who should get some of his money back, and it was fascinating to listen to Gratianus, with his intimate knowledge of the character and resources of every prominent citizen in the Diocese. When he was dismissed Felix had recovered his self-confidence; he looked forward to many more confidential interviews, as a full partner in the government of the Empire.

He was to come back at supper time to discuss the ceremonies of the formal inauguration next day. It was not until he was climbing into his litter that he realized he had heard nothing of Maria; presumably she was somewhere in the building, and he would see her at supper. In any case, if the Emperor had wished her to divorce her husband, surely he would have mentioned it in the course of their exhaustive conversation. Yet uneasiness returned. The Sacred Gratianus might think it amusing first to pick the brains of the veteran Praeses and then to hand him over to the torturers. He would not be safe until Maria returned to his roof; to-night he must find out how the land lay, and if she remained in the Praetorium when he left his wisest course would be to flee when the city gates opened at dawn.

There was no point in going to the office to-day. Most of the clerks would be in hiding, afraid of being lynched during the interregnum, and if they could be found and set to work no one would take a decision until more was known about the personality of the new Emperor. There was an infinity of work to be done at the end of the Indiction and these interruptions would make the pressure greater, but Felix needed rest before his second Imperial audience in one day; he went straight home. As he passed through the forum he noted that the market women had set up their stalls; the gates must be open; presumably they would be open to-morrow, if he decided to run away. There were no troops in the city; either they were under arms or confined to their quarters. The weak point of the new regime was that it had not been called into existence by soldiers; the senior officers had been bought at the last minute, and the other ranks taken by surprise when their leader was dead; but so far no soldier had offered to raise Gratianus on his shield.

At home Felix drank a flask of wine, and ate a few honey cakes. Bread and olive oil was the right food if you wanted to drink and still be sober; but oil came from over sea; what remained in the household was locked up, and only Maria knew the right key. The Praeses must put up with sweet cakes, unless he followed the Celtic habit of smearing his bread with a horrid white grease made from milk. When he had eaten what his nervous stomach would hold he went to the bath, and read in Epictetus while the eunuch massaged his legs. Eros had once been a handsome bath attendant, and his then master had mutilated him to keep his body young and boyish; unfortunately he had grown pot-bellied and wrinkled, as sometimes happened with fair-haired Celts; Felix had bought him cheap, considering his rarity, when his previous owner was ruined by pirates ravaging his estate. He was an unpleasant sight, particularly naked in the bathroom, but he was still an excellent masseur.

Felix relaxed in the warm steam; but he was not happy. He suspected that without any effort on his part he had climbed too high for happiness. He was now so prominent that the enemies of Gratianus would be his foes also, yet he had no certainty that he was in truth a favourite of the Emperor. He tried to consider the problem dispassionately. He was too elderly and prosaic to inspire Maria with love, and there had been no pretence of it even at the beginning; they had married because it was convenient that the weak administration should make an alliance with a wealthy business man. But his wife had nothing to complain of. In the social world of women, that ran parallel to that of men, she had been the most important lady in Londinium, and he had always rewarded her friends and punished her enemies. Presumably her father would not allow her to take half a dozen lovers even if she were a widow, and at present she had as much freedom as was consistent with her good name.

There was one obvious danger, although he could do nothing to guard against it. Maria might fall in love, to the point where she wished to marry some other man. If she had a discreet affair, and her father raised no objection, he must stifle his pride and pretend to see nothing; but the favoured gallant might be ambitious, and a suitable heir to the Purple. Then the elderly husband would be removed. That was an unpleasant prospect, but he thought it unlikely. Maria was too calculating to fall blindly in love with a handsome figure, and she must see that as wife of the heir she would lose the freedom she now enjoyed. Better to remain in the household of a husband who made no demands on her, where she was free to dismiss her chosen companion when she tired of him. But it was no good shutting his eyes to the weakness of his position; under the tyrant Honorius he gave Maria a social status; now she was Augusta in her own right.

It was interesting to lie in the steam and speculate about the actions of individuals, but civil servants should consider the future in a broader aspect. He was not very good at foretelling the actions of a politician; but he could plan for the good government of Britannia Prima, because that was what he had been trained to do all his life. There were two broad alternatives when a Province showed signs of giving up the exhausting struggle to maintain civilization in the face of constant barbarian raids; either the government made more regulations, and enforced them by confiscation and torture; or they could acknowledge the perpetual economic distress, reduce the taxes, and show that there were advantages in remaining part of the world-wide Oecumene. The first plan came naturally to the mind of an official, and Felix thought it really was the wiser, since it is absurd to expect gratitude from the governed. But the Sacred Gratianus intended to follow the second, as was to be expected from an escaped Curialis who had made a fortune in trade. It would need a lot of thought.

When it was time to dress Felix had recovered some of his spirits. He was in deadly danger, of course, but agents might at any time arrest the most loyal Praeses, and he had grown used to that. Meanwhile nothing puts more courage into an official than a few hours' meditation on the stupidity of the governed, and on the mess they would get into if the guiding hand were withdrawn. In a cheerful voice he summoned the family litter, certain that Maria would return to his roof that night.

There were a few unarmed troopers in the city, loitering at street-corners and whistling at passing slave girls; they were sober, for they had spent their pay, and they seemed to be in good humour. At the Praetorium the sentries still stood at a ceremonial attention, confident that peace reigned. The Sacred Gratianus had worn the Purple from sunrise to sunset, and no sword had been drawn against him; his rule might endure.

A supper table had been placed in the private office; beside it were three couches, with the Emperor on one and Maria on another. This was a shock, for Felix had never permitted his wife to recline; it exposed her ankles, and by the custom of the ancients ladies sat on chairs. But he was not so foolish as to show displeasure; in fact, after a prostration to the Emperor he began the same abject salute in the direction of her couch. But the Sacred Gratianus intervened.

'Steady on, Caius,' he called, 'we know you have been trained in the etiquette of Mediolanum, and you get your old bones down very gracefully. But we can't have you giving your wife the Imperial salute. Now draw up that couch, and let's have no more formality. I'm half-dead for want of sleep, but we must get things organized to-night. After the inauguration to-morrow I can rest for as long as I like.'

As Felix complied Maria addressed him in a casual but friendly tone: 'I hope you had a good night, dear husband; although I gather you were very properly upset when you considered the mortal danger that faced your intrepid wife. I heard a full account of it from that silly maid you tied up when it would have been much easier to silence her for ever. She was brought here this afternoon, to answer some questions. But no matter what the agents did to her she insisted that you had not touched her. So, as she doesn't appeal to you, and I never liked her, and anyway she would always have been a cripple after the questioning, I burned her an hour ago. The guard were impressed, and it frightens off possible assassins. Now I can take anyone's maid, for no one will refuse the Emperor's daughter.'

'My dear, I leave the management of the household to

you. There is no need to inform me when a servant is punished,' answered Felix, as though it were a matter of no importance. All the same, this was a significant development. The Sacred Gratianus was at heart a jolly fellow, who preferred happy faces round him; but obviously his daughter had tortured the girl for her own amusement.

But they had not come together that evening, after a sleepless night, to discuss the discipline of servants; the way to put Maria in her place was to start a conversation on politics, of which a woman must be ignorant. Felix coughed, and caught the Emperor's eye; at Mediolanum no one spoke to the Divine Theodosius until he had spoken first; but these provincials would not know the etiquette, and the Emperor was his father-in-law. Boldly he asked:

'What news from the Littus? If we do not hear from the Comes to-night would Your Sacred Majesty consider marching on Rutupiae at dawn? Probably Constantinus is unwilling to commit himself until he sees the cavalry actually obeying your orders; but his troops will not fight for him at odds of five to one, and when your army marches he must submit or fly.'

'I have heard nothing so far. If he had answered at once the message would have reached us by now, but I admire his good sense in waiting for confirmation. Marcus might have sent news of his own death as a trap, to see if the old drill-master suffers from ambition.'

'But Your Sacred Majesty fears no trouble from that quarter?' Felix persisted. It was easy to seize power by a palace revolution; but once swords were drawn, even in a skirmish, soldiers bargained and changed sides until you had to buy each man all over again once a week. It was important that a civilian Emperor should have no fighting.

'There is nothing to fear from Constantinus,' Gratianus replied lazily. 'I rather like the old armour stand, and I think he likes me. But in any case an intelligent man can foretell how the military mind will work in any given situation. If I wasn't sure I could look it up in the official manual of tactics. He has seen one change of government, and it raised him from command of a numerus to the rank of Comes. Now he is the only officer in a position to make trouble; he will want promotion, and I am willing to let him have it. Young Marcus did the work of the Comes Britanniarum and the Dux, and ruled the Empire in his spare time. Now those offices are vacant, and I am untrained to perform their duties. I shall offer Constantinus the combined commands, on condition he takes only one salary. I suppose the Comes Britanniarum draws the highest pay? Then he will be supreme over every soldier in Britain, which ought to content him, and I shall be freed from a mass of tiresome detail I don't understand.'

'Is it wise to give him so much power?' said Maria sharply. 'The Divine Diocletianus thought it too much for one man; that is why it was divided among three in the first place.'

'That had occurred to me, my dear,' the Emperor answered, 'but no matter how these things are arranged I must rely on some soldier to run the army. I am a merchant, and I have never killed even one man with my own hands; as you did with such skill and determination. I could keep the three commands separate, which would mean paying three salaries, but then I must appoint a Magister Militum to compose their quarrels; the Divine Diocletianus had to. In this way I save money.'

'Even so, Your Sacred Majesty must recognize that such a command is a temptation to any soldier,' said Felix, in a humble voice. His ruler might be annoyed to hear him underline the obvious when he should be giving intelligent advice, but it would show Maria that her husband took her opinion seriously.

'Not every soldier thinks himself worthy of the Purple,' said Gratianus, smiling at his own cleverness. 'If every officer snatched at power whenever he got the chance there would be no discipline in the army, instead of the very little we have at present. No, the command of the army was a problem, since I cannot undertake it myself. I thought it over, and this seems the only solution. I hope Constantinus is not the most brilliant soldier in Britain; if he is, the Saxons will prosper. But he is good enough for my purpose. Consider his past life,' he went on, in the self-satisfied voice that an Emperor picked up very quickly, when he found he was never interrupted. 'The old boy spent something like thirty years in a second-rate numerus of limitanei, the Barcarii Tigridenses, and eventually commanded them through sheer length of service. In the normal course he would have remained in this Praetorium for another ten years, and then retired to nurse his rheumatism. Because I let him into the secret of a coming revolution he put Marcus under an obligation, and he was rewarded with the rank of Comes. I have looked up the agents' reports on his behaviour at Rutupiae; they make amusing reading. It seems he was baffled by all the paper work of the Littus, ration-strengths and requisitioning and reliefs for the various forts; he left all that to the quartermaster, who has bought a fine estate and is ripe for confiscation. What really thrilled him deeply was a stable full of horses; these limitanei have it impressed on them in early youth that they will never be the equals of a dashing trooper. Do you know, he takes riding-lessons in the seclusion of an abandoned fort, and inspects the squadrons on horseback, with his feet in iron stirrups? When he comes to Londinium I shall let him ride through the streets beside my litter, and he will regard that as an apotheosis. Can an old fool like that be a danger to my Empire?'

'With great respect, Your Sacred Majesty,' said Felix, 'the danger is not quite negligible. Granted that Constantinus himself has no ambition except to peacock about on a quiet charger, there is the possibility that the soldiers will hail him Emperor against his will. Many revolts start in that way, and a few have been successful.'

'Yes, that danger must be considered,' Gratianus said fretfully. 'But it is a risk that must be run, whoever commands the army. I can't command it myself, and the next best thing is to give it to an elderly man with no energy and no ambition. He can't think he has been promoted on his merits, and in his heart he must know his present job is beyond him. He won't want more responsibility. Naturally, any commander has a certain influence over his troops, but I have hit on rather an amusing scheme to reduce it. At a ceremonial parade we shall find an excuse to make him change horses, and our gallant Comes will be bucked off while inspecting the cavalry. The comitenses are snobbish about that sort of thing; they will never hail as Emperor an officer who can't ride.'

At length the Sacred Gratianus stopped talking, and his two listeners dutifully laughed. It would be wrong to stick to his point after the Emperor had told him the danger was foreseen, but Felix was not convinced. They should disperse the army under junior commanders; and if there must be someone at headquarters to make final decisions that duty should be undertaken by the Emperor himself. Certainly he was a citizen, without training in that work; but he was not a fool, and it must be easy, considering the intelligence of some officers who did it quite well.

As the Emperor went on to discuss the eternal question of finance Felix tried to make up his mind about the real strength of the new regime. Gratianus was a clever man, especially in all that concerned money, and his view that what the country needed was lighter taxes and less administration would make him popular among the citizens. But civilian support was useless if the army turned against him, and he treated that danger too lightly. He had been extremely lucky to come out on top after two revolutions; that had called for skill as well as luck, but it would be fatal if the Sacred Gratianus got the impression that it was easy to hold his dangerous position; it seemed to be in the back of his mind at present. A clever man with plenty of money had a good chance when he conspired against the central government. That was all Gratianus had done in the first place. The removal of Marcus had been a fluke, unplanned; any Emperor could be assassinated by his mistress, if she was brave enough to risk the penalty of failure. The real strain was only beginning. It is always more difficult for a gambler to keep his gains than to win in the first place. Yet how could he convey all this to his father-in-law without appearing disrespectful, or, worse still, disloyal?

One danger was already apparent. Now that his ambition was satisfied the Sacred Gratianus revealed an underlying laziness. An energetic ruler would even now be learning enough drill to make a show of commanding the great force encamped outside the city. This Emperor thought he could find a commander-in-chief who was at the same time competent and lacking in ambition. Such a creature did not exist.

Felix reclined on his couch, eating steadily and drinking very little, for lack of sleep might send the wine to his head; the surface of his mind assented respectfully to the ingenious financial schemes of this ruler from the world of commerce. It was a good idea to confiscate the wealth of the army quartermasters; previous governments had feared to touch any wearer of uniform, lest the soldiers should spring to the assistance of their comrade; but Gratianus saw that soldiers hated their own administrative branch quite as much as they despised the civil power. They would be delighted at the execution of these greedy men. Yes, Gratianus was a clever financier. But deep down Felix felt uneasily that this civilian regime, with a commander-in-chief picked almost at random, was extremely insecure.

Unfortunately he must stand or fall with it. He was the husband of the Emperor's only child, and if Gratianus was overthrown the next ruler would certainly add his head to the pile. Unless, of course, he led the revolt himself. ('Yes, Your Sacred Majesty, that plan is a master-stroke.') But after some thought he saw there was no safety even in leading a rebellion. He would find himself in the position his father-in-law now occupied; a civilian, with an empty Treasury and an unpaid army. Besides, he did not think he could plot successfully. He did not know the identity of the chief agents, which was always a carefully guarded secret of the central administration; although Gratianus, by lavish brib-ery, had discovered it before the first revolt. Gratianus had outwitted him once. It would be hazardous indeed to conspire against this cunning and well-informed Emperor.

It was an anomaly that the secret service was not under the control of the civil or military authorities of the Diocese; although of course that had been deliberately arranged, since civil and military authorities were the principal quarry it hunted. Some of the lesser agents were known, for they displayed their credentials when they made an arrest; but the superiors never came into the open. They were paid from the Sacra Largitio, so it was impossible to trace them through the Treasury of the Province. It was a job that would only appeal to a twisted mind, Felix reflected; very hard work, possibly dangerous, and the reward a secret power which could not be used openly to earn bribes; the chief agent must ostensibly get his living by other means, and live according to that income; he might save his pay, but it would do him little good; by the time he was ready to retire he would probably know too much and the organization would never let him go. It was interesting to speculate which of the leading men of Londinium held the post; but quite likely it was not a prominent man at all; some barber or bath attendant, naturally in a position to hear gossip, might have worked his way to the top. Felix was certain that Paulinus reported to the agents, and probably his footmen and litter-bearers made notes of who called on him and when; but they would not know the identity of their ultimate employer.

The system must be cheap, since the Emperor supported it from his privy purse and it never appeared in the estimates; and, judging from the report on Constantinus, the agents got hold of a great deal of information about anyone who might be dangerous. But, paradoxically, the result of all this hard work was a very small increase in the security of the ruler. This was because the agents had established the convention that they were above politics. A successful usurper naturally wished to keep on the network of spies he found at the disposal of the government, even though he himself had deceived them or he would not have been successful. So it had become the custom that agents obeyed the Emperor who held power at the moment, deserted him when he fell, and were never prosecuted for treason. Perhaps that was a better reward than their exiguous pay; they could mingle in the dangerous game of politics without staking their heads on the outcome.

The Sacred Gratianus had finished his exposition of financial policy, and there was silence at the table. Felix, dreaming of spies and treason, had not followed what was said, though he pulled himself together and murmured his admiration at the ingenuity of these proposals. It was always the same, with every new broom; anyone could see the taxes were too high, and each Emperor who seized the Purple announced his intention of reducing them; but then he came up against the demands of the army, the prop on which rested his own power and the civilization of the Oecumene; it was impossible to reduce the cost of defence, and therefore the taxes must remain at their present level. For an intelligent man, the Sacred Gratianus was taking a long time to discover this elementary fact.

It was late, and they had not slept the night before. Maria yawned openly, and Felix struggled to keep his countenance alert and respectful. But the Emperor showed no sign of retiring, and began to discuss the feasibility of building a Palace in Londinium; he seemed to be in a nervous condition, that could only be soothed by the sound of his own voice. Felix remembered, with a start, that they still had not heard from the Littus; at this very moment two first-class alae might be marching against the large but unenthusiastic army that lay round Londinium.

Suddenly Maria sat upright; a moment later the two elderly men also heard the trampling of horses. Within the city men were riding fast to the Praetorium; it was a troop of horse, not a solitary courier, but it must be the answer of Constantinus; they had entered in peace, and that meant either that they recognized the new Emperor, or that all his men had deserted him. Felix told himself grimly that it was an even chance which was the right explanation; they would know in a minute.

The horses were ridden at speed to the parade ground of the Praetorium, and the three nervous and exhausted civilians listened keenly to the unfamiliar sound of the guard turning out. They heard running feet and the clank of armour; Gratianus turned pale and splashed unmixed wine into his cup; the Bodyguard might make a formal show of resistance, to save their honour, but they would not go down fighting against hopeless odds for a civilian who had murdered the leader of their choice; even if they did their duty there was no escape from the stockaded Praetorium. Then the noise died away, a voice cried an order, and there followed the three rhythmic crashes of the General Salute. The horsemen of the Littus were come to swear allegiance to the Sacred Gratianus.

There were more orders from the parade ground. Really first-class troops could not get off their horses without a multitude of shouted commands and the thud of smart arms-drill. The Emperor gulped his wine, until his cheeks turned a most Imperial purple, Maria pulled her gown over ankles, and Felix let out the belch that had troubled him for the last half-hour, without being observed in the rising tension. Then the door was flung open and a guardsman shouted at the top of his voice: 'The Comes Littoris Saxonici per Britannias, reporting to the Sacred Emperor.'

Constantinus lurched in very stiffly. He was so bruised that he could hardly stand, but sitting down would be even more uncomfortable, and he leaned gingerly against the wall; there was half an inch of white beard on his cheeks, and everywhere he was spattered with mud; the stain on one shoulder of his cuirass and all down the leg of his padded barbarian trousers showed that in addition to the ordinary discomforts of a long ride in the dark he had come down at least once on the road. But he was a veteran of the parade ground, if not of the battlefield, and in a moment he straightened up.

The Sacred Gratianus was so relieved that he rose from

his couch (Felix wearily jumped to his feet, but Maria lay back and closed her eyes). He spoke with genuine affection:

'Well, well, I see you have become a horseman. I am glad our old friendship will continue, and you will find me a liberal master. You and I will defend this island together. Now tell me frankly, are your forces loyal to me?'

'I tell Your Sacred Majesty quite frankly, they are just as loyal as I am,' Constantinus answered at once. He was not the man to think of such a reply on the spur of the moment; Felix, who was intensely interested in the exchange, guessed he had been working it out for the last twenty miles of his journey.

'I ask no more, my friend,' the Emperor said cheerfully. 'I have been discussing with my advisers the command of the army, and we agreed that the troops in Britain need a single head. I am ignorant of the routine of soldiering, though of course I shall lead my men in battle; so at present that head will be you. Will you arrange for the army in Londinium to take the usual oaths at the inauguration to-morrow? Then we must appoint a deputy for the Littus, since I want you to command here.'

'I am grateful, Your Sacred Majesty. I shall give orders to-night for the ceremonial parade to-morrow. But I must set out for my headquarters before midday.' Constantinus looked a shade embarrassed, but squared his shoulders and plunged on. 'You see, Your Sacred Majesty's letter took me by surprise. It was difficult to judge the situation at long range. So I turned over the command to Constans, and gave orders that if I had not returned by sunset to-morrow he was to march to the assault of the city. I shall send a message at once, announcing my promotion. But a courier will not satisfy him. He must see me at liberty in the open, or he will bring his troops against you.'

Felix was trying to remember every word, that he might

reflect on it at leisure; Constantinus was sure his troops
would follow him, whether he obeyed the new ruler or
resisted; that was a point on which commanding officers
were sometimes mistaken, but it was important, none the
less. Surely the sensible way to arrange such an affair, when
the head of an independent force bargained with a newly
established Emperor, was for the Comes to shut himself up
in his strongest fortress, and send an intelligent but
expendable secretary to carry on the negotiations. By
leaving his army on the coast, and entering Londinium with
a petty escort, he had put himself in the power of the Sacred
Gratianus. True, he had threatened that his death would be
avenged; but the threat had been made crudely, in the
presence of the Imperial family, before there was need to
make it at all; if the ruler was already feeling the
intoxication of supreme power (which intoxicated very
quickly), such an answer would be enough to send him to
the fire. Constantinus was not a practised politician, not
even a clever man, but there was a problem here all the
same.

The Sacred Gratianus kept his temper; as a business man
he was used to negotiating with opponents whom he
disliked, and the Comes had only stated rather bluntly the
true position of affairs. He agreed pleasantly that the parade
should be held early the next morning, so that the Comes
could start his return journey before noon. He even offered
the weary rider his own litter, or a carriage with posthorses,
but this was refused. The veteran of the limitanei was
determined to ride home like a Comes and a warrior, if he
split in half on the way.

There was no more to be done. The Sacred Gratianus was
now recognized by every soldier in the Diocese; details
about salaries and donatives could be settled later, when
they saw how much the confiscations brought into the

Treasury. Constantinus withdrew, and the weary Emperor announced that he must sleep before he appeared in armour for the ceremonies in the morning.

This was the decisive moment that Felix had awaited since the beginning of supper. Would Maria come home with him? If she remained in the makeshift discomfort of the Praetorium it would show that she was finished with the husband who no longer gave her influence and position; and he might consider himself already dead. Yet if he inquired what she proposed to do it might seem as though he were giving orders to the Emperor's daughter, and if she had not finally made up her mind that might just tilt the balance against him.

When he rose from the prostration that had kept his eyes on the floor while the Emperor left the room, he glanced at his wife; she was standing out of filial respect, though she made no extra obeisance to the sacred ruler. Maria stared back in silence with an expressionless face; then her mouth twitched into a vulgar giggle, and she held out her hand.

'Poor old Caius,' she said happily, 'wondering whether he is son-in-law to the Emperor or a faggot for the burning, and much too frightened to inquire. Isn't it time you led home your loving wife? You may share my bed tonight, and I shall tell you the whole story of how, single-handed, I slew the tyrant.'

In a daze of weariness Felix escorted her to the door; his life was safe for the present, although Maria had shown him she was now the master.

In the litter, at first he could do nothing but draw great gulps of fresh night air. But it was a mistake to sit silent, waiting to be spoken to, like a confidential servant. He was more intelligent than his wife, and much better educated. In privacy, where it did not impair her dignity, he must gradually re-establish his superiority.

'My dear,' he said weightily, 'there is something odd about the behaviour of the Comes. Why did he ride into a trap, when he could have bargained from the safety of Rutupiae? It passed off peacefully and he seems loyal for the moment; but there is something behind it. He may be negotiating with the Bodyguard. That looks bad, but I cannot think of any other explanation.'

'He left orders that he should be avenged, if anything happened to him,' Maria answered lazily. She was not very interested.

'Yes, darling, that sounded impressive when he said it.' Felix was worrying at the sort of problem that often faced high officials, and the sound of his own measured voice gave him increased confidence. 'But in actual fact soldiers never avenge anybody. There has been no movement to avenge Marcus, whom they really liked; why should the cavalry on the Littus avenge a strange infantryman? No, armies will fight for their leaders, or to earn a donative; but when the general is dead they look round for another candidate, if they are still bent on rebellion. Constantinus spoke as though his men were hereditary retainers, not regular troops who watched with the utmost indifference when their last commander sailed away. This is something I don't understand.'

The answer came as a surprise.

'You never wanted a son, did you, Caius?' Maria said in a weary voice. 'I can't blame you, in these unsettled times, and I also feared the pain of it. But Constantinus is a father, with a fine young soldier son, and I think that explains everything. Can't you see? Constans is popular; if his father were killed the army would follow him. The old Comes risked his life to give his son a chance of the Purple. That is why he put himself in our power, and I think it rather touching.'

Felix murmured a polite agreement, and was silent for the rest of the journey. He had tried to impress his wife with his superior skill in politics, and this was the result. It was going to be very uncomfortable living at close quarters with a woman who had the ear of the Emperor, was all-powerful in domestic matters, and now showed that she understood a great deal about the workings of the human mind. Perhaps he ought to escape while he could. Presently he might get hold of a reasonable sum in ready cash, and disappear without warning. In Spain or Italy the authorities would execute him for treason to Honorius, but he might accomplish the long voyage to the dominions of the Sacred Arcadius; there he would be remembered, if remembered at all, as a faithful servant of the Divine Theodosius, who had been rewarded with a small appointment at the ends of the earth. Or he might dodge the barbarians and find some untouched corner of Gaul, where a stranger with a bag of gold could buy a small estate and no questions asked. In these troubled times the authorities would not make the exhaustive inquiries about new settlers that were laid down in the regulations. The difficulty would be to get hold of the money, with the Treasury in its present condition.

For the short remains of that night he shared his wife's bed. Perhaps, if he had not been so tired, he might have established his authority over her as she lay muttering to herself in bloody nightmare. But he slept without touching her, and in the morning told himself sadly that he had not been a cheerful companion; if she disliked a lonely bed she would soon find another partner to share it. He never did hear a first-hand account of the slaying of Marcus.

The inauguration of the Sacred Gratianus passed off uneventfully. The troops swore allegiance, the Bishop preached a sermon, and a Banquet was held in the Basilica of the Treasury. This Banquet gave the only sign that the Oecumene was in disorder; there was not enough wine, even Gallic wine, and the less important guests were served with Celtic barley drink; the tables were heaped with bread and beef, but there were no olives or anchovies from over sea. The Comes Littoris Saxonici per Gallias still held Gessoriacum and a small district round it, and took orders from Londinium as the only means of paying his men; but the rest of the Gallic coast had submitted to the barbarians, who were now reported in the foothills of the Pyrenees.

Gratianus no longer needed the seal of the Vicariate, and the post was allowed to lapse. There was no room for an official between the Emperor and the Praeses of Britannia Prima, for the Diocese of Britain had in practice contracted to that one Province. The foederate Kings had undertaken the protection of the rest of the island, except for a few fortresses still occupied by sedentary limitanei who were little better than armed peasants. Everyone knew the loyalty of a foederate, and its limits; he would not ravage the territory of the Empire, in a crisis he would fight under the Labarum, once in his reign he might send a deputation to headquarters bearing presents that could be called tribute; but he collected the taxes in his realm, and kept every penny for himself. The Emperor might describe himself as lord of the Diocese of Britain, but his commands would be obeyed only in the south-east.

One of the new Emperor's good qualities was that he saw things as they were, not as they were described in official reports. He joked about the small extent of territory that must support all the expense of a large army and an Imperial court, but it did not seem to worry him. He passed his time in the Treasury, where he read all the files and saw every important minute as it was written; but he would very seldom give advice and never issued a definite order. His presence caused great inconvenience. The clerks could run their Province if they were left alone, or they could carry out orders that reached them in proper form from their superiors; now they were afraid to take a decision without instructions from the Emperor, although the Sacred Gratianus only laughed and told them to use their own judgement when they applied to him. He seemed to take an impish delight in making things difficult, though he did not punish mistakes. Felix decided he was getting his own back for the many occasions in the past when an official had stood between him and some remunerative but illegal stroke of business. There were traces in him of the cruelty that was now a marked feature of his daughter's character, but it took the form of laughing at the worries of intelligent men faced with insoluble dilemmas, rather than delight in physical wounds and blood.

On the 25th of September, the first day of the financial year, when the new reign had lasted a fortnight, Felix plucked up his courage to ask for a frank exposition of Imperial policy. As usual, the Sacred Emperor had wandered unattended into his private office in the middle of the morning; he was looking through a list of criminal cases, while the Praeses, unable to get on with his work, stood respectfully in a corner.

'Your Sacred Majesty,' he began, in a firm official tone, 'we are doing all we can to collect arrears, as you see from that list of charges. But it is a waste of fuel to burn these humiliores; they can't pay, and they have no property to confiscate. In fact, we are coming to the end of our tether. If the Treasury were given a free hand we might find something to sell, or even raise a loan in the north, where taxes are no longer collected. But no one likes to take action without your consent, and you never give us a definite answer. Please, either govern Britannia Prima yourself, or allow me to do so, or at least tell me frankly how long this state of affairs will continue.'

This was a strong speech, but Felix was so harassed that he hardly cared if Gratianus did lose his temper; better to be dismissed than to sit powerless in the Treasury until unpaid troops plundered the city and the whole Province slid into anarchy. The Emperor took it with a good-natured smile, and rose from his chair; he had a habit of striding about the room as he talked, which was a nuisance, because of course his audience had to remain standing also.

'My dear Caius,' he said with a chuckle, 'you ask me to be frank, and I will. We are in a very awkward fix. You will just have to scrape up enough to keep the soldiers faithful until spring. Melt the statues in the forum, or sell tiles from the roof of the Treasury, but find the money somehow. It doesn't matter very much if the soldiers are not paid in full; they are sensible men, and know that two Emperors have been inaugurated in one summer. See they have enough for a few drinks on pay-day, and we can make up the arrears presently. The harvest is in, and you can give them good rations. At least there is no one else in the Diocese who can bribe them away from their allegiance; if you hear of anyone rich enough for that, confiscate his property without delay. Perhaps things will be easier next year.'

'Perhaps,' Felix answered with a sigh; for more than ten years he had been hoping to turn the corner next spring. 'But it is my duty to point out to Your Sacred Majesty that one Province cannot for long support an army which was a heavy strain on the resources of the whole Diocese. Would it be possible to dismiss some soldiers to their homes, or conquer a larger territory, whose taxes might increase our revenue?'

The Emperor frowned; either alternative was distasteful, and so was deciding between them. Then he made up his mind, suddenly, like the gambler he was.

'I dare not discharge any soldiers, I can't pay them in full, and they would never go without their money. In the taverns they talk as though they were longing to retire, and envy the citizens who lie abed in the morning; but really they are very proud of their calling, and would revolt if I told them to go home and grow cabbages. Besides, they have made one long march this year, and now their families have joined them they won't want to move before next summer. Naturally I have considered your other suggestion. There are only three armies in the world. Arcadius has the strongest, but it is busy on the Euphrates; Stilicho leads the great Army of the West, and he is now marching against Alaric. I command the only force of trained Roman cavalry that is not fully occupied by a barbarian foe. Eventually I must conquer the West, if not the whole Oecumene. But I must proceed step by step. Next year I shall tour this Diocese, collect tribute from the foederate Kings, and enrol their tribesmen in my army; when Britain is reduced to obedience I shall liberate Gaul. Then I can negotiate either with Stilicho or Alaric, and link up with a friend beyond the Alps. I see my way clearly, if only we get through the winter. Find the money for that, and next year everything will come right,'

Gratianus strode about the office with flashing eyes, as though he already saw himself riding in state through Mediolanum. But Felix stubbornly brought him back to earth.

'It will be very difficult to get through the winter. Would it be possible for Your Sacred Majesty to subdue the foederate Kings this autumn? You could march now, while there is corn in every barn, and pay your men from the tribute you collect. It would encourage the citizens of Londinium if they saw someone else paying a share of the taxes.'

Gratianus checked in his walk, and stood by the chair as though ready to sit down. He looked curiously deflated, all his majesty replaced by an expression of friendly but anxious cunning.

'My dear son-in-law,' he said, 'there is a difficulty which I have kept secret. I don't mind revealing it to a member of the family. The fact is, I cannot give orders to the troops; whenever I try to shout a command I begin to stutter and giggle. So for the winter I must remain in the Praetorium, practising on my orderlies until I can bellow like a drill-master. Don't let this be known; ridicule would weaken my position. As to tactics and strategy I shall have no difficulty. Remember the Divine Julius was forty before he commanded in the field.'

Felix bowed respectfully, for there was nothing to be said. The Emperor sat down again and fussed with the papers on the table, but the revelation of his insufficiency had made him uncomfortable; it was not long before he wandered into the outer office, where he could pester junior clerks who dared not answer him.

At last the Praeses could sit in his own chair. He sank down, his head in his hands, and gloomily contemplated the future. Gratianus was a very intelligent business man, and he had plotted with courage and skill; he should have been a good ruler. But he was suffering from an advanced form of the dangerous occupational disease that attacked so many Emperors: delusions of grandeur. He was unable to give the simplest command in the drill-book to the guard outside his door; yet he thought he could drive the barbarians from Gaul whenever he wished, and negotiate as an equal with one of those mighty antagonists, Stilicho or Alaric. How long before he built a temple for the worship of his own Genius?

Yet everything he said was plausible, and not demonstrably untrue. He really had a good army, and no enemies to keep him busy at home; in Italy and Asia the two main armies were so equally matched against their foes that twelve alae of good horsemen should turn the scale. As a matter of historical fact Julius Caesar had been a politician who never commanded in the field until his fortieth year. Gratianus was sanguine, but his aspirations were not absurd.

This would never do. If the occupational disease of Emperors was the delusion of grandeur, courtiers and officials must be on their guard against the infection. It was much easier to emit convincing flattery, and so win safety and promotion, if one believed the Emperor was invincible in war and the loving guardian of his people in peace; it was possible to convince oneself, for the human mind is easily swayed by self-interest. But then the administration of the Province suffered, for a civil servant with delusions was not a competent governor. It was playing with words to say Gratianus commanded a great army because twelve strong alae saluted his name every morning; they followed their officers, who had been bribed into obedience; but if ever it came to real war they would not follow a merchant. An intelligent man with an open mind might pick up the simple trade of arms, even in middle life; it was nine-tenths luck, anyway. But the Sacred Gratianus was not trying to learn, for all his boasting talk. If his mind had been as busy as when he plotted the original revolt against Honorius, he would have spent his whole working day drilling large bodies of troops, and getting to know the junior officers; he might whisper his commands, and his men would not mind, so long as he led them to victory. The lazy brain of the

Emperor had been seduced by a daydream, in which he passed over all the hard fighting against tough and swift-marching barbarians, to dwell on the glory that would be his when he stood in triumph on the Rhine.

What had really annoyed Felix was the implied comparison between Gratianus the rich trader and the Divine Julius, saviour of Rome and founder of the Empire. Julius entered the army at the top, and commanded in his first action; but when there were forced marches he went on foot, farther than his men, and in a tight place he drew his sword and jumped into the front rank. It was disgusting to hear the fat merchant compare himself with such a hero.

A good Praeses must look facts in the face. The Sacred Gratianus had no plans for the better government of his dominions, and masked his indecision with glorious visions of conquest in the future. Presently the soldiers would discover him for the sham he was, and then his son-in-law would share his fate.

Felix continued to sit at his desk, staring into a bleak future. Last year he had been planning the production of many industries, keeping the hereditary guilds at their unpopular occupations, granting or refusing a mass of permits for imports, for exports, for building, for the sale of land or the felling of timber; now all that had come to a stop. There was no trade with Gaul, and very little with the rest of the Diocese, since the subjects of the foederate Kings feared to come within reach of the Imperial tax-gatherers. All the money in Londinium had disappeared into the pay-chest of the army, the citizens could not settle their debts even if they were solvent, craftsmen no longer made anything beautiful or lasting. Economic planning was a waste of time, and the subordinate tax-gatherers could be trusted to seize anything of value without instructions from their superiors.

There was no more work to keep him busy, but he was reluctant to leave the office.

For at home he felt extremely uncomfortable. His wife took complete charge of the household, although her behaviour was outwardly correct, and she asked his formal approval of what she had done. This, of course, was never refused; but he was continually afraid that she would commit him to something so outrageous that he must put his foot down; then she might prefer the independence of widowhood.

In one respect luck was on his side. Maria was only twenty-five, but so far she had not fallen in love. He was not compelled to wear the horns without a murmur, or in danger of death to free her for another marriage. But that was because she was satisfied with the substitute of cruelty. Nearly every day she found fault with a servant; then she would shut herself up with the culprit, and spend hours tormenting her. So far the victim had always been a woman, which was more horrible but reasonably safe; he dreaded the day when she would begin to torture men, for from that it was a very short step to adultery.

Felix had no sympathy with servants; all citizens were his fellow-men, but there was a bigger gulf between a Roman and a slave than between a slave and a plough-ox. By all means inflict any punishment that made them more useful, or kill them without mercy if it increased your convenience. But to be actively cruel was to hate them, which was as degraded as to love them. Nobody hates a horse or a dog.

He supposed, as he stared at the cracked plaster on the wall of his office, that Maria had always wished to torture people with her own hands, though when the Empire was better governed she had been denied the opportunity. As a mere matter of economics it was rare for a house-servant to be killed, or so punished as to be unfit for work. A stringent

law forbade anyone, slave or free, to leave a productive
occupation to minister to useless luxury. There had been a
shortage of household slaves for many years, and they were
so expensive that even the richest man would think twice
before he killed one for pleasure. Also there was a law
against it, although these Christians laws, repugnant to
educated opinion, were not often enforced against honestiores. But a year ago, if Maria had behaved like this, she
would have faced the disapproval of her equals, and
presently found her household understaffed. Now she was
the Emperor's daughter, and no one dared to murmur
against her conduct; while she replaced her servants by
asking her friends to send her their maids, as a gift.

Felix had been continually afraid for a long time, and the
fear was now a nagging dull discomfort to which he was
accustomed, as luckier men grow accustomed to rheumatism
or corns. But he was also lonely and bored; he must talk to
an understanding friend, or he would break down. He
reminded himself that the son-in-law of the Sacred Emperor
could talk as long as he liked to anyone; at the same time, he
could not expect truthful answers, for he would be
regarded as a member of the government. He was as isolated
as any tyrant, without the consolation of power.

Presently there was a knock on the door, and Paulinus
came in with a bundle of papers. The secretary started when
he saw his master, and began to apologize:

'I am sorry, lord Praeses. I thought you had gone home.
These are some drafts I thought you might read to-morrow,
but they are not of great importance. If you wish to rest I
can take them away.'

'No, Paulinus, don't go away. I'm lonely. Sit down and
talk Greek to me until I forget my worries.'

Like all Africans Felix spoke Latin as his mother tongue,

though he had learned Greek at school; in the East he had spoken it fluently, if inaccurately, for shopping and on social occasions. But the language of the administration was Latin, and even in Constantinople he had never used Greek in the office. In fact, he had sometimes pretended to understand less than he did, just to make those easterners use the language of Augustus and Rome. But in Britain the citizens felt they were making an effort for civilization if they spoke Latin instead of Celtic, and except for the Christian clergy very few knew even a few words of Greek; with a quite understandable perversity Felix now used that language as often as possible. Paulinus was the only clerk in the office who spoke Greek more accurately than the Praeses, and it was good practice to chat with him sometimes. Their minds were in sympathy, and if only he had been a free citizen he might have been a good friend.

The secretary sat down shyly and made a banal remark about the weather, in laboured but correct Attic. Like all freedmen, except a few brazen toughs, he was shy in every company; he could never forget that once he had been an animated tool, and that no citizen could regard him as an equal. But Felix was irritated by this humility; polite small-talk would not help him to forget his troubles. He answered roughly, in the fluent Koine that he could speak without taking thought:

'Let us discuss something serious. The weather in this island won't bear talking about, anyway. We are quite private. Tell me whether you think the Sacred Gratianus will enjoy a long reign.'

Paulinus looked up with a startled expression. Then his face went quite blank, and he answered smoothly: 'To doubt that would be treason.'

'I know, I know. But I shall go mad if I don't talk frankly to someone. In any case, I stand or fall with my father-in-law. I don't want you to denounce anybody, but I should like to know what an intelligent onlooker thinks of our chances.'

'Very well, lord Praeses. We cannot be overheard, and I doubt whether any of the freeborn clerks understand us. The position of affairs is extremely precarious, but interesting to watch from outside. The Sacred Gratianus is running risks that make me shudder. No civilian has held the Purple since the days of the Divine Diocletianus. I don't count Eugenius in Gaul, or the sons of the Divine Theodosius, figureheads for powerful soldiers. On the other hand, it is right that power should return to the educated civilian. If we get through this winter without a military revolt, in the spring we can disperse the army, give land in the north to most of the comitenses, and let them dwindle gradually to the status of corn-growing limitanei. That will lessen the present intolerable expense, and the taxes could be reduced. I assume the Emperor won't really undertake the liberation of Gaul, although if he leads the army over sea the saving in money would be appreciable.'

'Then you are really a Carausian, eh, Paulinus? You think this Diocese can stand on its own feet, and that we owe no duty to our fellow-citizens in Gaul?'

'I am not a Carausian in sentiment, my lord. I come from Pontus, and I have no particular feeling for Britain. But the only chance for this Diocese is a few years of peace. The citizens of Gaul did not resist the barbarians, because they preferred a German landlord to a Roman tax-gatherer. Unless we get some relief the citizens here will begin to make common cause with the Scots. Civilization is not native to this island. It is only kept in being by constant work in this office. We need the support of at least part of the population, and they are very near giving up.'

This was a gloomy presentiment that occasionally

haunted Felix, although he suppressed it as firmly as he could. He did not really want a frank discussion of the future, he wanted reassurance. He gave Paulinus an indication of the line he should take.

'Next spring we shall kill two birds with one stone,' he said cheerfully. 'As the army disperses the foederate Kings will be reduced to obedience. With the other Provinces paying their quota of taxes Londinium will prosper.'

But Paulinus had been told to speak frankly, and he refused to play up. This talk was so treasonous that it could never go beyond the private office, and for once he could say what was in his mind without considering the feelings of his superior.

'The Diocese may prosper, if the pirates leave us in peace,' he said doubtfully, 'but Londinium will go downhill so long as we cannot trade across the Channel.'

'Are you assuming that Gaul is for ever lost to civilization?' Felix asked in an angry tone.

Paulinus hesitated, while a strange expression flickered across his face (men who had been born in slavery did not always love civilization as they should). 'My lord,' he said quietly, 'we have both spent many years in the service of the State; we should see things as they are, and make our plans accordingly. It will be a long time before Gaul is restored to the Oecumene.'

'Good Heavens, why do you think that?' Felix asked, too surprised to be angry. 'Stilicho is the finest soldier in the world, and the Sueves could not withstand the Army of the West, even led by a fool. Why, Constantinus is confident his Army of Britain can beat them, although he may not get the chance.'

'Don't you see, that is the point.' Paulinus was excited, and he spoke as frankly as anyone could wish. 'Constantinus will not be allowed to conquer Gaul, because the

Emperor would be jealous of him; Gratianus knows he cannot do it himself, and therefore he will keep the Army of Britain on this side of the Channel. That is certain. But Honorius is in the same position. Stilicho will never be allowed to cross the Alps, and if he tries against orders he will be assassinated. No, it won't be safe to liberate Gaul until an Emperor commands his own army; and since in Italy even the subordinate posts are filled by barbarians, it will be a long time before a genuine Roman soldier attains the Purple.'

There was sense in this argument; Felix reluctantly abandoned hope that Londinium could grow rich by trading with the Continent. But if they were in a corner of civilization, cut off from the education and craftsmanship of the East by a German desert, there was one vital point on which he longed to be reassured. He had lost confidence now that his life depended on this unstable regime, and he felt the freedman would give an honest opinion.

'I suppose you don't think Honorius will lose Italy as he lost Gaul? Alaric is on the march, and those Goths defeated an Emperor thirty years ago, at Adrianople.'

'Oh no, lord Praeses. There is no chance of that,' Paulinus answered promptly. It was an absurd question, which showed that his patron was losing his nerve. 'Gaul was overrun because the army was in Italy, not because we were beaten. We cannot afford nowadays to be strong every-where, and barbarians break in when the soldiers are called away. But our army must always be victorious over Germans; man for man, our troops are as brave and active as any Goth, and we can give them better armour, regular supplies, and all the tactics of civilization. If there is anything, even fighting, which barbarians do better than Romans, then the whole idea of civilization is a fraud. Of course Italy is safe, and one day Gaul will be liberated; but with the high command in its present hands there can be no reconquest for many years.'

It was comforting that Paulinus had no doubt of the efficiency of the Army of the West. Someone last year had talked about the narrow margin of superiority, and the utter disaster that would follow if Stilicho lost a single battle. Of course, it was young Marcus, on his first visit to Londinium. So much had happened since that it seemed a lifetime ago. Marcus was a trained soldier, and Felix had accepted his opinion as that of an expert; but the fellow was really very foolish, and now he was dead; he had been killed easily by that brutal woman Maria, as though he were no more than a housemaid. Oh dear, I must forget that unpleasant subject; what can I say now, to keep the talk going?

'Then if we can tide over this winter without a military revolt you think we can settle down and wait for better times?' he said in a pleading voice; he was repeating himself, but he must not be left alone with his thoughts.

'There is always a danger that some soldier will seize the Purple,' Paulinus answered at once. 'The Sacred Gratianus has chosen as wisely as possible. Since he can't command the troops himself, Constantinus was the best man to put in charge. The old fool will not try to rise higher. But his son is of a different type. A young man in his twenties who is given command of a large force of cavalry sees nothing odd in aspiring to be supreme commander. *He* has not spent thirty years with a garrison of limitanei to remind him that he is not good enough for the comitenses. The Comes Britanniarum is extremely fond of his son, and he might make a snatch at the Purple for the boy's sake. Does the Sacred Emperor ever ask your advice? If so, suggest that Constans should be killed in a brush with pirates. But it will have to look like an accident. If the father learns his boy has been murdered he will revolt to avenge him, and the army would follow.'

This was just the sort of conversation Felix needed; now his mind could be busy, planning to send the young officer into an ambush; a genuine defeat would be easier to arrange than the alternative of getting him killed by his own men in the heat of action; you could usually find a trooper who was willing to murder his officer for a small reward, but so long as Constantinus kept his command the man would have a valuable secret, and that opened up a prospect of endless blackmail. He was so occupied with his plans that he did not remember how seldom Gratianus asked his advice, except on questions of finance.

Paulinus saw the Praeses had forgotten his worries. He liked his patron, and was glad to see him cheerful; but this treasonable conversation was very frightening, and supper was waiting at home. He got up and walked quietly to the door, where he bowed in silence; Felix replied with an absent-minded nod, and the freedman left the Treasury before he could be called back.

Felix forgot his personal troubles as he considered the more easily averted danger to the State; he could do nothing to make his wife behave like a civilized lady, but he could work out a plan to cope with Constans. It was true that the Sacred Emperor never asked his advice, but he could pass on his views by telling Maria. He sat for another hour, making occasional notes on wax, for it was not the sort of project to be written on enduring paper; then his stomach reminded him that it was supper time and he had missed dinner. He jumped up in much better spirits, and felt so energetic that he walked home with his litter following.

He was brisk and smiling as he told the porter that he wanted supper at once; then came the awkward moment when he tried to find out what his wife was doing, while keeping up before the servants the fiction that he was master of the household. The man looked uncomfortable as he said that the lady Maria was in her private room and had given orders not to be disturbed; but Felix was still feeling happy and confident, and he sent a message by Eros asking her to join him; a eunuch was such an abject creature that he could interrupt the most shameful occupation without disturbing a lady's dignity.

A husband must not wait for his wife before the servants; Felix began to eat, for he was very hungry, and Maria joined him in a few minutes. She modestly took a chair beside his couch, and ate in silence with eyes cast down, as a wife should; but more than once she signalled to the footman to refill her cup. Her face was flushed, as though she had been drinking already, but then she had a strong head.

When the servants had withdrawn came the moment that Felix dreaded. He licked his lips, and forced himself to ask the conventional question: 'Has the household behaved to-day?' just as he used to in the good old days when Mediolanum ruled Britain and he ruled Londinium. Then it had been the signal for Maria to repeat the mild gossip of the fashionable shops, now it often released a stream of horrors.

'Most of the servants behave well nowadays,' she answered in a casual tone. 'I have tightened up discipline all round, and they work harder than they used to. There was one fault I had to correct.' (Here it comes, I must approve anything she has done.) 'The new hairdresser is extremely incompetent. Her hands trembled so that she could hardly unfasten my curls, and then she jerked the comb through a tangle and hurt me. I let her finish my head, since there is no one else in the house fit to touch it, but I could not allow the fault to pass without rebuke. She is tied to the window-bars, and I was showing her that it hurts to have your hair pulled out when Eros said you were ready for supper. I may punish her a little more before I go to bed, or I may leave it until to-morrow. But in any case I shall need another hairdresser.'

'I am sorry your maid caused you pain,' Felix said politely. 'I hope you can replace her. Naturally it is for you to run the household; but this is the fourth time in a month that we have needed a new servant, and there will be a shortage of trained girls if you are very difficult to satisfy.'

'There will be enough for the Emperor's daughter, even if everyone else goes without,' Maria answered carelessly. 'Now tell me about the office. I can inform Father of anything he ought to know.'

Felix took it for granted that Paulinus was an agent; it would make a bad impression if that afternoon's discussion reached the Emperor in a secret report; better pass it on openly. In any case he was glad to get away from an unpleasant subject.

'I had a talk with my secretary,' he said, 'about the difficulty of paying the army from the taxes of Prima alone. Do please convince His Sacred Majesty that we cannot continue as things are. The soldiers must be moved in the spring, and there are too many of them. One other matter came up. Paulinus is a clever man, with no axe to grind. He says, and I agree with him, that although the Comes is loyal young Constans has risen so fast that he needs watching. It would make for the safety of the State if that young man met with an accident. Since the Sacred Emperor enjoys such excellent confidential relations with the Saxons it ought to be possible to arrange an ambush. Remember, it must be an accident, or his father will be troublesome.'

Maria looked demurely through her eyelashes. 'How

GRATIANUS IMPERATOR SEMPER AUGUSTUS

amusing, Caius,' she cooed. 'Your mind always agrees with mine, only I see things quicker than you do. Young Constans is a gallant soldier, and it is a shame to deprive Britain of his services. But Father has already decided to remove him. We discussed it the day before yesterday, and of course the plan we first thought of was a fatal encounter with pirates. But there are difficulties. You see, Father gave the Saxons false information when Marcus was proclaimed, and now they would not credit a message from him. In any case the scouts on the Littus know their job, and we could not arrange an ambush without bribing right and left. I thought of a better plan.'

'Indeed, my dear. Are you willing to let me into the secret?' Felix asked with a smile. It was absurd for a woman to meddle in politics, but he must keep on good terms with his bloody and unscrupulous wife.

'Why not? You won't approve, but you can't change sides. If Father was overthrown his successor would kill my husband before he killed me. You won't forget that, will you? Well, we made up our minds to repeat a plan that has already proved successful. No tampering with soldiers who won't stay bribed, or doubtful agreements with untrustworthy barbarians. He shall meet the fate of Marcus.'

'You mean to murder him with your own hands?'

'This time I shall not do the stabbing with my own hands. Here is the plan we made. The day after to-morrow Constans inspects remounts in Londinium. You must be away in the country, and he will be commanded to supper with Father and me, just the three of us. Then Father will be called out on urgent business, and presently I scream for help. The guards dash in and see Constans trying to rape me. When he is dead Constantinus will not feel justified in rebellion, and his men won't follow him if he tries. It's a curious thing, but though soldiers have the utmost respect for a seducer they despise a man with so little confidence in his own charm that he depends on force. The troops will be on the side of the attractive young lady who is defending her honour.'

'Thank you for telling me, my dear,' Felix said wearily. 'It is not a plan I would have chosen myself, but I imagine it is well within your capacity. Must I be absent? Couldn't I rush in and help to kill him? That would make the suggestion of rape all the more plausible.'

'No, Caius, we shall stick to our plot. Father didn't want me even to tell you beforehand, but you have been frank with me, and it seems a shame to keep you in the dark. However, there is no room for you at the supper party. It would look odd if you and Father both left me alone with a young man; but the Emperor might easily take it for granted that no one would touch his daughter. Constans will suspect nothing until I jump on his lap. He must be killed without a struggle, before he knows what it is all about. Now give me a good reason why you should go to the country.'

'That's not easy. I haven't gone on tour for years. Let me see . . . Verulamium is the birthplace of the Sacred Emperor. I shall summon their Curia to discuss the celebration of Games in honour of his birthday. They will think me mad to talk of Games when there isn't a penny to spare in the Province, but they can't refuse. We might even get a small sum out of them, as a bribe for dropping the whole idea. But I shall come back to Londinium immediately Constans is dead. And, my dear, there is one thing I beg of you: see that the young man meets his death before he succeeds in his wicked design.'

Maria leaned back in her chair and laughed. 'Dear husband, you are always so mindful of my honour! Perhaps I shall not call for help at the very first moment, but I won't let him go too far. I don't really like being pawed by young

213

men. I get more fun out of watching girls scream and wriggle. That reminds me, the hairdresser is waiting upstairs. I shall sleep late to-morrow, and you had better start your journey in the morning. So good-bye. When we meet again Father will be secure.'

CHAPTER V

CONSTANTINUS IMPERATOR SEMPER AUGUSTUS

Verulamium lay in a valley, but the imposing Church of Saint Albanus was outside the walls, on the old place of execution, and that served as a landmark. When the litter-bearers topped the rise Felix ordered them to halt, while he surveyed the second city of his Province from a vantage-point where he could see the layout of the streets inside the walls. The cumbrous family litter was set down and the bearers squatted by the roadside; Felix took in the whole landscape with a practised financial eye, then turned to Paulinus. (It was not in accordance with the custom of the ancients that a freedman should share the litter of a Praeses; but it was too far for a clerk to walk, and even more contrary to etiquette for him to have a litter of his own. Yet the financial expert was needed.)

'Well, well,' said Felix, in a brisk and cheerful voice, 'this looks better than I had expected. The walls are strong, and more than half the ground inside is laid out in streets and houses. What a pity I never found time for a proper tour of the Province; I always intended to make an inspection when I had cleared up my files.'

'Yes, lord Praeses,' Paulinus replied, in the extremely deferential voice that he used to express disagreement with his superior. 'From here it looks a fine city, and of course at one time it was prosperous. But they say it has decayed lately, though that may be nothing but lies to cheat the tax-gatherers. We shall know the truth very soon. Yet this is dinner-time, and I see very little smoke. Most of those fine mansions must be deserted.'

'If they are, it is because the citizens have run away from their obligations,' Felix said sharply. 'They must be caught and set to work again. Otherwise I shall get refugees from the north to settle here. They think that once they have reached Londinium they are entitled to live on government relief for the rest of their lives, and the guilds won't allow strangers to work at skilled trades. A deserted town is the very place for them. Make a note at once, and when we enter the city work out an estimate of the empty houses.'

Felix had enjoyed his journey. It was eight years since he had been out of sight of Londinium, although a civil servant who had travelled from Africa to Constantinople, and then to Britain, was not by nature a stay-at-home; but there was usually more work on his desk than he could get through in the day, and if he went on tour either a great mass of lawyers, agents and witnesses would have to follow him about or he would find a mountain of civil and criminal cases waiting when he returned. He had got into the habit of putting it off until there were no arrears of work at the Treasury, and that time had been slow in coming. Now he could travel with a clear conscience, and enjoy it all the more because his wife was legitimately left at home. These fourteen miles on a good road with stout litter-bearers had been a rare pleasure. His confidential secretary was spoiling it by taking such a gloomy view of the condition of Verulamium. As they dipped into the valley he looked about him keenly, annoyed with Paulinus, and determined to see the bright side of everything.

*

But a close view of Verulamium was undoubtedly disappointing. The walls were strong, although grass grew thickly on the rampart-walk and floods had silted up the ditch; as his litter passed under the arch he saw there was no gate; instead a dry-stone wall blocked most of the gap, and a tangled heap of stakes showed that even the remaining entrance was often completely closed; a rutted track led eastward outside the half-filled ditch, indicating that travellers to the north usually avoided the dying town.

Felix had seen cities in Gaul that had never been more than administrative centres for the agricultural tribesmen who lived round about; they contained public buildings, but no permanent dwelling-houses, and the ground within the walls was let out in market gardens. He had been prepared for something of the sort at Verulamium, but what he saw was worse. For the town had once been closely inhabited, and that not long ago; yet now it was nearly unpeopled. No watchman challenged at the gateless entry, and for more than a hundred yards he was carried between empty cottages of the Gallic build, their timbered gables leaning askew. He feared he would pass right through the place without meeting a soul, though he had sent a messenger to announce his coming; then he was aware of a knot of shabby peasants, huddled where the road widened into a small forum. Three seedy-looking men in patched togas came forward as the litter was set down, and one of them began to declaim in verse, marking the rhythm with a stamp of his foot as they did in the elementary schools. Panegyrics were normally reserved for Emperors or distinguished soldiers, and Felix was impressed by the trouble these dingy citizens had taken; but as he listened he realized the poem had not been composed in his honour; it was all about glorious victories over Scots and Caledonians. He interrupted:

'Many thanks for your gracious welcome; but you need not read to the end. I suppose you three gentlemen are the Curia of the municipality? I understood there were ten Decurions, though naturally I do not blame you who are present for the absence of your colleagues. Have you a town hall, where we can discuss our business?'

The chief Decurion folded his paper carefully and put it in his wallet. All three Curiales wore belts, with wallet and dagger, which was absurdly barbarous; but it was something that they had rummaged out their ancestral togas for this occasion, instead of wearing wolf-skins to meet the Praeses. The Curialis answered nervously:

'My lord, there is a town hall. It has been swept, and the holes in the roof won't matter on a fine day like this. We fetched a chair for your honour from the church, but there are no desks. However, I can write a little, if there is to be a written record.' As Felix descended from his litter and walked to the shabby building he babbled on; he was one of those unlucky men whose nervousness shows itself in a rush of words to the mouth.

'I hope you liked my speech of welcome. It was composed by my grandfather for Theodosius the Magister Militum. I have known it all my life, and that is why I can read all those long words. We keep it in the archive-chest, which in fact contains nothing else. Our records were sent to Londinium during the Pictish War. The city wasn't sacked after all, but we never got them back. They were mostly deeds about endowments for annual sacrifices, and I believe we ought not to sacrifice oxen nowadays, so perhaps it doesn't matter. This is one of the oldest cities in Britain, but at present everyone does his shopping in Londinium.'

'I see you have done your best, and no one can do more,' Felix said kindly. Sometimes a Decurion was unco-operative, and then it was necessary to threaten; but this wretched little man must be encouraged before he became incoherent with embarrassment. 'By the way, where are the others? It is hard for three to do the work of ten.'

'Quite so, my lord. In the old days there were ten landowners in the Curia. But one has now become the Sacred Emperor, another died without heirs, two were executed for concealing assets from the tax-gatherers, and three disappeared, run away to the barbarians or gone to work as coloni where they were not known. There are only three of us left.'

'The Treasury shall look into that. We may find the deserters. In any case we must fill your Curia. I am sure you would not mind associating with prosperous coloni if they are worthy of the honour.'

There had been a time when membership of the Curia was a jealously guarded hereditary privilege; but since Decurions were compelled to collect the taxes of their city, and make up any deficiency out of their private estates, the office was now very burdensome; these uneducated citizens would be glad of colleagues to share the obligation, even if they were barbarous coloni of servile descent.

The town hall had been a fine building, though the leaky roof was repaired with untidy thatch, instead of baked tiles. The throne-like cathedra from the church was the only piece of furniture, too grand to be suitable for a business conference; luckily anyone who could write at all was used to scribbling with the tablets held in the left hand, and they could manage without desks.

It was late in the afternoon, and the proceedings were brief; the Praeses outlined his scheme, that in return for the cancellation of all arrears of revenue the city should offer to its distinguished son, the Emperor, a sum of money for the celebration of Games on his birthday, or possibly, in the present emergency, for any other purpose. He then adjourned the meeting until the following evening, when the Decurions might report how they intended to fulfil this Imperial command.

There was just time for a walk round the town before darkness fell. It was enough to show that Verulamium was far gone in decay. The two gateless entries were left unblocked for the night, there were no watchmen and no curfew, and very nearly no inhabitants at all. The Curiales lived in substantial villas in the country, for no landowner liked living in a city nowadays, and all the merchants of the south were in Londinium. Round the forum the fine town houses were inhabited in a slovenly fashion by unwashed families of Celtic squatters, the descendants of refugees who had been too lazy or too stupid to get work on neighbouring farms; presumably they lived by theft and begging, and they must be in arrears with their poll tax. Felix made a note to order the arrest of these unproductive mouths; the able-bodied could be sent to the mines or the weaving sheds, and the children sold as domestic servants, if they were young enough to learn habits of cleanliness. Apart from these squatters no one lived permanently in the city, and there was no reason why anyone should. Verulamium had been founded on the site of a tribal fortress; it was on a main road, beside a little river; but nowadays there was practically no traffic with the north-west of the island, raided by Scots and Picts, and as a centre of trade it was too near Londinium.

None of the verminous squatters near the forum had heard of the theatre, but a Curialis had mentioned that it was beyond the North Gate; all Felix saw was a dimpled rubbish heap, from which protruded the capitals of two Doric columns, though the general lie of the ground marked roughly the limits of the auditorium. It was not really very interesting. All the same, the Emperor might one day wish to embellish his birthplace, and it would be simple, if the theatre were repaired, to insert an inscription implying that it had been built entirely at the charge of the Sacred Gratianus. A good official must always be devising such economies.

An empty mansion had been prepared for the distinguished visitor; the roof was weatherproof, and a good bed had been brought from a villa in the neighbourhood; there was a profusion of excellent food, which had been ruined by an unskilful cook. Altogether, considering the normal discomfort of the country, Felix had nothing to complain of. But he did not sleep well, for his mind was disturbed.

In the first place there was the ever-present feeling of insecurity, reinforced by a strange bedroom; at home, in the official residence where he had been powerful and respected for more than ten years, it was hard to realize that his life hung by a thread; here it was only too easy to see himself in squalid exile. Well, that was one of the disadvantages of a political career, which he had incurred, all those years ago, when he robbed the Treasury at Lugdunum to help the Divine Theodosius. An educated man should bear with fortitude troubles he had brought upon himself. Felix lay still and closed his eyes; he needed sleep if he was to argue with the Curia about a birthday present for the Emperor, and it was ridiculous to be haunted by such fears. He was the Praeses of Britannia Prima, a vir spectabilis, worthy of his ancestors; an agent might take his head at any moment, but then the roof might fall or he might be bitten by a mad dog; a servant of the State should plan as though he were immortal, and leave his desk in order when it was time to go. By an act of will he dismissed from his mind all fears for his own life.

But still he could not sleep; he was quite genuinely not

afraid for himself, but something was worrying him, something he was reluctant to face. He sat up in bed, squared his shoulders, and meditated on the Gens Sempronia. That consoled him, as it had often consoled him in the past. The great men of old faced facts, and sometimes overcame them; even when defeated they tried to comprehend what had beaten them; they were not barbarians, to be frightened by Something mysterious above the sky, or Luck hidden in a queer stone. The Divine Theodosius had announced that the old gods were dead, and the new God, though He had revealed to His ministers so many extraordinary details about the next life, seemed to take very little interest in this one; a true Roman should examine the world, so that when he understood it he might rule it. Very well, what was worrying him now?

When at last he pulled out the anxiety that had lurked all day at the back of his mind, and examined it fairly as a Stoic should, he realized why he had been reluctant to face it. For it made nonsense of his whole life. He had been wondering, unconsciously, whether Rome and Civilization and the Oecumene, everything that he had been brought up to serve as greater than himself, were inevitably dying by inches. The miserable vestiges of what had once been the second city of Britain were responsible for that, but of course there was an answer. Populations shifted, trade sought new channels, and established cities decayed; he had never visited Rome, but travellers said even the Mistress of the World no longer filled the walls built by the Divine Aurelianus; he had passed through Thebes in Boeotia, once the greatest power in Hellas and now a dusty hamlet. But as some towns decayed others arose; the glorious city of Constantinople was only seventy years old, and its swarming population and magnificent works of art had all been brought from elsewhere. The desertion of Verulamium was nothing to worry about, if some other city had prospered at her expense.

There lay the real trouble. With the exception of Londinium every city in Britain was shrinking. The whole Diocese was going downhill, and it was hard to think of any other region that profited by it; certainly Gaul had not gained, and now Gaul, just for the time being until things could be put right, was a desert of barbarians. Was the West losing ground while the East expanded? But although there were many flourishing cities in the East, there were also wide stretches of desolation; men said that in Moesia the wolves died of hunger. Then the whole Oecumene was growing weaker every day? Well, it might be so, but that was an incentive to all true servants of the State to work harder than ever; only a scoundrel left the losing side just because it was losing.

There is a gloomy pleasure in picturing yourself as the champion of a worthy but defeated cause; Felix felt a glow at his heart as he contemplated his own nobility. He very nearly went to sleep, but suddenly a deeper layer of anxiety was revealed to his conscious mind. Suppose the whole conception of Imperial rule was wrong? Verulamium was dying, and he had been considering the way to revive it; but perhaps it was the civil service that had killed it. Why had it been a city in the first place? Because a tribe of barbarians lived in a neighbouring fortress, obsolete when the Pax Romana was established. But why had they come together in a walled town, instead of living scattered on their farms? What did a city offer to an active young peasant who could grow his own food, and wear wool from his own sheep? Education, amusement, a measure of self-government? There had been a time when Verulamium offered something to the Belgae that they could not get on their self-sufficient farms. But now penury had destroyed education and amusement, and the civil service had abolished self-government; so farming, even with the risk of raiders, was preferred to a regulated life behind strong walls. That was the explanation; to these Celts, though not to the more cultured inhabitants of the East, regulation was the enemy.

But regulation was necessary. It was possible to imagine an ideal State in which each citizen pursued his own interest, and yet these private interests harmonized with the interest of the community; Rome must have been like that in the early days, before the Punic Wars. But the economic system, that had once been as plastic as a lump of fresh clay, had been baked into a rigid tile long before he was born. During the great struggles on the Danube, more than a hundred and fifty years ago, something had gone wrong with the currency; money lost its value until nobody counted individual coins and all reckoning was by sackfuls; business came to a standstill, and the State had to step in to compel people to work. Of course, once that started it could never be stopped. For it was the essential occupations that were subject to compulsion, and because they were subject to compulsion they attracted no volunteers. There was no going back, and the best a conscientious official could do was to make more regulations, to counteract the unforeseen results of the last batch (which always did have unforeseen results).

That was what Felix had been doing all his life, and his unremitting labour just kept the system working. But now, he told himself as deeper gloom descended on this unfamiliar bed, he was not even continuing the system of enforced production. Since the revival of the Empire of Carausius he had concentrated on taking the whole wealth of the community to pay the army. Of course there was an emergency, and this was not the normal method of administration. But could he honestly say that he foresaw an end to the emergency? For eleven years he had been in charge of what was on paper a peaceful and wealthy Province, and during that time he had not yet been able to start the schools decreed by the Divine Valentinianus; latterly he had been unable to spare money even for work on the roads, whose milestones bore a record of their last repair by the Divine Constantinus, more than sixty years ago.

He lay back and resigned himself to a wakeful night. All his life he had been upheld in his exhausting and dull administrative work by the knowledge that he was serving something greater than himself; first it had been the cause of Rome against the barbarian generals, when he had risked his head to support Theodosius in the civil war; then he had served the sons of his old leader, because they were his sons and representatives of Eternal Rome. But when Marcus rebelled he had merely struggled to keep his footing in unpredictable convulsions, without considering whether he served a worthy master. Now he was son-in-law to the Emperor, enormous promotion for the young Treasury clerk of Lugdunum. But not only was his position less powerful than it looked; in addition he had lost the stimulus of serving an ideal. Why should he wring money out of a bankrupt Province for the greater glory of this treacherous swindler, who had made his fortune by selling prohibited goods to the barbarians? At length he drifted into an exhausted sleep, and by long habit forgot his troubles, temporarily, in the morning.

The conference with the Curia was fixed for the evening, and he spent the day with Paulinus, inspecting the cultivation of the neighbouring farms. This was better than he had expected. Several fine villas were falling into ruin, and others looked as though they had not long been abandoned; although of course the damage was put down to the Pictish raids of forty years ago, that inevitable excuse which Felix was extremely tired of hearing. But even where the farmer lived in a makeshift hut beside his roofless house the fields were properly ploughed, and had been manured, which every official knew as the mark of permanent cultivation; peasants who spread manure would rather pay a heavy tax than abandon their land. The workers in the fields were lusty and well fed, and the children ran sturdily to hide from the strangers. No matter how strictly taxes were collected the men who actually grew food would not go hungry.

Felix had been invited to dinner by each of the three Curiales, but if he dined with one the others would naturally assume that he was also receiving a secret bribe; he preferred to picnic in the ruins of a deserted villa. The roof-beams had been stolen, as always when a house stood empty, but one wall remained as a shelter from the wind, and before he could stop them his litter-bearers had built a roaring fire on a rather decorative mosaic pavement in the principal room. He had brought wine from Londinium, for in these rustic parts even officials might be offered fermented barley, and a shepherd had given him a hare, a treat for a city-dweller. The sun shone as he sat happily on the windward side of the bonfire, trying to fit the Georgics of Vergil into this northern landscape. For the rest of his life he remembered the carefree atmosphere of that meal, the security and the leisure.

In the evening he returned to the town hall, and conferred with the Curia about the celebration of the Imperial birthday. The Decurions pleaded poverty, but he had a good idea of what their land should produce; it did not take long to get their agreement for an offering in silver, on condition they were excused Games. It was the sort of routine negotiation a junior clerk could have done; but of course, as he remembered with pain, this whole journey was merely a pretext to get him away from home while his wife committed another murder. At this very moment Maria would be twining herself in the arms of Constans, and calling to the guard to cut him down. Her cruelty made her already a most unpleasant person to live with, and when she had removed a dangerous menace to her father she would be less supportable than ever. But there was nothing to be done; he dared not divorce her, and she was unlikely to die before her husband. Was there a poison that could be got hold of quietly, which killed with the symptoms of natural disease . . .

It was late, and he sat over a brazier of charcoal, warming himself before he climbed into that strange bed. The servants had been dismissed, and as he took it for granted he would not be disturbed he had not bothered to bolt the door. Suddenly he was roused from idle dreams by the unexpected entrance of Paulinus.

Felix noted with sleepy surprise that the freedman carried a rough frieze cloak, such as peasants wore in wet weather, and a wallet from which dangled a stout pair of Celtic brogues. Then he saw something else, a short legionary sword in a plain leather scabbard, and his heart gave a jump. Paulinus was an agent, as he had long suspected; now he had come to take a head.

He rose with dignity; this was a scene he had practised before. At least they had granted him a quick death, or Paulinus would not be carrying that sword; but he hoped the agent would strike where he indicated, at the back of the neck, and not cut his throat in front and watch him bleed to death like a pig. He had been a kind patron, and his last wish should be respected.

'Sit down, Sempronius Felix,' said Paulinus in a casual tone. 'I am the chief agent in Britain, but I have not come for your head. I want a private talk with you, and if you are frank there is no reason we should not part friends. Now tell me, what was planned to take place in Londinium to-night?'

Felix collapsed in his chair, much more frightened than he had been at the prospect of a clean death by the sword. The chief agent wanted a private talk with him. That was how the interrogations began; soon he would be babbling any incriminating statement they chose to put in his mouth, and begging for the fire to end his agony. Desperately he sought to postpone the torture.

'You say you are the chief agent. I know you only as my freedman. Show me your credentials.'

The secretary put a hand to the neck of his tunic and pulled out a leaden bulla on the end of a string. Felix recognized the pattern, and now he had to think of something else to say. Very well, he would begin with the truth, though that could not be what the Emperor wanted.

'The lady Maria had plans that necessitated my absence,' he began in a shaky voice. 'She is to sup with her father and young Constans, son of the Comes Littoris Saxonici per Britannias. She will be left alone with the young man; then she will cry rape, and he will be killed by the guards. I only heard of the scheme the day before I left, and if you consult the account of my movements which I presume is kept by your subordinates you will see that I had no chance to warn the victim. I am a loyal subject of the Sacred Gratianus, who is the father of my wife. I would not warn a traitor. Are you certain your instructions authorize you to interrogate me?'

'You will not be questioned, Caius. I only want a private talk. I did not know what the lady Maria had planned for to-night. However, it all fits in. Come on, man! Can't you see

I am your friend? I have no instructions to arrest you, or to wring information out of you. On the contrary, I am telling you something which will at least save your life, though you must flee at once. But I don't suppose you will find a change of scene unbearable. I give you this chance because you treated me as a friend, in spite of my birth, and I think you served the Oecumene faithfully and well. Now pull yourself together, and listen carefully.'

Oddly enough, what struck Felix most forcibly in this speech was that a freedman addressed him by his praenomen. The shock of this impudence awakened his mind. His heart ceased to race, and he sat up to listen carefully. Something had happened in the high politics of the Empire, and he would have to make plans for his own safety; but here was a friend who knew all, and with inside information a politician could always save himself.

'To-morrow we shall have a new Emperor,' Paulinus continued placidly. 'And he will want the head of the son-in-law of his predecessor. My subordinates knew nothing of the arrangement to eliminate Constans, though he was an evident threat to Gratianus, and something of the sort was bound to come. But it was a mistake to forget your wife's reputation. The amusements of the Imperial family are a legitimate subject of gossip. When young Constans was invited to a private supper he very sensibly suspected danger. He got in touch with the commander of the guard, who is a cousin of his. Gratianus ought to have remembered that. No man can hold the Purple unless he knows the cousins of the captain of his guard. Anyway, these two discussed the rather surprising invitation, and decided it was a plot. As a matter of fact, they got that part of it wrong. They guessed the idea was to remove you, marry Maria to young Constans, and proclaim him heir to Gratianus. The young man would be unable to refuse, but the lady has such a reputation for atrocity that he did not relish the prospect. He decided instead to destroy the Imperial family. There were only a dozen guards in the Praetorium, and it was possible to bribe such a small number by offers of promotion. Constans hid his sword under his tunic; when the servants left the room he slew the tyrant and his wicked daughter. He is a pious son, without ambition, and he decided to give the Purple to his father. An agent has brought me word that the first part of the programme went off without a hitch. Gratianus and Maria are dead, and their guard helped to kill them. It is possible the troops may cheer for someone else, but probably Constantinus will be Emperor to-morrow.'

Felix tried to analyse his emotions. He ought to be filled with horror at the brutal murder of his pretty young wife; and Gratianus had been an old acquaintance, if not an old friend. But there was no doubt about it; he was glad they had been removed. It was time to make his own position clear.

'It is very kind of you to tell me this news in advance,' he said, with a shrug. 'I will not pretend to mourn. Anyone who enters politics faces sudden death, as I know personally; and what came to them was swift, and as dignified as these things ever can be. No one dies well if he is torn asunder by wild horses, or given to bears in the arena; but the sword can be met with fortitude. However, you did not come here in the middle of the night to tell me I am a widower. What is your advice? I am willing to serve Constantinus, and I have never done him harm. Shall I go back to Londinium to-night, or send in my allegiance in the morning?'

'No, no, Caius,' Paulinus answered vehemently. 'Listen to me when I call you by that name, and you will understand that you are powerless. Because of your marriage, you seemed to be an important ally of the tyrant Gratianus. I know you did not approve his rapacity, and Maria practised her disgusting amusements without your encouragement. But Constans never concerned himself with politics; he could have seized the Purple for himself, but he preferred to serve under his father. A man of such feeble spirit cannot know the true state of affairs; to him you are a member of the Imperial family, to be destroyed as soon as possible. Within the walls of Londinium you would not live a day. I am an experienced agent, and I can feel in my bones when a politician is ripe for the fire. It is only the accident that you happened to be away from home, for the first time in eight years, that has hitherto preserved you. Constans sent two guardsmen to your house as soon as the Emperor – I should say the tyrant – was dead.'

'Why are you telling me this?' Felix interrupted, in a fretful tone. 'I can't escape, for my litter-bearers will obey that bulla of yours, and so will the Curia of this city. Is it just that you want more information, so that you will be more skilful in your infamous job? I will tell you anything I know, in return for the promise of a quick and painless death. Is that a bargain?'

'Well, it would be interesting to know why you supported such a shaky ruler as Gratianus. But I suppose you were carried along by events. You were never so skilful in politics as you thought. And you could only get free by murdering your wife; perhaps your old-fashioned prejudices made that impossible. That is how I suppose you got into this mess; but the whole thing is now ancient history, and you need not correct me if I am wrong.'

Paulinus was enjoying a most amusing interview; how satisfying to see this pompous disciple of the ancient Roman virtues alternating between frenzied fear of the pain he had freely inflicted on petty criminals, and spasmodic efforts at a Stoic contempt for the rage of tyrants. But time was pressing.

'It seems I have not made myself clear,' he continued. 'I am the chief of the agentes in rebus, and it is the tradition of our organization to serve the Emperor for the time being. I like you, as I said before, but if I received an order from the competent authority I would question you until you died in agony, for that is my function. But at present I have no orders from anybody. For this one night Britain is without a ruler. So I am masterless, and on my own initiative I offer you the chance to escape. To-morrow I shall receive an order for your arrest, and if you are within reach I must carry it out. But in these days my authority holds good only in the Province of Britannia Prima. I have brought you clothing and shoes for a journey, and a sword if you prefer suicide to exile. Now I leave you. I hope, for your sake, that we do not meet again. If you decide to live, remember that you have this chance because you were kind to a lonely freedman, and treat all slaves as though they might one day save your life.'

In a single movement he dropped his burdens on the floor, and slipped out of the room.

Felix tried to think quietly. At first the blow to his self-esteem filled his mind to the exclusion of other questions. He had employed in his office the chief of the agents, and he had suspected nothing. True, he had supposed Paulinus reported his movements and spied on his private papers; but he had never guessed that his secretary was the head of the organization. What a golden opportunity he had missed! It would have been easy to get a hold over the man, as it was always easy, in that regulation-ridden State, to get a hold over anyone important. Then he could have denounced his enemies and rewarded his friends until he was all-powerful in Britain. But he could not be blamed for not recognizing the chief of the secret agents, when the whole point of the service was its secrecy. Yet even when he forgave himself that omission there still remained two bad mistakes. He ought to have overthrown Gratianus himself, as soon as he saw the regime was too weak to last; that was the only way to survive the wreck and keep his office. The second mistake showed even worse incompetence in a trained politician; when Maria explained her plan he ought to have seen it was dangerously two-edged. It depended on two assumptions: that Constans would come unsuspecting to supper, and that the guards would be faithful to an elderly merchant, with no money left for further bribes, when the alternative was support for a dashing young soldier. If Constans had to be removed the only safe way was to have him stabbed in the back by a competent and well-paid assassin; you could never trust the Bodyguard to murder a comrade. But he had been so overwhelmed by financial difficulties that he could not spare the time to watch over the safety of his father-in-law. That, of course, was the explanation. It was not that he was unskilled in politics, but that his mind had been occupied by more important matters.

Thus he won back enough self-confidence to make plans for the future. Paulinus had suggested he might prefer suicide to flight, but that was absurd. Suicide was preferable to prison and torture, and there might be circumstances in which it was a valuable public protest against misgovernment. But in Britain such a protest would be wasted, for the Celts had never heard of Cato or Thrasea; and in fact he had no reason to suppose the rule of Constantinus would be any worse than that of Gratianus, or Marcus, or for that matter of that Honorius.

He rose and examined the little heap that Paulinus had

left on the floor. If he wore the rough cloak and clumsy brogues he would look like a travelling peasant; though if he spoke the disguise would collapse, since he hardly understood ten words of Celtic. He brought out the little purse he had worn secretly since these political troubles first began. There were the ten gold solidi minted by the Divine Constantinus, first of that name; the best money in the world, pure gold, unclipped, well-struck and of even weight; any one of them would pass without question at its face value, while modern coins were of such doubtful metal and irregular shape that petty traders haggled endlessly over the value of each. Ten solidi would buy a passage to Spain; but to fly over sea he must find a ship ready to sail. He considered for a few minutes, and saw this plan was impracticable. Voyages to Spain were infrequent and irregular, since that Diocese also produced lead and was self-supporting in corn and wool. He remembered that last winter he had begun to plan more frequent sailings, before these rebellions made havoc of the normal routine of his work. And since Spain still obeyed Honorius any trade thither could only be unauthorized smuggling. If he hung about Londinium or the ports on the south coast, he would be arrested before he could get in touch with a reliable smuggler.

He must hide in the country, until he found a chance of escaping over sea. The choice was narrowed down; should he go north or west? Ten years ago he had followed Stilicho to Eburacum, when the great Magister Militum reorganized the defence of the Diocese; in so far as he knew any of the main roads it was the route to the north, which happened to pass through Verulamium. If he set out at once he might reach the dominions of King Coroticus before the agents caught up with him. It seemed obvious; without thinking he strode to the door to summon his litter-bearers.

But he stopped short. The plan might work if his bearers did not betray him, but of course they would. They would learn at the first tavern that a new Emperor sought his head, and would immediately hand him over; they might be freed, they would certainly earn enough blood-money for an evening's amusement, and in so far as they were not completely indifferent to the load they carried they hated their master. If he fled, he must abandon his litter here in Verulamium while the slaves still slept.

His nerves began to give way under the pressing fear of torture and the fire, as he strode up and down the bare ugly room. Presently he halted by the chest which contained his clothes for the journey, and tentatively hoisted a leg over the curved top. As a child he had often played at riding, and in later life he had occasionally been carried from place to place on the back of a quiet mule, with a groom at the bridle; but he had never mounted a horse. Educated citizens did not ride; they left such boisterous means of travel to barbarian mercenaries and uncouth soldiers. A few land-owning nobles in southern Gaul so far forgot their dignity as to gallop after deer and hares, instead of netting their game on foot after the respectable manner of the ancients; but civil servants did not hunt, even on foot, and very seldom journeyed beyond walking distance of the office. Of course, riding must be easy, when one considered the extremely foolish people who did it quite well; but there was a knack to it, all the same. A horse would be no more use to him than a litter.

Then he must leave Verulamium on his own feet. In that case it was no use trying to outdistance pursuit; he must hide by day and creep through byways at night. He was not a good walker, but then he did not have far to go, since the other four Provinces of Britain were now in the power of the foederate Kings. He sat down, his nerves more calm since he had made up his mind, and scratched a rough map on his note-book; without a map to look at, even the inaccurate sketch he could draw from memory, he was helpless to plan his route; for he was so used to living in Londinium that he could not picture in his mind how the country lay from any other starting point.

Gazing at the wax Felix had an inspiration. His knowledge of the great road to Eburacum was useless, since he would have to travel across country; and the agents would expect him to flee northwards, since he already had fourteen miles' start in that direction. But there on the sketch was the River Thames, only a day's journey to the south; by travelling upstream he would soon find himself, without danger of losing his way, in the territory of King Cunedda of the Otadini. Furthermore, there was one method of travel, other than walking, that he did understand. He had been born and brought up in the African port of Tingis, and as a child he had played by the harbour; swimming was an art one never forgot, and he could scull and paddle as well as his soft muscles would allow. There was the perfect way of escape. With an access of resolution he pulled off his light indoor slippers and wriggled his toes into the heavy brogues.

One of his litter-bearers dozed by the door, for the lodging of a high official must always be ready to receive a messenger; but this temporary billet had a small garden at the back, and it was easy to slip through a gap in the ruinous wall. Ten minutes after he had decided to strike up the river Felix found himself in a deserted side street of dying Verulamium, wrapped in the thick frieze cloak; the sword hung under his left arm, where it did not show, but Paulinus had also provided a stout iron-shod staff, sufficient protection against sheep-dogs; from this dangled the wallet containing his indoor slippers, flint and steel, and a few silver coins in a small purse. The slippers were a necessity, for these strange brogues would chafe his feet so that he might not be able to put them on again for the second night's march.

He had melted the map off his note-book, but he carried the lie of the country in his head. He must strike the river above Londinium, which was fairly easy so long as he kept to the west of the main road; but before he reached the bank he must cross the great road to Calleva, which ran north of the Thames as far as the famous bridge at Pontes; then it diverged southward to a ridge of high ground, well away from the thickets of the undrained river-valley. He did not know how far he must march, nor what speed he would make; he might cross the road before the world was awake, or he might have to lie up all day to the north of it. But by to-morrow night at latest he should be on the water; meanwhile the agents would not look for him so near Londinium.

The sky was full of stars, and he had no difficulty in keeping direction. This was the most closely cultivated part of Britain, the larder of Londinium, the only town which still had a flourishing population and a garrison who paid cash for what they bought. The high ground was all under corn or cabbages, and only the valley-bottoms with their slow-moving threads of swampy water were choked with thorn and rushes. He rarely crossed a stream, and when he did the heavy brogues protected his feet, while the holes in the leather let the water run out. There were no isolated cottages to avoid; all this countryside had been devastated forty years ago, and the coloni had rebuilt their miserable habitations in close-set villages; where raiders had been they might come again, and nobody nowadays dared to live by himself in an open field. The villages showed no light at such a late hour, but it was easy to mark them by the barking of the sheep-dogs.

An hour before dawn a mist came down, and Felix crouched in a hollow, fearing to lose himself. Both his heels were chafed raw, but the sore places were not yet inflamed, and he thought that a firm disregard of pain when next he set out would enable him to wear his brogues for another night. When daylight came he crawled into a clump of bushes on a slope, where he could look out towards the south; cabbages grew on both sides of him, so the sheep, with their alert and dangerous dogs, should not wander too near. He peered about with interest; he knew nothing of country life, but he was an educated man, who had read Aristotle and been taught to reason; he should be able to interpret what he saw, and recognize the position of the western road.

A few years ago that road would have been crowded with mule trains, bearing lead and copper from the western mines. Nowadays the mines paid tribute to King Cunedda, who shipped the ore from his own havens. In fact, when Felix came to think of it, there seemed no reason why anyone should bring anything from the west to Londinium; but the road was still there, stoutly paved and in good condition; if anyone did happen to be going that way he would follow it, and indicate its position to a careful watcher.

His luck was in. Soon after sunrise a heavy ox-wagon left a village a mile to the west, and lumbered heavily south, rolling like a boat as it lurched over the ruts of the unmetalled farm lane. It was laden with heavy sacks, presumably corn for Londinium. Felix tried to remember how corn reached the bakers of the city; a great deal came by barge up the river, but from the west did it come by boat or wagon? That was the kind of thing he forgot very easily; he nearly clapped his hands for a clerk to look it up, as though he were in the office. But he was cut off from the tools he had used all his life, books, and records, and the memories of his subordinates; he must work with his unaided brain. Surely a villa that sent its produce by barge would not possess such a strong and capacious wagon, or take six yoke of oxen from the plough to haul grain to the river bank; that could be done by donkeys at much less expense. The wagon must be on its way to the city.

Presently he could hear the driver shouting at his oxen; then the unwieldy machine swung round and headed east, bouncing and rattling along at a fine pace. That was it. They were on a well-paved stretch of main road. He was so pleased with his deduction that he felt quite brave. He remembered there had been complaints of bandits on this lonely stretch east of Pontes. At the bridge itself there was a small detachment of limitanei, for the protection of travellers; but they had been stationed there for several generations and no officer ever inspected them; probably they spent their time cultivating the land assigned to them in lieu of pay, and rarely buckled on their swords for a patrol. He could cross the road now, and reach the river. But then he must pass under the bridge; no boats ever went above Pontes, and watchers in the little settlement would guess he was a fugitive. With his new-found courage he preferred to get boldly to his feet, and walk openly westward, across the fields.

The brogues hurt him to begin with, but he set his teeth and pushed on, until the raw patches on his heels began to bleed and the pain eased off. It was now mid-morning, the time when men who have worked in the fields since dawn sit under a bush for a snack of bread and cheese; he might stumble on a group of peasants before he was aware of them, but a man who saw him in the distance would be reluctant to get to his feet and trudge over the clods to question him. In any case, as he remembered from many suits in the law courts, ploughmen were always tired and stiff, and too stupid to show initiative; the people he must avoid were shepherds, who usually had time on their hands, were insatiably curious, and thought nothing of walking a mile to learn the news from a stranger. He walked on, keeping as much as possible to the arable, and waved his staff to a few labourers in the distance. Probably they took him for a runaway, either a slave or a craftsman evading his obligations; but their sympathies were not with the law, and in his rough cloak he did not look the kind of man for whom a reward is offered.

He decided he had been too cautious. Couriers would have galloped down the great roads, bearing warrants for his arrest; agents would be searching, in the taverns and low lodging houses by the docks, for an educated man with money trying to buy his way out of the island; possibly a command had been sent to the foederate Kings to hand him over if he should be found in their dominions; but no one would seek him among the peasantry. Still, he must not rashly walk up to the nearest village and throw himself on the hospitality of his comrades in misfortune, for he might be recognized. All poor men were the allies of a poor man flying from the law, but an official was an enemy; a colonus who caught an ex-Praeses would be happy to watch him burn, if he did not first throw him to the village bull.

By midday he was out of the rolling ridges near Verulamium, on the northern margin of the flat Thames valley. This country of sodden clay was too heavy for the Celtic plough, and it was uncultivated. Goats and pigs foraged among the thickets, and he lay up once again to avoid their chatty and inquisitive herdsmen. A thin rain began to fall, which reduced visibility, though the weather remained warm for October. He wrapped himself in his cloak, and fell asleep.

When he awoke it was dark and the misty rain still fell. Before he slept he had marked the western side of the thorn bush which sheltered him, and he struggled to his feet, very stiff, to continue his journey. There should be a light in Pontes, and once he had passed it he could make for the river. But his feet were in no state for a long march, and he was very hungry. He could not get the brogues over his swollen heels; he hobbled along in his slippers, but they were flimsy things; at any moment he might run a stub into his foot, and then he would be helpless. After a hundred yards he decided that marching was impossible; he must make for the river at once, and find a boat. Also he must eat soon, or he would faint.

He did his best to make a right-angle turn to the left, though it was not easy to judge direction in the blackness. If he had come straight from the thorn bush, and if he had turned as much as he thought, he should now be pointing south. But it was easy to get lost in the dark, and he might wander in a circle. He felt a surge of panic fear; he longed to run until he could run no more; he could hear agents behind him, and smell the fire on which they heated their instruments. But thirty-five years of the Stoic discipline saved him; he knew that his body was taking command of his mind, and that he was lost if that happened. He sat down where he was, in the middle of a bog, and reasoned with himself.

'I am one of the few educated men in Britain; Paulinus is another, but he was born a slave, and the subservience of his youth ruins the character of every freedman. I don't know whether, when it comes to the point, he will hunt me down or allow me to escape; but I am a Sempronius, and I shall not be overcome by a Greek-speaking mongrel from

Asia. Apart from Paulinus there isn't an intelligent man in the government. I have now been on the run for a day and a night, and I am not twenty miles from Londinium. But there lies my safety. They will search for me in Eburacum, and far to the west. The peasants will not betray me if they think I am one of themselves. There is no immediate hurry, I must sit quite still until dawn, forgetting this tiresome body I carry in my flight. It is hungry and tired, but that is irrelevant. Whither shall I direct my mind? I wonder how the Sacred Arcadius is getting on with the embellishment of his Palace at Constantinople?'

He sat with his knees hunched into his stomach and his hands clasped round them to control their shivering, while his mind dwelt on the glorious white buildings that were springing up in the new centre of the Oecumene. Mentally he traced a block of porphyry from its quarry on the Upper Nile to its final resting-place in the Sacred Palace; they would fetch it by sea from Alexandria, but in the Hellespont there was an adverse current from the Propontis, and it must finish the journey by land. Would it be wiser to land it in Thrace, where a wagon could take it all the way but the hills were steep, or to put it ashore in Lycia, where a good road led to a ferry over the Bosphorus; if he was in charge of the undertaking which method would he choose? Presently he ceased to shiver, and sat in a heap, motionless, with his body asleep and only his mind awake.

He was brought back to the present by the crashing of some large animal in the bushes near at hand. He had often heard, whenever he planned to celebrate Games for the honour of the government, that there were no dangerous beasts in southern Britain; but it was hard to believe that now, when something with a thick skin that did not feel the thorns was blundering nearer and nearer; he sprang to his feet, his iron-shod staff held aloft. Then the beast made a snuffling noise, and even Felix the city-dweller recognized it for a hog. This was something he had not bargained for; he knew sheep were folded at night, and he had assumed that other animals were shut up also. But this was a valuable creature, and the swineherd would not be far off.

Sure enough, there was something else pushing through the scrub, and then a voice called. But it was the voice of a young girl. He made up his mind almost without conscious thought. He was armed, and could silence her if she called for help; but if she was friendly she could lead him to food, and he wanted food more than anything in the world, more even than safety. He forced his way in the direction of the voice, driving the pig before him.

A faint light seeped through the clouds; the pig was a moving shadow against the black ground, and then he made out the girl standing in an open glade. Presumably the pig had strayed; it was comforting to know the countryside was so peaceful that a small girl could be sent to search for it in the dark. Then the child was aware of a stranger; she called out in the local dialect, and ran back a few steps. But she was not so frightened as to run away and abandon the pig; she halted until he drew nearer, then took to her heels again; and in this manner they approached a cottage standing alone in the scrub.

An isolated cottage was just the place to get supplies; if the inhabitants proved unfriendly he could kill them with his sword, for coloni were forbidden to possess arms. But if he kept silent, and they did not guess who he was, they might help him willingly. The girl scuttled through the low entrance on hands and knees, followed by the pig. Felix halted beside the dark mass of the hut, whose thatched roof reached in one sweep to within a foot of the ground; to enter he must go down on his hands, and the householder could crack his head before he had a chance to draw his sword. But he felt keyed up to run risks, and at that moment he smelled grilling bacon, the most entrancing odour that can reach a starving man. He wallowed through the low entry with his knees stumbling over his trailing cloak, and sat back on his haunches, his right hand feeling for the sword under his arm.

The hut seemed bigger from within. Dry sticks had been laid on the ashes of the central hearth, and small flames were beginning to creep round them, for it was nearly morning; through the smoke he could see an old woman holding a skewer over the flame, with the delicious bacon sizzling on it, and behind her several pigs lay in a heap; to one side a mound of rushes suddenly erupted, and the man of the house crouched on his knees, with his head brushing the slope of thatch and a billhook in his hand. He shouted, and glared fiercely. Felix, dazed with fatigue, acted on the inspiration of the moment; he pulled out his sword, laid it beside the hearth, and squatted with empty hands on his lap. It was the classic attitude of a suppliant, which old-fashioned country people should understand.

The householder understood; with a deliberate ritual movement he placed the billhook across the sword, though he left the handle towards him, and if it came to a scuffle he would reach his weapon first. Then he repeated his question. Felix shook his head, and spoke a few words of Libyan that he remembered from his childhood. This visit would pass off more pleasantly if his hosts could not converse with him. He grinned at the man, then at the woman, and finally at the girl, whose head, with two other tousled little heads, now appeared from the tangle of pigs at the back of the hut; then he pointed at his mouth, to show he was hungry.

Peasants do not turn away a starving man, but he would

get better food from this hovel if he offered to pay. Yet he thought it unsafe to show his gold. Was there anything he could offer instead? He needed his weapons and his cloak; but his brogues were well made, though it would be weeks before he could put them on his raw and swollen feet. He scrambled over to the old woman, put the shoes in her lap, and took the skewer with its lump of bacon out of her hand; then he looked to the man, to see if he approved.

That was enough to make them all intimate friends. For the next hour, though he stuffed himself with bacon and barley scones, Felix had rather a trying time. He was desperately sleepy, but the others were just waking up, and they were convinced that if only they shouted loud enough they could get him to understand Celtic. Under his cloak he still wore the fine linen tunic that he had put on two days ago; the peasants noticed it with puzzled admiration. A runaway slave would not possess such a garment. Presently they decided he must be a fugitive baker, in his best clothes; for the old woman (she looked much older than her husband, but then she probably worked harder) made cooking motions at the fire and waved a lump of dough, while the man laughed and thumped him on the back. The baker was the stock example of a skilled craftsman held to unremunerative forced labour, all over the Roman world; it was the only city trade these primitive swineherds could imagine.

The woman tried on the shoes and liked them; to show her goodwill she rummaged among the pigs and children at the back of the hut and brought out a small jug of barley drink; but Felix refused it, for he guessed it would make him sick; and anyway this was no time for drinking, with the sun just rising.

But all this friendliness in pantomime had given him an idea; if he could make them understand, these new allies might lead him to a boat. He went through the motions of paddling, and pointed southward in the direction of the river. At first his hosts were merely amused at his actions, but presently they grasped what he was trying to convey, and there was a short argument between husband and wife; it seemed that she had some plan, which he considered too dangerous or too difficult. But it was time to let out the pigs; they could not talk round the fire in broad daylight. The man made up his mind with a sudden gesture of decision, and crawled out of the hut; his wife and the two small children gathered the cooking pots into a little heap, which they guarded as the girl drove out the swine; Felix also crawled through the thick pig-dung which daylight revealed in the entry, and waited outside for the next move. His light slippers were wet through and caked with greasy dung; they would be quite useless on the march. He must have a boat.

The swineherd stood jabbering in great excitement. He was trying to explain something, but of course he had never met anyone who did not speak Celtic; he found it very difficult to remember that even shouting was no use. His wife was more intelligent. She was wearing the brogues that had paid for breakfast; now she took them off, gave them for a moment to Felix, snatched them back and held out her hand for more; then she made the motion of paddling. Plainly there was a boat, but he must pay for it.

Once that was understood negotiations did not take long. Felix brought out the few silver coins that even a poor fugitive might possess, and held them on the palm of his hand; they should be enough, and anyway he dared not show his gold; ten solidi were a fortune, for which the peasants might be tempted to murder him. But these people were not only poor, they were honest. The man took less than half the silver, and set off south-west down a winding overgrown trail. Felix followed, after grinning good-bye to the rest of the family; a moment later he was overtaken by a small urchin carrying his sword, which he had forgotten, and a little bag of oatmeal. They were really a very nice family, in spite of their barbarous manner of life.

Through the bushes they caught a glimpse of the roofs of Pontes, and went cautiously; but after a couple of miles they reached the river. It was swollen with autumn rains, flowing through a maze of swampy channels. Hidden among rushes were a dug-out canoe and a round leather coracle. Both had evidently carried pigs since last they were cleaned, but the canoe was fit for a long journey; though it was hollowed from a single tree the sides had been built up with interlaced willows and clay. Presumably the coracle was used to take animals to market, and the canoe to chase any adventurous pig who went for a swim. The swineherd took a paddle from the fork of a nearby tree, laid it on the ground, and walked steadily away without looking back. From his experience in the law courts Felix understood; the man would have to swear before his master that the boat had been stolen in his absence, and he did not wish to offend the gods by perjury.

A month later Felix watched the canoe floating swiftly away on the narrow stream, and addressed himself to climbing the steep northern bank. He was no longer recognizable as a fugitive Praeses. The tattered remains of his tunic covered a weather-beaten body, and a beard was beginning to hide the shape of his chin; his cloak was folded over one shoulder, and he carried his sword drawn in his hand as his deep-set eyes searched the wooded slope. Any countryman who saw him in the distance would put him down for a wandering Bagauda, or the scout of a band of foraging Picts. He watched rooks settle in the trees above; that told him now, though once he would not have thought of it, that there were no men on the hill-top; he could look out to the north before he decided what to do next.

His elderly body had stood the journey surprisingly well. His feet were still raw, for in the canoe they had never been dry, but water had soothed the inflammation, and they did not pain him until he walked. His hands, on which his progress depended, had never quite given out, though on the third day it had been a near thing; but he had bandaged them with strips from his tunic, and forced himself to continue paddling until they began to harden. His worst suffering had been hunger, but there were hooks and a line in the canoe, and the fish of the upper river, unmolested by man, were not difficult to catch; he carried flint and steel, but often he had eaten his fish raw, for lack of dry fuel; however, everybody ate raw oysters, and he would have to endure worse among the barbarous foederati of the west; it was wonderful how a well-trained mind could control the revulsions of the body. He had been astonishingly lucky, and he tried to murmur a grateful prayer to the deity of the river as his canoe drifted round a bend. He had nothing else to offer, and to a river god it was an appropriate sacrifice. But though he had no difficulty in composing a suitable form of words, his speech stumbled when he tried to utter them. For a moment he was dismayed, at what seemed a bad omen; then he remembered that he had not spoken since he said good-bye to the swineherd, more than a month ago; his voice was out of practice.

For he had seen no sign of human activity since he embarked. Above Pontes the whole valley was a dense tangle of thorn and scrub, uncultivated. The Celts, with their light ploughs and badly tempered axes, had no incentive to clear the forest from this stiff clay, flooded every spring; and the great roads which linked Londinium with the west avoided these bottomless swamps. The country had not changed since the days of Caractacus; possibly it had never been trodden by the foot of man.

Was that a reflection on the administration? Ought he, in the ten years in which he had supervised all the economic affairs of Britannia Prima, to have ordered this forest to be cleared of its valuable timber, the land drained, and rent-paying settlers encouraged to plough for the benefit of the hard-pressed Treasury? While his arms automatically lifted the paddle for another stroke, he had plenty of time to consider the matter. He realized, and was ashamed of the realization, that he had been ignorant of the extent of this solitude; he was too busy to travel, and none of his city-dwelling subordinates would inspect such a desolate place without very definite orders. But ignorance was not the only reason; in fact, during his entire governorship he had not begun a new undertaking of any kind. He had worked hard and done his duty, but all his time was occupied in propping up existing things that would fall down if left alone. Frequently his thoughts returned to the little family who had sold him the canoe. They lived among pigs in the utmost squalor, but a philosopher would call them virtuous; they had mercy on the fugitive, fed the stranger, lived in peace and kept their bargains. In what way was that family better off because he had worked eight hours a day for ten years to keep his Province civilized? Well, so far no raider had taken their pigs, and that was something on the credit side. But when he gave the matter more thought he realized that was an argument in favour of government, but not of Roman government. Every hairy King of a barbarian tribe did his best to protect his subjects from marauders.

That family were untouched by the civilization which Rome offered to the city dwellers. They never heard Latin spoken, did not wish to learn letters, seldom used money.

Under a Celtic King they would have lived the same life, but their taxes would have been very much lighter.

He began to see that the apparatus of government, which had once genuinely tried to elevate its subjects into civilized men, had now become an end in itself. The coloni were ground down by heavy taxation, so that the army might be paid; because without soldiers the taxes could not be collected. It was a vicious circle. Probably the peasants in Gaul were quite happy under the Germans, once the bloodshed and pillage of the actual invasion had come to an end. He had devoted his life to serving an intricate but useless organization.

Now he stumbled up the steep hillside on sore feet, seeking the protection of a barbarous ruler; later he would make his way to the civilized lands of the Mediterranean, where Rome still offered something to her loyal followers; there some governor would give a trained administrator a desk in his office. The forum, the Basilica, and the Acropolis were native to those lands, and where they were appreciated they were worth defending; but it had been a mistake to introduce these blessings to the barbarous shores of the Atlantic. The good life could not be lived where the olive trees of Pallas could not thrive. When he reached the crest of the hill he was full of resolution, ready to make a fresh start. He was also very hungry.

Northwards he looked over tumbled slopes of open grass, sparsely dotted with patches of arable. The soil was limestone covered with thin turf, infertile, but easily worked by the Celtic plough. In the distance a stockade crowned a rise, and smoke showed it was a village, not an empty fort; no one moved among the fields, but somewhere near he heard the tinkle of a sheep-bell. He left the shelter of the trees and walked down the northern slope.

*

Although he had seen no one, others saw him as soon as he
emerged; he had not gone a hundred yards before a large
sheepdog bounded up with bared teeth; there were sheep-
dogs in Africa, and he remembered from his childhood how
to behave. He sat on the ground with his drawn sword in
his lap, and the dog checked when it saw the steel. The
shepherd appeared from a hollow, blowing an alarm on his
horn. Felix continued to sit, for if he rose the dog would
risk its life to attack even a sword-bearer in defence of its
sheep; but the shepherd came no closer. In these parts
strangers were approached with great caution, and he was
waiting for reinforcements. In the distance another horn
took up the call, and the shepherd sat down to watch. It
was rather absurd, and Felix hoped someone would be
brave enough to offer him hospitality before he fainted from
hunger.

Then he heard the gallop of a horse, and a single rider
climbed from the valley. The horse was only a native pony,
but it had been groomed until it shone, and the rider was no
village headman; he wore trousers patterned in startling
checks and a short cloak of brilliant red; except for the
cloak his body above the waist was bare, but it did not look
naked because of the designs wrought in the skin; on his
head was a leather helmet decorated with eagle feathers,
and he carried a long barbarian sword and a bronze shield
enamelled in red. He galloped up to the seated figure and
reined his pony with a savage jerk. But when he had gazed
keenly for a moment he called out in very fair Latin, with
the usual Celtic accent: 'The dog will not molest you. If you
come in peace drop that sword and stand up with empty
hands. Then tell me who you are and why you travel.'

Felix had decided to tell the truth. He could not stay long
in the west before his hosts guessed he was a fugitive from
the Emperor, and it would be as well to let them know at

the start that he was an important fugitive. Accordingly he answered:

'I certainly come in peace. I carry this sword for protection, but I am not a soldier. I am Caius Sempronius Felix, vir spectabilis, late Praeses of Britannia Prima.'

The young man whistled in surprise. 'Well, well,' he said at last, 'so that's how you got away! They have been hunting you for a month, but no one thought a fat pen-pusher could make his way through the thickets by the river. Don't worry, I shan't send you back, though I must take you to my father. But it is rather odd the first person you meet should be me, for I am the new Praeses of Britannia Secunda, come to inspect the boundary of my Province. My name is Pelagius son of Cunedda son of Aeturnus, and my father is the King of the Otadini, who protect Secunda and Valentia. Can you ride? or walk on those sore feet as far as the village? No? Well, there are no litters in these parts, but the shepherd will carry you on his back.'

In this undignified manner Felix reached the first Celtic village he had ever visited. The young man rode beside him, and kept up a constant flow of chatter. Felix saw that his journey was regarded as a gallant exploit; the other was not interested in boats and the hard work of paddling, but kept on asking how he had dealt with the evil spirits of the forest. The Otadini had come from the open moors beyond the Wall, and feared dense woods, notoriously infested with ghosts; that a civil servant, untrained either in arms or magic, should have traversed them alone was worthy of admiration. When they arrived the young prince's follow-ing crowded round to hear the tale. There were more than a score of them, all young and gaily dressed; they looked so prosperous, to a traveller just emerged from the wilderness, that it was a shock to discover none of them understood a word of Latin; they were not exactly soldiers, for socially they were the friends of their lord, nor were they officers, for they had no subordinates to command. In fact, as Felix realized with a stirring of his historical imagination, they were the comitatus of a barbarian chief, as described by the ancient authors such as Tacitus.

The village was squalid, and its inhabitants went in fear of the Otadini. But there was plenty of food; even the old women were fat, which said much to a trained administrator. Felix thought it wise not to seem too inquisitive, and only Pelagius could understand his questions; but he gathered that the district had been no-man's-land for the past summer, since Marcus had withdrawn the garrison of Secunda; the villagers had not seen a tax-gatherer for months, and were beginning to hope they would keep their harvest for themselves when the emissaries of King Cunedda arrived to collect all they could. The peasants stood about with worried expressions while the gaily dressed horsemen rummaged in their corn-pits. Even so, Felix considered, the village would be better off than in the past, for these Celtic nobles would be more easily cheated than a professional tax-gatherer with written records to guide him.

Pelagius had brought no wagons to carry his tribute; in Valentia few roads were fit for wheels, and his native home beyond the Wall was a range of heather-covered hills. But there was a large herd of pack-ponies, and a few sure-footed mules to carry anything breakable. After a good supper and a night's rest Felix was placed on a quiet mule, led by a footman; his backside had been hardened in the canoe, and he found that riding was not difficult if someone else controlled the beast. He looked to the future with a fair amount of confidence. Pelagius was willing to give him asylum, or he would have sent him back to Londinium at once; he ought to know his father's views on such a matter, and even if Cunedda decided to sell him to the Emperor there were still his ten gold solidi, to buy his escape. His chief discomfort was loneliness. He was the only Roman in the caravan, where even the horse-boys were Otadini; and there was no one he could talk to except Pelagius, who was too grand to ride beside a mule and bore the responsibility of command; for they rode with military precautions, scouts and flankers and a rearguard, since they were within range of Scottish pirates and this convoy was a valuable prize. He wondered whether to start learning Celtic, for he was likely to spend some time in this country even if he reached Italy in the end; but he was too exhausted to begin just now, and there was the added difficulty that apparently the language of the Otadini was not quite the same as that spoken by the coloni. The oaf who led his mule soon found that his remarks were not understood, and could not be bothered to make things easy for a foreigner.

On the third day they reached Corinium, the capital of Britannia Secunda, and at present the seat of the wandering court of King Cunedda. From without the city seemed undamaged, but as they entered Felix noted many deserted houses; the south gate was walled up, leaving only a narrow passage for pack-horses, as though traffic on wheels was a thing of the past. The council house facing the forum had been burned, probably by accident since there were no signs of plunder, and a fallen column from its porch lay across the main street; already the sure-footed pack-ponies were beginning to wear a groove in the stone. What little life remained was concentrated by the North Gate, where the King had fixed his residence in a mansion whose roof still kept out the rain.

This would be an important interview, and Felix wished to rest and prepare a speech; but Pelagius was eager to show off his remarkable visitor, and without even a wash they went straight into the reception room as soon as they dismounted. An enormous and smelly warrior took Felix by the elbow, ran a hand over him in search of concealed weapons, and suddenly, without a word, twisted his arm to make him kneel. There was a blast on a horn, and the King entered from a side door. A big chair stood against the wall, but he did not sit in it; with an angry word to the guard he strode over and raised Felix to his feet. Then he said, in excellent Latin:

'Welcome, vir spectabilis. I must apologize for the roughness of my cousin, who thinks the whole human race should kneel to my majesty. He has never before seen a distinguished civil servant. What can I do for you? Three weeks ago I had a message from Londinium, asking if I knew where you were; I answered truthfully that I did not, and now that the Emperor is over sea I see no reason for a further reply. You will not be delivered up to the agents.'

Felix murmured his thanks. He was glad to be safe, but at the same time he felt a twinge of outraged patriotism when he heard a foederate announce that he intended to disobey the Sacred Emperor. The King had taken his seat on the throne, composing his limbs to look as Roman as possible. He seemed to be not yet forty, young to have grown sons, though of course these barbarians began early; he wore the same gaily checked trousers as his followers, which were a sort of uniform for all the Otadini, but his breast was covered by a decent tunic, under a Roman military cloak; hanging from his broad barbarian belt was a Roman officer's sword, in a chased bronze scabbard; but the most foreign thing about him, which gave Felix a delicious sense of seeing the wonders of the barbarian world, was the thin gold circlet on his head. Fancy conversing with a man who wore a diadem, like Romulus or Xerxes!

'I suppose you have plenty of money,' said the King, 'since you were in charge of the Emperor's treasure? No? That is unfortunate. But of course your flight was sudden and unexpected. However, if you can't pay for my protection, what can you do to earn it? I won't send you back to Londinium, but I cannot afford to keep in idleness every fugitive from the Emperor's tax-gatherers. Can you fight in the Roman fashion?'

'No, my lord.'

'Then are you a skilled farmer? Could you make my coloni grow better crops? Or teach my smiths any tricks they don't know already? Or curse my enemies until they wither away? Or bake pottery? If you can't do any of these things, why on earth did the Emperor pay you an enormous salary?'

It was not easy to explain to this barbarian exactly what he had done all day in the Treasury of Londinium. Cunedda collected his tribute in person, or sent a trusted member of his immediate family. (His immediate family, because in a loose sense all the Otadini were related. A fairy seal had once carried off a maiden of Manau Gododin, their land north of the Wall; she was the founder of the tribe, and in consequence every member was cousin to all the others.) He did not understand economic planning, and allowed his subjects to earn a living in any way they chose; nobody was paid a salary in money, although his warriors expected to be fed; he possessed a treasure of gold and silver, but it did not come from the taxpayer; it was the spoil of successful war against the plundering Scots whom he had expelled from Valentia. He had no need of a civil service.

Eventually it was arranged that Felix should live in the royal household, and make himself useful by writing a history of the famous deeds of the Otadini, and any other letters that might be needed. No other foederate King had a vir spectabilis to preserve his memory for posterity, and that made him a valued possession. (The scheme was successful, and Cunedda now stands at the head of the best Welsh pedigrees.) The idea of going to Italy he eventually dismissed as impossible. He had his ten solidi, but no chance of getting more; and ships no longer sailed to Spain. Meanwhile he was an honoured courtier of a powerful King, and he would eat three meals a day until he died of old age.

There were things he missed in this barbarian life. He never saw a book and rarely met anyone who spoke Latin as his native tongue; the Celts thought it unmanly to bathe in hot steam, though the better classes sometimes washed. The only representative of culture was a hereditary bard, whose compositions were highly regarded; but his language was so high-flown and allusive that Felix could not understand it, even after he had picked up enough Celtic to express simple ideas. He could not learn a language properly without written grammars and passages to construe, and northern Celtic had never been written.

But he settled down and made the best of it. He was safe from the Emperor's vengeance, for the Sacred Constantinus had taken the whole Army of Britain across the Channel, though rumour said that instead of fighting the Germans he was marching up the Rhine to attack Honorius. The King waited that winter at Corinium, and when it was certain that even Prima was denuded of troops he sent a young nobleman of the Demetian Celts to govern Londinium as his viceroy; Vortigernus was a drunkard whose other hobby was adultery, but he was a gallant warrior, and the western mountaineers flocked to his comitatus. Cunedda was too cautious to attempt to rule the whole Diocese, for his army of trusted cousins was small. He withdrew to the old Legionary fortress of Glevum, where he could keep an eye on his chosen Province of Valentia.

*

Five years after his flight, when he was sixty-one, Felix accompanied the King on a deer-hunt; it poured with rain, as it usually did in the west, and he was soaked to the skin on a bleak hillside. None of the Otadini thought anyone could take harm from this weather, so much milder than in their original northern home, and the King held him in conversation about the Roman method of driving game into nets while his teeth chattered and shivers chased up and down his back. That night he had a chill, which presently turned to pneumonia. For twenty-four hours he raved in delirium, but on the second day he came to himself. His bed was made up on the floor in the Celtic style, but there were plenty of blankets and he felt quite comfortable. The only annoyance was a woman grinding corn on a squeaky saddle quern next door; the rhythmic rattle and thump got on his nerves until he wept with rage. But it was no use complaining to his attendants; they genuinely meant to be kind, but they could not understand what worried him. In every Celtic dwelling the squat women of the lower classes worked unceasingly at these tiny mills, and the warriors were unconscious of a sound which they had first heard in their cradles. As he drifted off to sleep the noise wove itself into his thoughts, until his sick mind identified it with the Parcae spinning on their everlasting wheel the fate of Rome. At nightfall the noise ceased, and he fancied that Atropos had cut the thread.

For Rome was finished. Nowadays there was no foreign trade, but intrepid Christians sometimes dared the pirates of the Channel to bring the latest decisions of the councils to the isolated church of this remote island. Sooner or later Felix heard what had happened in Gaul or Italy. Now, in his last hours, his mind turned to the welfare of the State, as was fitting in a lifelong civil servant. His youth had been overshadowed by the great defeat at Adrianople, until the two soldiers, Theodosius the Magister Militum and his son the great Emperor, chastised the barbarians and restored the prestige of the army. Then the Vandal mercenary Stilicho led it to fresh triumphs. In the end it was not the barbarians who destroyed the magnificent Army of the West. The Oecumene had been betrayed by the intrigues of ambitious politicians, and he was as much to blame as any of them. If he had denounced the conspiracy of Marcus the Sacred Honorius might still be ruling over a peaceful and undiminished realm, instead of lurking behind the swamps of Ravenna. It was ironical that Honorius, the childish trifler who never drew the sword, had outlived all the dashing soldiers who rebelled against him. Constantinus had very nearly conquered the West; but after three years' warfare, when he had won Spain and those parts of Gaul which were not in the hands of the barbarians, he was cornered in the city of Arelatum. Eventually he was taken to Ravenna and executed in the presence of the Emperor. Meanwhile someone had murdered young Constans, the gallant horseman who had bestowed on his father the Purple he might have worn himself; most of the Army of Britain had been destroyed by fellow-Romans on the walls of Arelatum, and not a single trooper ever returned. The Germans plundered unchecked in Gaul and Spain, and in Britain there were no soldiers, only untrained Celtic warriors serving hereditary Kings. That was not the worst. The Empire could get on without Britain, as it did under the Divine Augustus. But the whole West was overrun while everyone was too busy fighting for the Purple to defend the frontiers; at last even Italy had fallen. When Stilicho had overcome all his enemies Honorius, jealous of the mighty soldier, had him murdered, and in disgust the barbarian mercenaries deserted to Alaric. Then Mediolanum was sacked, and the records destroyed, so the government was bankrupt and the remnants of the army dispersed for lack of pay. Last winter came the news that Alaric had plundered Rome Herself.

Perhaps the future lay with these foederates, who knew civilization in a dim sort of way, and yet kept their barbarian loyalty to hereditary Kings, the head of the family directing his kinsmen. (For it was no disgrace for a free man to obey the paterfamilias.) Perhaps the Germans would conquer everywhere, and the world revert to savagery. In any case there was no place left for a Sempronius, a competent civil servant who knew the routine and took a cautious but decisive part in high politics. He was quite ready to die.

Only seven years ago the Empire had seemed invincible.

HISTORICAL NOTE

The disturbances which took place in Britain in the year 406 are not described in detail by any contemporary historian; what is definitely known is conveniently summarized in Oman's *England Before the Norman Conquest*, pp. 172, 173. Stilicho's great victory over King Radagaisus is historical, and Niall of the Nine Hostages, High King of Ireland, was drowned off the Isle of Wight at about that time; the date cannot be fixed with complete accuracy, and I have made the two events coincide to emphasize the fact that in 405 the Empire was in a flourishing condition, victorious over all its enemies. Misled by the scale of Gibbon's great history, we are accustomed to think of the Fall of Rome as an age-long decline; actually, the Western Empire was destroyed in the seven years covered by this novel, and its destruction was as sudden and unexpected as the fall of the twentieth-century European Empires in Asia.

As regards Britain the sequence of events seems to have been this. On New Year's Eve 405–6 the barbarians crossed the frozen Rhine; they were never expelled from Gaul, and this island found itself cut off from the central power in Italy. In the following autumn the Army in Britain proclaimed as Emperor one Marcus, of whom nothing is known. He was soon murdered, and Gratianus reigned in his place. Of Gratianus nothing is known except that he was a native of the Diocese and a 'municeps'; that vague and non-technical word ought to mean a Curialis, but the Curiales were a very depressed class at that time, and it is difficult to see how he could have become prominent unless he had escaped the obligations of his office. I have made him an honorary Senator, which is fiction, but usurpers did sometimes found a Senate before they had conquered Rome. After four months he was murdered, to be succeeded by Constantinus, a soldier of British birth, old enough to have a grown son, Constans, who commanded the British troops in Spain; he invaded the Continent with the whole Army of Britain, and died as this book relates; none of his troops returned to this island, and Honorius sent word from Italy that the Britons were to govern themselves until the barbarians were expelled from Gaul and communications re-established.

King Cunedda of the Otadini is an historical personage, whose tribe was moved from the Lothians to Wales to protect the West from Irish raiders; perhaps he did not wear tartan trews and trace his descent from a fairy seal, but perhaps he did.

The regular Roman army abandoned the Wall c. 390. In the later fifth century St Patrick had dealings with a Christian King Coroticus who reigned in Carlisle and adjoining districts. I have assumed that he had a father of the same name, who defended the Wall as a foederate for Honorius. It is purely a conjecture, but a reasonable one.

The laws of the later Empire were as I have described them, though to what extent they were enforced is an open question. The *Notitia Dignitatum* tells us a great deal about the military organization of Britain, and from the same document we learn that there were now five Provinces. No one knows where these lay, but it seems reasonable that Prima should include London; Valentia used to be placed

between the Walls, but Oman made the ingenious suggestion that it should be in Wales, whence the Irish were
driven out in the reign of Valentinianus, not in the north,
where archaeology shows no Roman occupation at this late
period.